HOME and OTHER HIDING PLACES

HOME
and
OTHER
HIDING
PLACES

JACK ELLIS

ultimo
press

Lyrics from 'The Indian Pacific' on page 206, and lyrics from 'The Biggest Disappointment' on page 209 are reprinted with the kind permission of Joy McKean.

Published in 2022 by Ultimo Press,
an imprint of Hardie Grant Publishing

Ultimo Press   Ultimo Press (London)
Gadigal Country   5th & 6th Floors
7, 45 Jones Street   52–54 Southwark Street
Ultimo, NSW 2007   London SE1 1UN
ultimopress.com.au

 A catalogue record for this
work is available from the
National Library of Australia

Home and Other Hiding Places
ISBN 978 1 76115 007 4 (paperback)

10 9 8 7 6 5 4 3 2 1

Cover design
Amy Daoud
Typesetting
Kirby Jones | Typeset in 13/19 pt Adobe Garamond Pro
Copyeditor
Simone Ford
Proofreader
Libby Turner

Printed in Australia by Griffin Press, part of Ovato, an Accredited ISO AS/NZS 14001 Environmental Management System printer.

 The paper this book is printed on is certified against the Forest Stewardship Council® Standards. Griffin Press holds FSC® chain of custody certification SGSHK-COC-005088. FSC® promotes environmentally responsible, socially beneficial and economically viable management of the world's forests.

Ultimo Press acknowledges the Traditional Owners of the country on which we work, the Gadigal people of the Eora nation and the Wurundjeri people of the Kulin nation, and recognises their continuing connection to the land, waters and culture. We pay our respects to their Elders past and present.

For Anne Brooksbank

CHAPTER ONE

Fin extended the handle of his suitcase, and it reached right up to his shoulder. He had to tilt the bag almost flat to make it move. Lindy knocked on the boot of the taxi, and its headlights swept across front lawns as it turned.

'Why didn't you tell him to drop us out the front, Mum?'

'Gran would have come out to pay.'

They pulled their suitcases along the street. Most of the houses had their curtains open, and the glow of evening lights shone out onto the parked cars.

'That would have been nice of her to pay, wouldn't it, Mum?'

'She gave us the money to buy our car.'

Lindy paused at the gutter outside Gran's. Fin straightened up his suitcase and, still hidden by the dark, they looked through the scruffy bushes either side of the path.

The house had always looked to Fin like it was facing the wrong way. The ridge of the roof ran parallel to the street, and you had to walk around the side to reach the front door.

It was two years since he'd last been there, and now the high gutter was sagging down so it covered the tops of the two upstairs windows.

Lindy took a deep breath, and they began clunking along the path, past the tangle of nasturtiums. A lamp was on beside the downstairs window, and he saw Gran getting up from her computer. The door swung open just as they reached the front step.

Lindy straightened her posture. 'Hello, Mum.'

'Darling.' Gran pulled Lindy into a quick hug. 'And who's this tall young man? I'm not sure we've been introduced.'

'It's me, Gran.' Fin pushed past her into the corridor. 'It's only a haircut.'

'But you're so big all of a sudden! You're not getting past me without at least one kiss.'

Fin let his case topple over. 'Where's Josie?'

Gran led them into the old living room, which was filled with the smell of cloves and cinnamon. Fin saw Josie's narrow frame at the kitchen bench. Even though it was summer, she was wearing a pink jumper and she had made her Christmas-time mulled wine. She stuck out her lower lip and blew her silver hair out of her eyes as she poured the steaming liquid into teacups from a little saucepan.

'Well, well. What sort of time do you call this?'

Fin jumped onto the couch and began bouncing left and right. 'It's only nine o'clock. The bus had to wait for heaps of cows.'

'Shoes!' Gran pointed at Fin's feet.

He flung his legs out and his bum thudded onto the old cushions.

Gran turned and spoke quietly to Lindy. 'Bus? You should have told me.'

'We got a cab from Sydney Central. It wasn't much. It's fine.'

'Yeah, the car wouldn't have made it, Gran. Not that old rooster.'

'Cock-a-doodle-doo!' Josie tucked her hands into her armpits, stuck her bum out and pecked at the fridge.

'I've told you before, Jocelyn. The Alverton residence is a strictly chicken-free zone.' Gran shook her head.

'Baaah!' Josie raised her hands to her forehead and pointed her fingers like horns.

'And goats! We'd never get a thing done.'

Josie handed around the little brown mugs. 'And here's one for you, Mr Fin.'

'Josie, for the love of… The boy's eight years old.'

Fin corrected her. 'Eight and a quarter.'

'It's only a small one.' Josie winked.

'We are simply not teaching this boy to drink. Especially not!'

'Will you have a cup of coffee then, Mr Fin?'

'Josie!'

The three women circled the couch and clinked their mugs above Fin.

'Merry Christmas.'

~

Gran insisted on helping Lindy and Fin get their suitcases upstairs, even though she was the least fit of them all. She was sixty-two years old with a round middle and skinny legs. Fin had never seen her without a full face of make-up, and it was usually cakey around her bluey-grey eyes. Her silver-grey hair was always set firmly in curls. 'I've put you on the pump-up mattress in your mother's bedroom. I thought the downstairs room might be a bit far at first. We've got time, and it's still a couple of weeks until Christmas. So we can move you when you're ready for something more comfortable. Don't jump on the thing. You might tear a hole!'

'Thanks, Mum.' Lindy heaved her suitcase up onto the bed.

The room was decorated with music posters and cut-outs from magazines; the walls were painted uneven purple.

Gran spoke as she backed out of the room. 'I'll let you get settled in. There are towels for you both in the... You know where everything is.'

Fin flopped down on the pump-up mattress to test it.

'So here we are, little man. Back.'

The way his mum said 'back' made it sound like they were leaving Gustav's forever.

Lindy stepped in front of the long mirror on the wardrobe and parted her feet. She lifted her mousy-blonde hair and twisted it into a knot above her head. Fin had noticed she'd started checking for grey hairs. If she found one, she'd loop it around her finger and yank it out. Lindy pursed her lips into her kissy mirror pose. She had just turned thirty-three and still had a young-looking, freckled roundness to her face. But there were lines at the corners of her mouth and beside her green eyes.

Fin stood up and cuddled into his mum's side. He was still getting used to his new reflection. The week before, Lindy had clipped off his dreadlocks because Ms Minter had found them full of lice.

Lindy squared her shoulders. 'You're almost tall enough to be my brother.'

Fin stood as tall as he could beside her. The top of his head now almost reached her shoulder. They shared the same green eyes, but she was fairer than him. His skin was more olive coloured and his hair was more light brown than blond. Lindy let her head fall to the side and he could feel her cheek through his new spiky hair.

Josie appeared at the door. 'I'm toasting you some jaffles. I don't know about you, but buses always get me screaming for melted cheese.'

Fin knew that Josie was a few years older than Gran, but she looked younger. Her eyes were bright, and they could catch you from anywhere in the room.

'Thanks, Josie. It's lovely to see you.' Lindy pulled her into a hug.

'They'll be ready when you are.' Josie darted back towards the stairs and Fin noticed her tracksuit pants clinging to her skinny legs.

Lindy shoved her suitcase aside to make space on the bed, then sat on the edge and let herself fall backwards. Fin rolled over on the squishy pump-up so they were both looking up at the plaster ceiling.

Lindy took a loud breath in through her teeth and held it. The outside sounds of cicadas and distant traffic seemed to swell to fill the silence.

She emptied her lungs in a steady hiss. 'Back.'

∿

As he was just dropping off to sleep, Fin had the sensation of falling backwards and cried out.

'Finny?' Lindy whispered like she was talking after lights out.

'It's okay, Mum. It's okay. I was just dreaming.' At Gustav's, Fin was extra slow and careful if he had to get up in the night. Once his mum woke up, it could take all night for her to get back to sleep.

'Why don't you come up? Mummy would love a cuddle. It'll be like camping.'

As far as Fin was concerned, the uneven squishiness of the pump-up already felt too much like camping, but he commando-rolled onto the old shagpile in the dark and Lindy lifted the doona for him. He could feel her breath on his scalp as he fell asleep.

∿

Fin was tucked under the doona on the wall side of Lindy's bed when he woke up. Through half-open eyes he saw his mum unpeeling sticky tape and taking the old posters and cut-outs down from the walls. At Gustav's she'd hum to herself while she patched and puttied to keep the rain out for another week. But she was moving quietly now so he could sleep.

Once she'd stacked the last posters, she stood back and looked at the purple walls. Gran appeared at the door with a tray and Lindy lifted a finger to her lips.

Fin sat up. 'I'm awake too.'

'In that case.' She laid the tray down on the bedside table. There was white toast, a tea, two glasses of apple juice, and a mini jar of marmalade. 'I wasn't sure what you liked lately so I asked Josie to whizz up a bit of a mix.' Gran lifted the pile of crinkled papers Lindy had made on the bed. 'I'll deal with these.' She carried the little posters out of the room.

Fin took a big bite of dry white toast; it was soft and cakey. At Gustav's they only had Lindy's homemade wholemeal. Lindy tore the corner off a piece of toast, but she didn't put it in her mouth. She twisted her neck to look at each of the empty walls, and her eyes moved up and down like she was planning where new pictures might go. Now that the posters were gone, Fin noticed that the purple paint was thicker and then thinner in patches, like the walls had been painted with a small brush.

~

7

Fin sat on the patio with Josie while she smoked. The cicadas were in full fizz, and Lindy and Gran were out Christmas shopping. Although they called it a 'patio', it was really just a layer of bricks that had been arranged in a zigzag pattern and pushed into the dirt. Beyond the back lawn, there was a stone ledge before the land dropped away into a narrow valley full of gum trees. Lindy had once told him that the house was built over a spring; it was why the air inside was damp and the paint peeled off the walls. But Gran and Josie were just letting it slowly fall apart because they didn't have enough money to fix anything. Lindy had also said that the house stopped the spring from bubbling up, so the water seeped below the surface all the way to the river at the bottom of the valley.

Josie turned her head to blow the smoke away. 'Well, young man. Back.'

If he'd known there was even a chance they were staying forever he would have packed differently. He'd only brought the newest of his *Star Wars* books.

He and Lindy had lived at Gustav's for most of his life. The only other place he could half remember was a caravan and the day a pelican came to the door. He couldn't remember what his dad looked like, just the smoky smell of him as he leant over to feed the pelican a sardine from a tin.

Gustav's was a wooden farmhouse on a few acres. It was at the end of a narrow dirt road near Old Binnalong, a little Northern Rivers town about an hour inland. The locals called it 'Old Bin' and it was rolling, hilly country, worn smooth by dairy cows. They had the whole valley to themselves; the only other house was way up on the eastern ridge. The rest of the landscape was small paddocks and a few almond-coloured Brahmans that were allowed onto their part on 'agistment'. It was Fin's favourite word, the sort of word that made your mouth feel good – *agistment*.

Gustav had died, and his son who lived overseas hadn't wanted to deal with Gustav's stuff. So the son had rented it 'as is', with the dark-wood furniture and photos of people standing in front of old buildings. One of the walls in Fin's room had shelves almost to the ceiling filled with records – operas and songs, all in German. Sometimes, he and Lindy would build a fire and listen to the records on the old player in the living room. They had to promise to take care of it all in exchange for cheaper rent until the son could decide what to do.

Apart from the school and the shop, Gustav's was an hour's drive to anywhere, and their car didn't like the heat. It made a noise when it was about to cut out, and Lindy had to find some shade to park in so they could wait for it to cool down.

'Have you ever been all the way down there?' Fin pointed into the narrow river valley.

Josie stubbed out her cigarette in her little ashtray and turned her head away again to exhale. 'Poked around a bit. But the path's a bit of a bush bash and you'd only have to scramble all the way back up again.'

'Where does the river go?'

'To the sea, I suppose. It'd be a pretty funny river if it didn't.' She pointed at Fin's heart with her skinny forefinger. 'Everything all right in there, mister?'

'Yeah. Homesick maybe.' He hoped Josie would tell him what was going on.

'Homesickness? After one night? Well, that's fair enough. I know just the thing for that.'

They heard the front door unlock and then the sound of heavy plastic bags thumping down in the kitchen.

Josie said, 'Starts with C and ends with E, with icing too.'

Gran appeared in the back doorway, and Josie slumped in her chair.

'For the love of. He's only a child, Jocelyn. Have you never heard of passive smoking?'

Josie tucked her ashtray behind a plant in the raised garden bed.

Gran stepped through the doorway and Josie sank even lower in her chair. He'd heard that, if you put salt on a slug, it shrivels and turns inside out. Gran seemed to do a similar thing to Josie. It looked like she was expecting Gran to slap her.

'You'd think by your age you would have come to your senses.'

Fin said, 'How old are you, Josie?'

'I'll get back to you.' Josie stood quickly and elbowed past Gran to get into the kitchen.

After lunch, the three adults drank coffee at the kitchen bench and picked at the remains of the cake. Fin padded across the squelchy back lawn, and he could smell the steam rising out of the earth as he crawled into a little tunnel through the bushes that separated Gran's place from the tidy yard next door. A couple of Christmases ago he'd found a plastic soldier with a parachute in there. This time there was only a golf ball.

He heard the crunching of leaves, and a boy's face appeared a few centimetres away.

'That's mine.' The boy looked about a year older than Fin, maybe nine years old, with reddish-brown hair cropped short into a flat-top. The freckles on his nose and cheeks were the same light brown as his eyes.

Fin held the ball out and the boy grabbed it.

'It's a Penta, you know? A TaylorMade. At least twenty bucks a dozen.'

'Yeah?' Fin didn't understand what he meant.

'Do you live here? I haven't seen you.'

'It's my gran's house. I live in the country.'

'I live here. Next door with my pop. But I've got chickenpox or something maybe. But I don't really reckon I've got chickenpox because they say you can only get it once. I've got spots anyway. Not many. It's not bad though. Can you get out of my way?'

Fin crawled to the side and the boy pulled himself through the narrow tunnel in the bush. Fin could see a few purplish spots around the boy's ear and down the side of his neck.

'The fence at the back on my side is too high so I come through your gran's to get down to the river.' The boy crawled onto the lawn and made his way to the rock ledge at the back. 'You coming?'

Fin looked back at the house, uncertain, then he lowered himself over the ledge and down onto the path that led into the bush.

The boy was already far ahead, springing between rocks as he went. Fin struggled to match the boy's pace as he ran between the tall gums, and he didn't slow until he reached the bottom. By the time Fin caught up, the boy was sitting cross-legged on a large rock near the edge of a mudflat, tossing the golf ball from hand to hand.

'It always stinks down here.'

Fin sniffed the air, but there was only the freshness of gum leaves and river.

The boy looked out, like he was searching for something. Then he tucked the golf ball into the pocket of his shorts, pulled off his dirty sneakers and picked up a long stick that was wedged under the rock. He began crossing the mudflat to where the river flowed deeper before another hill rose up on the other side. 'Watch out for crab holes. Muddies can nip your toe right off through the bone.'

Fin pulled his shoes off. His feet sank in and he felt the mud holding on each time he lifted his foot. When he reached the boy, he crouched beside him near the water.

'There.' The boy pointed. 'I put rocks in so it floats just below the water and no-one will get it.'

Fin could make out a plastic milk bottle just under the brown surface.

The boy hooked his stick around a rope below the milk bottle and hauled it towards them. 'You grab the rope!'

Fin reached into the water and wrapped his hand around the slimy rope below the bottle. 'Got it.'

A flimsy cage made from thick sticks and chicken wire appeared at the surface. There was a silver-grey fish inside, about the length of Fin's forearm. It flung itself against the wire as he dragged the cage onto the mud.

'Not again! How am I going to catch anything if these stealers keep sneaking into my crab pot to nick my bait?'

'It's a pretty big one.'

'Funny-looking crab though.' The boy looked at Fin as though he was challenging him to disagree.

'Yeah. Pretty funny-looking for a crab.'

The boy laughed as he rough-handled the crab pot. 'Funny-looking crab. That's a classic!' The boy was laughing so hard at his own joke he looked like he was going to fall over. He unpicked a wire from the corner of the crab pot and flopped the fish out onto the mud. It flapped and curled, and Fin could see its gills flaring.

The boy shouted, 'That'll serve you right, stealer!'

The fish continued to strain and twitch, trying to fling itself towards the water. Each attempt only yielded a gain of a few centimetres, and the fish seemed more desperate with each one. Fin saw the moment it gave up.

'I'd chop him up for bait if it would do any good. Crabs don't like stealers, not stinky enough. The birds will get him if the water doesn't come up before he dries out.'

Fin took a few steps towards the edge of the deeper water. He didn't want to look, but he couldn't help glancing back to see if the fish was still moving.

The boy saw his look. 'Don't get shirty. That fish stole my chicken neck.' The boy paused as if he was waiting for a sign of agreement.

Fin wanted to let the fish live, to slip it back into the water before it turned into a piece of fishy garbage. But he nodded once. He'd learnt from birthday parties up at Old Binnalong that there were rules about these things – if it's your place, you get to decide what happens. This was the boy's place and they'd only just met.

The fish's gills stopped moving.

The boy spoke quietly, looking away. 'You can chuck him back in if you want. He's no good for bait.'

Fin looked up quickly to make sure the boy meant what he said.

'Only I'm not doing it. He's a stealer.'

Fin could feel his heart beating in his ears. He and Lindy had helped one of the agistment cows give birth, but he'd never touched a live fish. It had spines along its back and pointy teeth that looked like they would latch onto him.

He hurried closer and crouched down. It was probably best to grab it by the tail, but he was worried he might pull the tail right off. It was barely moving now.

He wrapped his hand around as much of the tail as he could. The stealer twitched but didn't struggle. Its solid flesh felt cold. Once Fin had it off the mud, he headed for the flowing part of the river, keeping low so the fish wouldn't get hurt if it slipped out of his hand.

As soon as he felt the water on his toes, he flung it forward. The stealer slapped into the water side-on and stayed on the surface, not moving. He glanced across at the boy, who also had his eyes fixed on the fish. It was completely still as it began to sink into the dark water.

Then, as though a jolt of electricity had struck it, the fish came alive. It flicked its tail and disappeared below. Fin trembled with relief and excitement. The boy looked away, retrieved another chicken neck from his pocket, secured it with wire and closed the gate before tossing the crab pot into the river.

They crossed the mudflat and pulled their shoes onto their muddy feet before the boy led the way up the hill without speaking. As they moved through the shadows cast by the branches high above, Fin understood that the fish had been a test, the boy's way of deciding if they should be friends. And, as had happened each time up at Old Bin, Fin had made the wrong choice.

As they neared the rock ledge behind Gran's, the boy turned and said, 'I was always going to. I just wanted to see if you'd do it.'

They stepped out from the shade of the trees and climbed over the ledge. Just as the boy crouched to crawl through the bush, he rolled the golf ball out onto the lawn. 'You keep it.' He disappeared into the tunnel through the bush.

'What's your name?'

'Rory.'

Fin thought he'd be in trouble for going to the river without telling anyone. So he tried to look casual as he stepped from the patio into the kitchen, and then into the dark of the living room. Gran was sitting stiffly on the couch with her back to him, sipping from a cup of tea. He took shorter strides so his footsteps landed softly on the old carpet, and he managed to get past without her noticing. He climbed the stairs and found Lindy on her bed with the sheet wrapped tight around her.

She was crying again.

CHAPTER TWO

Lindy had started crying around the middle of winter. The bouts of sobbing, rocking and fist-clenching would often last a whole day. The first time, Fin had waited for her to pick him up from the main-road bus stop. He'd smiled and waved at the few cars that passed, but then he'd hidden in the ditch behind the bus stop so people didn't think there was something wrong. When it started getting dark, he walked for over an hour to get back to Gustav's.

He got home after dark and the fire wasn't lit. Lindy was wrapped in her doona with the pillow soaking and her lips dried out. She said one of the women in town was trying to kill her. The woman was driving around 'like an assassin' so she could run Lindy over, and she'd heard the woman's car revving and skidding on the little dirt road out the front.

He asked who the woman was and said he'd call the police. Lindy repeated herself like she was telling him things for the first time, and she seemed to change the details. The more questions he asked, the more upset she became. It was like she'd turned into a different person. Fin wanted to help, but he had no idea what to do. She said they couldn't call the police because 'cops only make things worse'.

So, Fin had lit the fire, and fed her milk and cold baked beans. Then he cuddled in beside her, staying still until she slept. And she seemed more or less like her old self in the morning. By the time she picked him up from the bus stop the next day, she'd dug a whole new spot for a veggie garden.

A week later, she started again. It was like the bed would get hold of her and refuse to let go. Apparently, Deirdre from the general store had decided to kill her because Deirdre's husband was 'obsessed' with Lindy. She told Fin she'd done nothing to encourage it, but she couldn't help if he found her 'naturally attractive'. It got to the point where she was too afraid to drive into Old Bin because Deirdre might try to ram the car. This meant it took a full hour to get to the supermarket in Ballina every time they needed food.

It wasn't the first time someone had tried to hurt Lindy. In the past they'd just pointed the evil eye or wished bad luck on her. And Lindy told him stories of when other women had 'wanted her dead' because of the way their husbands felt, but this was the first time someone had actually tried to kill her. Deirdre's two kids went to Fin's school, and Lindy told Fin to stay away from them because 'this sort of thing runs in families'.

Lindy's fear and anger seemed to ebb and flow over a cycle of about four or five days. She'd be fine, even playful and happy, and then the bed would take hold of her again; Fin stopped waiting before he began the long walk from the main road to feed her and cuddle her to sleep.

About two weeks before they left for Gran's, Fin had arrived home after another walk from the bus stop. It had turned suddenly cold in the afternoon, and a gusty south-westerly was tossing the long grass in the ditches either side of their dirt road.

He'd seen smoke coming from the chimney – a good sign – and when he'd got in, Lindy was sitting in front of the fire with her rune tiles laid out on the rug.

She looked up, a little teary but smiling, and said, 'Look, little man. It's going to be all right. It's going to be okay. It's over.'

ᚺᛈᛉ

He recognised the symbols: ᚺ – Hagalaz – *when you can't go back*; ᛈ – Wunjo – *joy*; and ᛉ – Algiz – *the life-and-death rune*. He knew the names of the symbols, and he especially knew the distinct feeling of each one. The tiles were black and white, but it felt to him like each symbol had a colour of its own. He could recognise them, but only Lindy understood what they meant when they were drawn together.

Lindy had pulled him into a hug and kissed the top of his head. 'Thank you, baby. You've been the best little man a mummy could want. Any mummy.' She unpeeled herself from him and stood up. 'And how about a nice spaghetti for the man of the house?'

It sounded like a great idea.

They ate dinner and Lindy said she was going to sit up for a while and listen to Gustav's records. Fin climbed into his bed and drifted off to the sound of a German opera singer.

About an hour later, he was woken by Lindy's screams. He ran to find her frozen in her bedroom doorway.

'It touched me!'

The covers on her bed were drawn back and a black snake was moving across the sheet towards the window.

'It touched me! Kill it! Kill it!' Lindy ran barefoot through the dark.

Fin heard the car door slamming as he stepped through the doorway into Lindy's bedroom.

The light from Lindy's reading lamp shone yellow across the white sheets, and Fin could clearly see the grooves that outlined its leathery scales. The snake was still for a moment, and then it raised itself to curl over the windowsill. It tried to push its flat head through the tiny gap that Lindy had left for fresh air, but it was too big to fit through. So it pulled itself half up onto the windowsill and began nosing at the glass.

Fin jolted backwards as he caught a glimpse of another snake climbing the leg of Lindy's bed; it was only the lamp cord coiling down to the broken power point that was half pulled out of the wall. He looked over Lindy's clothes and stacks of books for something he could hold, something long and heavy enough to crush the snake's head. Then he darted into his bedroom to grab his cricket bat and hurried back.

He began taking small steps towards Lindy's bed. The snake was swaying, like it sensed the new danger, and a smell like horsehair and wet school shoes filled the room. Fin swept the bat across the bed so the snake would climb right up onto the wide windowsill. He thought he'd have a better chance of killing it there; it wouldn't work on the soft bed. The snake pulled itself up and folded its body along the windowsill. It twisted its head and tried to squeeze through the narrow gap of night air.

Fin stepped closer, raised the bat and waited. He'd have a clear shot once it turned back for its next search along the windowsill. Fin knew he'd break the window if he swung hard, but there was no other way. And, if he let it climb down, there were too many hiding places under things on the wonky wooden floor.

He tightened his grip. The snake turned. He swung the bat down hard at its head, but it darted forward, arching up against the glass, and the bat jammed between the wooden frame and the sill. He swung again, this time managing a half hit on the snake's body.

The room began to fill with a new smell, a smell of sickness, like a bandaid that had been left on too long. Fin swung at the snake another two times; the dirty-wound smell was becoming overpowering. The snake coiled and bit at the bat again and again, and each strike was getting faster and better aimed. He thought about grabbing one of Lindy's cooking knives to try to stab it, but that would mean getting his hand very close.

Fin tried a last thrusting jab with the bat, but the snake was too quick. It dodged left and bit the bat again. He now knew that it wasn't going to work; he wasn't strong or fast enough. He angled the bat to raise the timber window just enough so the snake could fit out into the dark. He heard it flopping onto the grass outside and kneeled on the bed to pull the window shut.

He tucked the bat under his arm and ran outside to find Lindy.

She wound down the back window to speak to him. 'Did you do it?'

'Yes, Mum.' He was crying and, after all that, he hated lying to his mum.

'How?'

He showed her the cricket bat.

'Where did you put it?'

'Just chucked him round the back. The birds will…'

'Come here.' She'd opened the door and pulled him on top of her. He could feel her tears on his neck, feel the warmth of her beneath him.

When they woke up it was just before sunrise, and the car was dewy with their breath. He was trembling with cold.

Now they were at Gran's, and all the adults seemed to think they were staying. He wanted to know what was going to happen when school went back, and to all their stuff. He sat on the floor beside his mum's bed and looked at the patchy purple walls. He interlocked his fingers with hers and hoped it might settle her tears.

Lindy whispered, 'It's nothing. It's just typical Gran criticising me. I'm all right.'

He had noticed that Gran gave advice as a way of pointing out that Lindy was doing life wrong. He wanted to ask what it had been this time, but he had learnt that words never made her better. He kept still until he heard the familiar, even breathing of sleep, then he untangled his fingers and went to find Josie.

The living room was empty. He followed the smell of cigarette smoke through the kitchen and onto the back patio. Josie was sitting with her back to him, looking out at the gum trees.

'Josie?'

She turned and smiled with her eyes. She looked older and more tired than usual. 'You just wait there.' She disappeared inside and emerged with a metal stand fan attached to a long yellow extension cord. She licked her finger and held it up to test the direction of the wind, and then placed the fan pointing away from her on the other side of her chair. 'Now you can sit on this side.'

Fin squatted on the zigzag brick paving beside her. 'What happened with Mum?'

'You know your gran.'

Lindy had sworn they were 'never ever going back' after the fight two Christmases ago. It started because Gran didn't think Fin should have dreadlocks. He would've preferred to yank them out himself rather than he and Lindy spending Christmas Eve at a youth hostel.

'What did she say?'

Josie lit another cigarette and blew the smoke forcefully into the back of the fan. 'Just the usual, I expect. Another solution to all our problems. If you ever find me completely repaired, you'll know where to point the finger.' She curled her narrow finger over her shoulder to point into the house.

They continued talking as Josie lit cigarette after cigarette, and then they stood at the kitchen bench to make sandwiches with margarine, tomato and salt. After lunch, Fin unfolded a ratty deckchair and sat beside her on the patio until the shadows cast by the gum trees fell over the back of the house. Lindy and Gran didn't appear again until it was nearly dinnertime.

Fin peeled potatoes while Josie got the chicken ready for baking. Gran drank two more cups of tea and went to type on her computer in the front room. Lindy stretched out on the couch, watching TV and playing with her phone. She only seemed to look up during the commercials. Everything had settled down. The only bump was when Lindy said 'hypocrite' under her breath after Gran began to say grace. And Gran said, 'Grace is something it would do you two ladies well to cultivate.'

CHAPTER THREE

'Is the boy here?' Rory's voice echoed through the house. Fin ran towards the kitchen.

'What sort of a boy do you mean? We've got a blue boy, a red boy or a…golden one. Let me think. Yes, I'm sure we've got a golden one.' Josie was cutting up fruit at the bench.

'He's a sort of golden colour, I suppose. With the golf ball. It's a Penta, TaylorMade.' Rory was untroubled by Josie's question.

'Mr Fin, you have a visitor. He's looking for a golden boy.'

'Hey.' Fin felt shy as soon as he saw Rory in his boardshorts and stained blue T-shirt. He was wearing a cap with a flap at the back to cover his neck.

'Your gran says that you've got all different coloured boys in here. How come I've never seen them?'

'She's not my gran. Josie's my…' Fin faltered, realising he didn't really know what Josie was. He looked up at her for help.

'Wait a minute. I need to take a deep breath for this. I'm your great-step-grandmother.'

Fin looked back at Rory, hoping he understood what it meant.

'And you two growing gentlemen aren't going anywhere without some nice fruit salad inside you.' Josie retrieved two bowls from the high wooden shelf.

'I hate fruit salad.' Rory was matter-of-fact.

'Not today you don't.' Josie stepped out through the back door and set the bowls down on the patio table. Rory obediently swung his skinny legs over the bench seat to start eating, and Fin sat down beside him.

It had never made sense to Fin that Josie was, in fact, Gran's mother – sort of. She looked so much younger. Lindy had once explained that Gran's real mother died when Gran was a baby. Gran's dad, Albert, was so busy running his spectacle business that Gran was raised by nannies. Albert was in his forties and Josie was twenty-six when they got together.

Gran married Lindy's dad soon after; he ran one of the optometry shops. But Lindy said he drank too much beer and the police kept coming so Gran broke up with him. Lindy was only three when she and Gran came to live with Josie and Albert in the big house on the edge of the bush.

Albert and Josie moved up to Coffs Harbour when Albert retired, and Gran and Lindy stayed living in the big house in Sydney. A few years later, Albert died of a heart attack on a cruise ship, and when Josie and Gran tried to sort out his will, they discovered there was almost no money. Even the fancy place in Coffs Harbour was owned by the bank. Once the debts were paid, the Sydney house remained, but there was no other money. Albert's will said that he'd left the house to Gran, but he'd given Josie a 'life tenancy'. This meant Gran owned the house, but Josie was allowed to live there until she died.

Rory lifted his bowl and drained the last of the fruit-salad juice. 'Come on.'

After Fin shovelled in a few more mouthfuls, the boys ran across the lawn to the bush.

Fin sprang from rock to rock behind Rory until they reached the river. The water level was higher today, and there was a shin-deep layer of brown water spread over the mud. The boys tossed their shoes onto the rock and Rory led the way. The cold water was a shock after the warm air.

The slimy rope half slipped through Fin's hands as he hauled up the pot and, when it neared the surface, he could see two green-grey mud crabs in the bottom.

Rory raised his arm into the air for a high thumbs up. 'You absolute beauty!'

Fin lifted the pot out of the water, and Rory grabbed it and wrapped the rope around it before setting off through the shallow water and mud.

Rory thumped the pot down on top of the rock and began rifling around in the hollow where he kept the stick. He also grabbed a bent and gunky pair of barbecue tongs, an old cigarette lighter, and a rusty tomahawk.

He squatted on the rock beside the crab pot. 'Do you want to chop or hold it steady?'

'What do you mean?'

'We've got to get the guts out. The gills taste like actual poo if you eat them.'

It hadn't occurred to Fin that they might eat the crabs straight away.

'Come around this side.' Rory held the tongs out to him.

Fin climbed up onto the rock and took the tongs. The crabs were about the size of Fin's hand with his fingers spread out, and they were climbing on top of each other.

'Careful. These buggers will nip something right off if you let them.' Rory untwisted the wire and flipped open the gate. 'Okay, you reach in with the tongs and get him. Make sure the other one doesn't go for you.'

Fin imagined the red jet of blood that would spray out when the crab cut through his knuckle.

'Come on! Just get him onto the rock. But don't let go.'

Fin struggled to control the shaking of his hands as he reached in. The crab nipped at the tongs and Fin instinctively recoiled. Rory looked at him without speaking. There seemed to Fin to be a wordless challenge in Rory's eyes – *come on, chicken out, I dare you.*

Fin poked the tongs back in. He slipped one of the flat ends under a crab and squeezed down. He pulled the crab out and Rory slapped the wire gate closed.

'Now bring him over here on the rock.'

Fin squeezed the tongs as tight as he could and swung the crab around to a flatter area of the rock.

'Turn him over so his belly's up.'

Fin did as he was told, twisting his arm as he squeezed tight. Rory hurried around with the tomahawk until he was opposite Fin on the other side of the crab.

'Okay. I'm going to count to three. When I say "three", you move the tongs away, fast. Just straight back towards you.' Rory raised the tomahawk up with both hands. 'Okay. One! Two! Wait, wait. I mean right on "three", not after it, okay?'

'Okay.' Fin felt like he was going to throw up.

'One! Two! Three!'

Fin pulled the tongs away and Rory brought the tomahawk down hard on the crab's belly. An involuntary fart exploded out of Fin as the crab was cut in half.

The crab stopped wriggling as soon as Rory lifted the tomahawk.

Fin felt a slight wetness on the back of his underpants. 'Sorry.'

'Don't worry. I reckon you're good luck. I've never got two before, especially big ones.' Rory grabbed each half of the crab by its big nipper. 'Anyway, it could've been worse. You looked like you were going to poo your pants when I had the axe!' Rory was laughing.

Fin laughed too and hoped the wetness wasn't showing through.

'Let's get the other one.'

They repeated the same steps to chop the second crab. Rory explained what to do and then sent Fin down to the water's edge to clean out the gills and guts with a stick. Rory snapped up some kindling and built a fire in the hollow under the rock. Once the initial flames died down, Rory used the tongs to lay the pieces of crab on their backs in the coals.

'Beautiful. Now it's time to get the pot back out.'

When they returned from baiting and sinking the pot, Fin could smell the rich smokiness of the barbecuing crabs.

Rory inspected the crabs. 'Not bad, eh?'

'Yeah.'

Rory inhaled deeply through his nose. 'Serious. Your farts don't smell bad.' Rory's freckles rounded into a smile.

Fin was flooded with a safe, almost golden sense of relief. He wasn't sure, but he thought it felt like love.

They sat on the rock and dug the crabmeat out with sticks. Then Rory cracked open the nippers with a pointy rock. The flesh was slippery and tender with a rich saltwater-and-butter flavour that coated Fin's lips and the inside of his cheeks.

When they'd scraped out the last of the crabmeat, they chucked the pieces of shell into the water and rinsed off their hands and faces. Rory made sure the fire was out and tucked the tongs, tomahawk and cigarette lighter back under the rock.

They exchanged a silent thumbs up on the back lawn at Gran's, and Fin hurried past Josie up to the bathroom. When he saw his undies on the floor, he decided that Rory was just being nice, maybe because he knew.

CHAPTER FOUR

Lindy started muttering in the dark and the fear of what was coming next kept Fin awake. At Gustav's, it was only the two of them, and he knew how to look after her when she got bad. It couldn't be Deirdre this time; she was still up at Old Bin.

He drifted off in the early hours, and Lindy was curled into him on the blow-up mattress when he woke. The warmth of her armpits and her sweaty-toast smell reminded him of how she would cuddle him to sleep when he was little. His bed at Gustav's was unusually high and made of old metal with a big space underneath; he was certain a monster lived there. Each night, Lindy would crouch down to check and then she'd say 'monster count zero' before climbing in beside him. She'd say he could check for himself, but he was scared that the monster might grab him. On his fifth birthday, Lindy handed him a long box wrapped in yellow paper. He tore it open to find a length of gutter pipe with a little torch taped through a hole. She explained it was a 'monster checking periscope'. She'd cut holes into the sides at the top and bottom and glued two angled mirrors inside. He could see behind him when he looked into one of the holes. Lindy secured it to the leg of his bed with twisted wire. So, if he ever got worried, he could click the button on the little torch and see the whole space under his bed. He only used it a couple of times. But he was never scared of monsters again.

'Don't worry, little man. It's going to be okay.'

'What do you mean, Mum? What's going to be okay?'

'I'll make it right,' Lindy whispered. 'One way or another, I'll make it okay. She won't come after you anyway. Not until she's taken me out.' She winked. 'I've got your back.'

'Who, Mum? Deirdre's not here,' he whispered back.

'Deirdre was only part of it. The whole thing was about getting me back in arm's reach. Yes, I know, Finny. I fell for it. I should've known. We can't leave yet or she'll know something's up. You just wait for me to work it out. When the time's right.' She squeezed him tighter.

Fin didn't want to believe that the danger had followed them from the Northern Rivers. 'Who, Mum?'

There was a gentle knock at the door and Gran edged it open. She had a tray of toast and tea. 'What on earth are you doing on the floor?'

Lindy smiled sweetly. 'Just catching up on a few odds and ends.'

'I suspect that your progress in this world would have been much swifter if you'd engaged with fewer odds and more ends.' Gran looked at Fin like they were sharing a joke.

'Tea! Yummy.' Lindy sprang up and took the tray from her. 'We'll be down in a sec.' She closed the door, nearly banging Gran in the face. Lindy set the tray down on her bed, opened the window and poured the two full teacups out onto the roof. 'Do not drink the tea. This is absolutely classic Gran.'

Fin didn't ask; he'd learnt that questions only made things worse.

~

Over the next few days, Fin noticed Gran pulling Lindy away for whispered conversations. He'd hear words like 'ambition' and 'momentum' before Lindy responded in a hissing gush, like she was shouting through clenched teeth.

Sometimes Gran would ask Josie to confirm the 'good sense' of a new plan or suggestion, and Josie would respond with something like, 'All this is out of my league,' or 'My Ps and Qs won't mind themselves,' as she crept back to the patio. Once, Gran also tried to convince Fin.

He and Josie were on the patio listening to Josie's little radio when Gran stepped out. She told Fin she was 'in the best position to know' and that 'it was beyond her how such promise had turned to tribulation'. And then she said, 'Unless your mother can locate some get-up-and-go, I feel I'll be forced to do it for her. Not just for her sake.'

At this point, Josie stood suddenly and said, 'You sound like you've got room for a hot cup of tea.'

They were silent for a moment, and then Gran stiffened before she turned and went back inside.

Fin spent most of each day on the patio or in the backyard. He avoided the TV because of the feeling in the house; the couch was Gran's place. And while he chatted to Josie or tossed his golf ball on the lawn, his eyes kept returning to the little tunnel through the bush. A few times he got down on all fours to peep at the tidy lawn next door. But something, a feeling like he would cause serious trouble, stopped him from crawling through.

After the third full day of waiting, he began to accept that Rory was just gone. Fin felt like he was back at school, hoping that someone might call out to him or kick the ball in his direction. He had talked to Lindy, and he had tried the things she suggested. But whenever he managed to get a smile out of one of the kids with a joke or story, it never quite worked out. Sometimes they got as far as Lindy making a phone call. He would sit close and hear things like 'play date' or 'getting the boys together', but it never happened. And soon, when Fin approached, he'd notice his new almost-friend turning to look away.

~

The path down to the river seemed more hidden and dangerous without Rory. Fin took each step carefully; he was trying not to mash up the sausage wrapped in newspaper he had stuffed into his front pocket with his golf ball. It was so quiet that he could hear the distant rumbling of the centre of Sydney and the sound of far-off trains. Even the birds seemed to have disappeared. Fin thought they were probably tucked in the shade, hiding from the midday sunlight and the sharp eyes of eagles.

He pulled his shoes off and checked under the rock to make sure everything was there – tongs, lighter, tomahawk. He'd decided, if there was a crab in the pot, he was going to cook it and eat it himself without Rory.

He took a minute to let his feet adjust to the shallow layer of cold water over the mudflat. He was careful with each step; there was no-one to help him if his foot went into a crab hole. The sun was directly overhead, and the rippling surface of the water had a busy sparkle to it, like static on Gustav's old TV.

He hooked the milk bottle and hauled up the pot. There were two smallish mud crabs and a stealer inside. Fin whispered to himself, 'You absolute beauty.' But it didn't sound right without Rory's shouty enthusiasm. He tried again, louder. 'You absolute beauty!'

He carefully lifted the pot onto the mud, and the stealer flapped over the crabs when it felt the open air. It already had a couple of chunks taken out of it, and ribbons of guts were hanging down. He untwisted the wire on the gate as fast as he could. The two crabs reared, lifting their claws towards him. Fin wished he'd brought the tongs from under the rock, but he knew he didn't have time to get them. He reached inside the pot. The stealer looked up at him and flipped itself on top of one of the crabs.

'Stay still! Please stay still.' Fin could see the stealer's gills straining.

Fin reached in again. He managed to grip its tail. One of the crabs took a nip at his finger, and his hand opened and pulled away. 'Arrgh! You stupid crab!'

He reached in again. Both crabs were nipping at each other, as well as towards Fin's skinny fingers, but he managed to restrain the urge to recoil. He wrapped his hand around the stealer's tail. He could feel the fish trembling as he pulled it out. As soon as it was clear, Fin took a step towards the flowing water and dropped the stealer. It flicked its tail and disappeared below.

'Good luck, fish.'

He wired the gate shut on the pot, bundled up the rope and the milk bottle, and carried everything over to the big rock. His ribs seemed to shudder with each thump of his heart.

He felt the compressed smoothness of the bank, and he dug his toes into the mud to stop from slipping as he climbed up towards the rock, holding the pot away from his legs so the crabs couldn't get him through the wire. He settled the pot onto the surface of the rock. The two crabs were still now. They squatted, gripping the bottom of the pot, waiting to attack. He retrieved the tongs and the tomahawk. One of the crabs reared up, pinching left and right like a boxer as Fin untwisted the wire on the gate. The other tried to climb the side of the floppy wire cage and flipped itself over. The wind dropped and left a deadly stillness behind. The trees were quiet. Fin focused. The silence seemed to intensify the ugliness of what he was doing. He thought about how, if Rory ever came back, he'd tell him it had been easy to do it on his own.

The tongs rattled in his grip as he guided them through the open wire. He decided he'd go for the crab that was belly-up; it was safer than risking a nip from the one that was fighting back. He tipped the cage slightly and slipped the tongs under the crab. The other crab locked a claw onto the upper arm of the tongs. Fin tried to shake him free without letting go of the other one. He withdrew the tongs and the fighting crab continued holding on, rising up with its friend until the chicken wire of the top forced its grip to slip.

Fin kept the tongs firm on the slidey surface of the crab's shell. He was also careful to keep the crab away from his bare feet in case it slipped free and got a hold of one of his toes. He placed the crab down on the rock so he could see the rounded shell between the crab's eyes and raised the tomahawk high. Then he swung the little axe in a slow-arcing practice swing to the spot where he would open the top of the little creature.

'One.' Another slow practice swing. 'Two' He flung the tongs away behind him and brought the axe down hard.

'Three!' The crab dodged and the little blade hacked off one of its nippers. The injured crab hurried towards the edge of the rock. Fin kneeled and stretched his arm to bring the axe down again. This time he landed a glancing blow on the top of the shell; it propelled the crab further towards the edge. He now remembered that Rory had told him to hold the crab upside down.

Fin thought about how he could simply stop, let the crabs go. He could still tell Rory it had been easy. But nothing about this was easy. Rory was supposed to be his friend and now he had vanished, or he was ignoring him like the kids at Old Bin.

The scurrying crab had made it to the edge of the rock and launched itself over the edge. It was hurrying but making slow progress through the unfamiliar terrain. Fin jumped down and swung the axe hard, but the crackling bed of sticks compressed under the belly of the crab and absorbed the shock of the blow. He brought the blade down again. The crab stopped running. Again and again, he brought the axe down until he was mashing the insides and the broken shell into the dirt. He struck each blow harder until the crab's mushy grey gills smeared on the dried leaves. The crab was dead, broken up and dirty. He tasted the weak saltiness of his own blood; he'd bitten into his lip. All was quiet. The crab was no use to anyone.

Slowly, using the blade of the axe, he scraped a shallow grave and pushed in the mushy pieces. He covered it with an ugly mix of dirt and leaves and climbed up onto the cool surface of the rock. The other crab was crouching at the bottom of the pot. It raised its claws as Fin came close.

Fin spoke to the crab. 'Your friend's chopped up down there.'

The crab examined the air with his claw.

Fin placed the little axe beside the crab pot and sat down. 'Rory's gone now, crab.'

The crab stretched his claws upward, reaching towards the sound.

As he sat there looking out at the empty water, he craved the rickety familiarity of Gustav's. And he began quietly singing the opening lines of one of the songs on Gustav's records. '*Muss i denn, muss i denn, zum Städtele hinaus, Städtele hinaus...*' He trailed off. It looked more beautiful here, but he missed the worn predictability of the landscape around Gustav's.

It occurred to Fin that, like the stealer, maybe the crab couldn't breathe out of the water, and that while he was sitting there wishing for Rory, the crab was quietly choking on the bush air. Then he remembered seeing the little crabs hurrying over the rocks on the inlet beside the caravan park when he was little. When his dad was still there. Narrabeen. The name had become like a place that didn't exist, like heaven. Those little Narrabeen crabs seemed to live most of their lives on the rocks. So maybe it was the other way around. Maybe crabs had to come up for air like tiny whales? They didn't study much about sea creatures at school in Old Bin.

He decided the crab could breathe. 'Don't worry. I'll let you go, but in a minute.' The thought of returning to the horrible tension of the house kept him sitting on the rock. 'Where's Rory, crab? Where is he and why did he go without saying?'

He carried the pot to the muddy bank and gently shook until the crab splashed into the shallow water. It held still for a moment and then crept towards the deeper part of the river.

Fin heard the crunching of sticks and leaves further up the hill. The footfalls were heavy and fast, like a big dog running and not taking care to follow the path. Fin dropped the pot near the water's edge and hurried behind the big rock. He crouched down low so the intruder couldn't see the top of his spiky head. He felt soft earth beneath his feet and realised he was standing on the crab's grave, but he couldn't move without being heard.

Everything was suddenly quiet. Fin knew the stranger would have seen the crab pot and the tomahawk – *the tomahawk*. He imagined a bush murderer raising the axe and chopping it down hard, cutting into his shoulder. Or maybe it was Deirdre, the woman who had tried to run over his mum. And it seemed obvious now. If Deirdre was going to look for them, she'd look at Gran's first. Her address wouldn't be hard to find. She had probably already finished off his mum, Gran and Josie. And now she'd run through the bush to cross the last name off her list. He was the last one alive in his family and, if he was going to survive, he'd have to fight back. Running would do no good with all these hills around. And she probably had her big ridgeback with her, and it was making all the noise down the hill.

'Golden Boy?'

Fin scrambled out of his hiding place. He could feel little bits of dirty crab guts in the wrinkles where his toes joined his feet.

Rory was there on the rock, closer than Fin had expected. He had the tomahawk held high with both hands, ready to strike.

'Cripes! I thought a murderer had got you. Why were you hiding?'

'I didn't know who it was.'

'What the jolly hell happened here?'

'I checked the pot. There were two in there. I got them up here and I was going to chop them. I caught two.'

'Well, it wasn't really you who caught them. I was the one who baited the pot, actually. Where are they?'

'I couldn't do it without you.'

'So you let them both go?'

Fin hesitated, then nodded. The lie had slipped out and now he couldn't take it back.

'That's classic, Golden Boy. Two again! You must be good luck.'

'I brought some sausage. It looks really stinky. We can bait it and put the pot back out now. Where were you, anyway?'

'Two crabs!'

Fin persisted. 'Where were you?'

Rory spoke casually, like it wasn't a big deal. 'Up visiting my mum.'

'Where?'

'In the country. She had her graduation. She's going to be able to make heaps of money now. And...' Rory stopped, like he was thinking of something he wasn't supposed to talk about.

Fin pulled the mushy newspaper out of his pocket and held it out to show Rory. 'Anyway, this sausage looks really stinky.'

'Like Pop says, it's just the ticket.'

Up to that point, it hadn't really occurred to Fin that it was strange Rory lived alone with his grandpa.

Rory removed his shoes and baited the pot at the water's edge. They walked out through the shallow water, Rory carrying the pot and Fin trailing with the slimy rope and milk bottle. When they reached the edge of the mud bar where the cooler, deeper water of the river ran, Rory held the pot out to Fin. 'You set it. You're good luck. And you owe me two runaway crabs.'

'They didn't run away. I let them go.' Fin launched the pot out and wiggling bubbles spiralled up as it sank.

~

Fin turned on the tap in the bathroom sink and the cool water ran down the sole of his foot. He felt a panicked sense of urgency to hide any evidence of what he had done, but the sink was so high that he had to stretch up onto the ball of his other foot to wash away the dirt and any leftover crab mush. He overbalanced and fell hard into the old green bath. He reached out for the little ceramic soap dish and it snapped off in his hand, making a horrible grinding sound as it grazed its way down.

'What are you doing in there?' Gran tried the handle, but Fin had slid the little silver latch across to lock the door. 'Griffin, are you all right?' She began shoving at the door.

'Yes, Gran. I just fell into the bath.'

'I know you're up to something in there. Open this door!'

Fin hauled himself back up onto his feet. He unlatched the door and Gran pushed her way in. She looked in each corner of the room as if she was searching for something he'd tried to hide before settling her pale blue eyes on him.

He held up the broken soap dish. 'I'm sorry, Gran. I only bumped it. But it came right off.' He handed her the broken chunk of porcelain.

She weighed it in her hand as if she was deciding whether to keep it. 'Oh well. It's only one more broken thing.' She carried it out and Fin closed the door. Rather than risking another fall, he used a scrunch-up of thin toilet paper to wipe between his toes and clear the remaining crab mush away.

When he entered the bedroom, Lindy was sitting with her back to him on his pump-up bed with her rune tiles laid out in front of her. She gathered them up quickly when she heard him. He couldn't see them all but he clearly saw ᚺ, the tile that comes when you can't go back, and Ⴤ – *the life-and-death rune.*

Lindy held the little cloth bag out to him. 'Take these away. Don't let Mummy throw them, little man. They do me no good.' She flopped facedown onto his mattress and lay there breathing deeply for a moment, then flipped over onto her back, opened her eyes and looked at each corner of the room. 'I hate purple. Don't you?'

Fin knew, if Lindy told Gran she wanted to change it, there would be a fight over choosing the colour. 'I don't know, Mum. It's just like that.'

'Come here.'

She opened her arms and he lay on top of her. He could see her heart beating in a little blue vein on the side of her head. He tried not to wriggle too much as he tucked the bag of rune tiles under her bed.

'There's something about the air in the place. It always feels…too close.'

'Yeah. Not like Gustav's. When are we going back?'

'It's not even Christmas yet.'

Fin knew Christmas was supposed to be a happy time. But he also knew there would be arguments over how he and Lindy could be 'improved', and more of Lindy's tears, and Josie sitting outside all day, and tea poured out windows. He wanted the road home. Gustav's didn't need improving.

CHAPTER FIVE

The sausage bait hadn't worked. It had only been stripped into stringy ribbons of skin. Rory said it was yabbies; they are small enough to get through the spaces in the wire. He baited the pot with a chicken neck and tossed it back into the water. They climbed up the hill through the sticky heat of the bush.

Rory perched on a rock about halfway up and pointed out into the valley. Fin could see an arrow-shaped line of silver-grey over the horizon. There were three thick columns of gnarled cloud pushing up into the sky above it.

Rory pointed high. 'Thunderheads. And it's a nor'easter so it'll be a thumper.'

The last time he'd heard the word 'nor'easter' was after a really big one up at Gustav's. Lindy loved storms. They'd pulled off their shoes and crunched their way out into the hailstones. Fin remembered looking at the blue of the ice against the grass and then up at the suddenly clear sky. His toes were so cold they ached, and he'd climbed onto the bonnet of the car to get some warm blood back into them. He watched Lindy scoop up handfuls of the melting hailstones and rub them on her bare arms like she was washing herself. The electricity had gone out, so they sat in quiet candlelight after the storm and ate a whole big tub of half-melted frozen yoghurt for dinner. Lindy had said, 'It was a nor'easter,' as she licked her spoon.

Rory turned to run up the hill. 'We'd better get back before it hits. I could murder a sandwich anyway.'

Fin had noticed that Rory didn't talk like the kids that lived up at Old Bin. He seemed to use different words for everything.

Fin followed him over the rock ledge, through the tunnel in the bush and onto the lawn at the back of Rory's house.

'You wait here. Pop doesn't like people... I mean, he doesn't like them coming in.'

Fin sat down on the soft grass and watched the storm move closer. The tall thunderheads seemed to approach in a coordinated relay, first one and then another pulling ahead. He could hear thunder echoing in the narrow valley.

Rory appeared with two untidy white-bread sandwiches on a plastic chopping board. 'Wrap your laughing gear around that.' Rory began trying to stuff the whole sandwich into his mouth.

Fin took a bite and tasted the sweet sourness of tomato sauce.

'Pickles and tomato sauce. It's my own recipe. Pop says I should put it in a cookbook.'

'Or maybe on the internet.'

'Pop doesn't like the internet.'

A sudden gust of wind surged through the tops of the trees below. The rain followed heavy and fat just as Fin was finishing his final mouthful. Although the wind was warm, the rain was ice-cold.

'What do you reckon? We ride it out?'

Fin didn't know what Rory meant. 'All right.'

Rory reached out and intertwined his fingers with Fin's. They squeezed their hands tight, sitting with their faces angled down against the stinging rain. The wind and wet washed over them like ocean waves, and the lightning seemed to fry the heavy air before each roll of thunder. Fin held tighter to Rory's hand, as though he might be washed away without their combined weight to hold them down.

The storm moved overhead, lightning and thunder arriving as one. The light was blinding and Fin's ears rang.

'Whoa!' Rory screamed.

The wind stopped and the rain grew drizzly.

Rory untwined his fingers from Fin's and wiped the rain out of his eyes. 'I told you it was going to be a thumper.'

Their wet clothes clung to their skin.

A happy chorus of frogs began knocking and croaking. Fin heard the door open behind them and turned to see the pink face of an old man. He had close-cropped silver hair and was wearing a grey tracksuit. 'Boy, get out of it. You'll jolly well catch a death.'

Rory pushed past and went inside without saying anything. Pop's face was expressionless. He looked at Fin without speaking.

Fin held out the wet chopping board. 'Thank you for the sandwich.'

Pop took the chopping board and stepped inside. Fin walked away, noticing the two patches of dry grass where his and Rory's bums had been. He crawled through Rory's tunnel in the bush.

Josie was smoking on the back patio. 'You look like a drowned rat, twice drowned. Best not let your mother see you like that. She's got enough on her plate with…' She pointed towards the house.

Fin could hear the straining voices of Gran and Lindy in the living room.

'You're always telling me to get a job, Mum. And then when an opportunity like this comes up, you won't support me.'

'But, dear, that's not what you're asking. I do support you. You've got my full support. But you're not asking me to support you, you're asking me to give you money.'

'It would only be a loan.'

'Asking me to loan you money then. Who are these people, anyway?'

'They've been around for ages.'

Fin pulled off his wet T-shirt. 'What's going on?'

Josie took the T-shirt and began wringing the water out of it. She spoke with her cigarette between her lips. 'You know how they are. They're going to kill each other one day with all this. It's heart-attack stuff.' Josie stretched Fin's T-shirt over the edge of the little table. She took the cigarette out of her mouth and blew the smoke away from him. 'Nothing for you to worry about.'

After an almost silent dinner of shepherd's pie and cauliflower cheese, Lindy and Fin retreated to their room. Lindy flopped onto the pump-up with all her clothes on and explained that she'd found an 'amazing opportunity'. She'd met a lady who makes heaps of money selling vitamins from home. 'Not the chemist ones. These are more natural vitamins that really work because they haven't had all the effectiveness processed out of them.'

Fin lay down beside her. He knew of a couple of places Lindy had worked – the supermarket and then the pub in Ballina. And she'd worked as a school cleaner, and at the shop at Old Bin. Fin had loved the days she worked at the supermarket; she'd always bring him home a special treat. But the jobs never lasted. Something always happened, an argument, something broken or gone missing that wasn't her fault. She had tried making kids' clothes to sell at the markets, but it turned out the stalls were too expensive, so the kids' clothes stayed on hangers around the house and in boxes in the laundry. The veggie garden and the cheap rent at Gustav's meant they could manage on Lindy's government payments.

'You have to spend money to make money. You have to buy the vitamins for a start. And get business cards printed. You know, start-up costs. But once you get going you can sell the vitamins for two or three times what they cost you. It's called wholesale. You should've seen this woman's car.'

'But what's the fight about then?'

'Gran won't help me with the start-up money. It's only twelve hundred, and I'd pay her back after the first week. Shannon, the woman with the car, makes three thousand a week, and she does it all from home so there's no overheads. Well, almost no overheads.'

The word 'overheads' reminded him of the big powerlines up on crisscross metal towers that ran along the ridge near Gustav's. Each one looked like a giant goat's head, with two horns and little ears sticking out. They had so much electricity in them that the wires hummed.

'What's overheads?'

'It means, you know, buying things, bills and stuff.'

'Why can't Shannon just lend you the money?'

'Business doesn't work like that. I've already booked my meeting with her. She's so busy, and she's especially made time for me before Christmas. I can't cancel. She's coming on Wednesday to do my business plan. Then we'll see. It's such great timing with everything. It will have to work out. No such thing as a coincidence.'

An involuntary burp bubbled out of him and he tasted the creamy saltiness of the cauliflower as well as a hint of Rory's tomato sauce. He knew that he probably wouldn't see Rory again if Lindy and Gran had a big fight, and the thought of it was so upsetting it was scary.

'Ribbit. Ribbit. You sound like a cane toad.' Lindy spoke with a growly cane-toady voice.

'Ribbit,' Fin croaked back.

Lindy pulled him into a tight hug. 'Thank you, little man. You make all this stuff…worth it.'

CHAPTER SIX

It was five days till Christmas. The morning air was sticky by the time Fin woke up. Lindy was already up and she was wearing her nice clothes, a black skirt and white shirt with the sleeves half rolled up. When Fin asked her where she was going, she said, 'Just to see a man about a dog.' Fin hated it when Lindy disappeared like this. At Old Bin, when she got home from these vague journeys, there would usually be a new problem.

Josie invited Fin to sit on the patio. She brought her little radio out, and they listened to classical music while she blew smoke into the back of the fan. Fin told her about Rory's sandwich recipe and offered to make them both one, but Josie said there were no pickles in the house because they 'repeat on' Gran.

He made himself a tomato sauce sandwich and rolled his golf ball between his bare feet, checking the backyard again and again for any sign of Rory. He thought about climbing through the tunnel in the bush and knocking, but Rory had said that Pop didn't like visitors.

'Waiting for your friend?' Josie asked.

'Yes. Rory.'

'I know. That's a nice name for a boy. You seem to miss him a whole lot all of a sudden.'

'Yes.' Fin remembered how he'd felt when Rory had disappeared the first time, like his stomach had been cut out.

'Friends are good. About as good as it gets, I'd say. Well, maybe marriage is better. Yes, finding someone you want to marry is even better. They're like a friend but you get to live in the same house.'

Fin could tell Josie was missing her husband, Gran's dad. 'If it's better, I'd like to marry Rory.' The idea filled him with a warm feeling, like runny sunlight. 'Boys can get married, can't they?'

Josie thought for a moment before speaking. 'Not here. I heard something about them changing the rules, but it's still only in New Zealand.'

The conversation went quiet.

'Your great-granddaddy was happy as a pig whacking those things all day.' She pointed down to Fin's golf ball. 'He used to get me out sometimes when we were living up at the Harbour.'

Coffs Harbour – *the Harbour* – was Lindy's happy place. She was always in a hurry when she got behind the wheel of a car, but she took her time at the Harbour. And she made a point of talking about Fin's great-granddad whenever they passed through. It seemed deliberate, as if she was trying to keep his memory alive by putting stories of him into Fin's head. Each time they were passing, Lindy would park at the beach and she'd stomp her bare feet in the sand so it squeaked and clucked; she said Great-Granddaddy told her there were chickens buried there.

They'd buy banana bread and look in the windows of the real estate agents. Fin knew she dreamed of moving to the Harbour, but Old Bin was as close as they could afford.

'I couldn't see much point in it. All that aggravation just to hit a little ball into a hole. But he always made up for it with lunch afterwards.' Josie winked at Fin.

'You still miss him, Josie? Great-Granddaddy?'

'Every day.' Josie took a draw on the cigarette and blew it out in a slow stream into the back of the fan. 'Funny thing is, I'm the older of the two of us now. Doesn't seem right.' Josie looked out into the far distance of the valley. 'I talk to him sometimes. It still feels like he can hear me. You'll know what I mean one day. Some things *are* real even when you know they aren't.'

'So you think Great-Granddaddy can hear you, in heaven or whatever?'

'I don't know about heaven and all that...' Josie stopped herself. 'You'd study it at school, wouldn't you? Evolution?'

'I know the stuff about the old monkeys. Not about heaven, just the science part.'

'I don't know that there is any other part.'

It seemed strange to Fin that Josie smoked if she believed in science.

'God's supposed to hear you when you pray, isn't he? So maybe Great-Granddaddy can hear you too.'

'His hearing was never that good. Anyway, I think those blasted caterpillars eating up my nasturtiums at the front know as much about all this as I do.'

'But Gran and you go to church.'

'Your gran goes. She sits there. But there's daylight between your gran and me on most things.' Josie paused, like she was deciding whether to continue. 'It just doesn't seem to fit together with the other things I know, that's all. And the more you hear on the news about the things they're finding, genetics and all that, the less room there seems to be for angels and devils. And all the terrible singing about it.' She stubbed out her cigarette. 'Don't think for a minute I'm telling you what you ought to believe. Not likely. I'm just telling you the opposite. I don't have a clue. I'd ask the caterpillars if I were you.'

Fin looked down into the narrow valley, and he could see hints of the river through the gaps in the gum trees. He tried to imagine how God would have done it. How he would have added all those details, put the bones in the fish and the shells on the crabs. And made the trees breathe out just the right air for animals. He imagined a hand descending from the sky holding a paintbrush with multicoloured bristles. The whole thing seemed pretty unlikely. But maybe it didn't matter if the story was real. Because, if people thought God was always watching, they wouldn't do bad things. He didn't feel like God was watching when he bashed that crab, but he sort of felt like Rory was watching.

The words tumbled out of him. 'But if there's no heaven or hell or anything then it wouldn't really matter what you do, would it?'

Josie's eyes softened. 'When you get to my age, it doesn't do any good thinking about questions like that. They just rattle round and round in your head until they make you dizzy. And the last thing these crumbly bones need is me dizzy. Anyway, I'm old. I'm not the right person to work out the answers anymore for that. But, knowing you, you're the sort of person who just might.'

'Golden Boy!'

Fin felt his stomach leap. Rory was on all fours, pulling himself onto the grass through the bush.

'Rory!'

'Tell your grandma or whatever she is that there's no use feeding me. I'm all full up from breakfast.' He held his hand out towards Josie like he was stopping traffic.

Josie nodded towards Fin as though the name made sense to her. 'Golden Boy.'

Fin looked up at Josie with wide, hopeful eyes.

She nodded and reached for another cigarette. 'Off you go.'

Fin discarded his golf ball, and the two boys ran across the lawn towards the bush.

'You be careful down there with no shoes on,' Josie called. 'Could be redbacks.'

Rory sat down on the grass to pull his shoes off. Fin took it as a powerful display of friendship, and it gave him the runny-sunlight feeling. Was it love? If Fin was going to get bitten by redbacks, Rory wanted to be bitten too.

Rory was more cautious today over the knobbed sticks and leaves of the path. When they pulled up the pot, the bait was gone and all they'd managed to catch was a black eel. Rory untied the gate and tipped the pot until the eel slapped onto the surface and disappeared below.

Rory baited the pot with a chicken neck, and they moved back to the gum-tree shade of the rock. Fin thought Rory might hurry off as usual. But, instead, he lay back on the cool surface. Fin lay down too, making sure to stay between Rory and the little crab grave. He'd thought about coming down to bury the crab properly so there was no chance of Rory discovering the lie, but the thought of having to scrape up the mushy corpse was too upsetting.

'Did you know all eels come from the same place?' said Rory, looking up at the gum leaves.

'What do you mean? The same river?'

'I don't know if it's a river. I think it's an island maybe. Yeah, they all come from the same place. All over the world. All the eels come from the same island then they swim all over the world and they go back to that island to have babies. I think it might be America.'

'So you think that eel we caught was swimming back to America?'

'Could be. Anyway, he was American either way. He could have been swimming back.'

'Sounds like a long way.'

'Well, it can't be that far if that eel swam here, and not if he has to go all the way back again. It couldn't be that far. There's more muscle in one of my feet than in a whole eel. I've seen it on a map. It doesn't look that far.'

Fin looked down at Rory's feet. He imagined the eel folded into the shape of a foot and he thought that Rory was probably right.

'My mum read it in a book about eels. She reads heaps of books.' Rory looked at Fin as though he was expecting some sort of challenge about his mum.

'My mum reads too. All about the stars and runes.'

'Ruins?'

'Runes. They tell the future.'

'Oh. That must be handy.'

'Where's your mum?' Fin wanted to understand, but he sensed it was a sore point for Rory. 'It's just you and Pop in there, isn't it?'

Rory's jaw tightened and the muscles in his neck strained. 'I already told you. She's in the country at college.'

'So you have to go up to the country again then? I mean for Christmas.'

'No. There's no Christmas happening this year.' Rory paused to assess Fin's reaction to the idea. 'It makes sense, though. She'll save heaps of money getting a ride straight to the music festival rather than coming down first. If she came for Christmas, then she'd have to fly up, and plane tickets are absolutely murder this time of year.'

'Yeah, makes sense.'

'It doesn't mean I have to like it, though.'

Fin wasn't sure what he was supposed to say. 'No.'

'I *hate* Christmas, anyway, especially this Christmas.'

Fin couldn't help feeling a little pang of sadness. Now that he'd met Rory, it was looking like it might be Fin's best Christmas ever. His worst Christmas had been two years earlier, when Gran and Lindy had their last big fight and they'd stayed at the hostel. When he and Lindy had arrived at the hostel, Fin asked if they should text Santa to let him know their plans had changed. Lindy sounded like Gran when she'd said, 'It won't be necessary.' One of the other guests dressed up as Santa in the morning, but he was so drunk by lunch that Lindy wouldn't let Fin sit on his lap.

The boys continued looking up through the blanket of gum leaves to the big summer sky. The sound of the cicadas swelled, and Fin felt the pressure of the silence between them. He had to say something, and it almost didn't matter what. 'I know what you mean about Christmas. I sort of hate Christmas too.'

'I think we're on the same page with that one. I like you, Golden Boy. You're a realist.'

Fin felt like he grew a little taller in that moment.

The silence between them returned and Fin worried that Rory might spring onto his muscular feet and disappear up the path into the house that didn't like visitors. He needed something interesting to say, something similar to Rory's thing about eels. He thought of some of his mum's books, but they were about astrology and runes and harnessing power. 'Did you know boys can only get married in New Zealand? Not in Australia.'

'That sounds like a jolly silly rule to me.'

'Yeah. Jolly silly.' Fin didn't feel right saying 'jolly' the way that Rory did all the time. He kept talking so it didn't stand out. 'Do you want to get married?'

'What? To you? Well, I don't know... I suppose, if you really want to. Yeah, okay, I'll marry you if you want. But it'd be good if it was before Christmas.'

Fin had meant 'do you want to get married ever' or 'do you want to get married one day'. He hadn't expected Rory to take it as a proposal. And now he had said yes.

'Oh, okay then...' Fin had no idea what to say. 'I suppose we'd have to... I'm not sure we'd be able to.' He dreaded disappointing Rory.

'I've got a boat. You should see it. It's a beauty. It should do the trick.' Rory gave Fin a confident thumbs up.

'How far do you think New Zealand is? I mean, how long do you think it would take in a boat?' Fin thought this would be enough to dismiss the idea.

'It doesn't look that far on the map. As the crow flies anyway. Just leave early.'

'Do you know which way it is?'

'By the looks it's due east. It looks pretty much straight east. And that's where the sun comes up. So, if we leave early, we just paddle straight for the sun. Anyway, your grandmas would have internet, wouldn't they? We don't. Pop won't have it in the house. You could print out a map to make sure.'

'Yeah, Gran's got internet.' Fin was concerned by Rory's use of the word 'paddle'. He'd assumed Rory was talking about a motorboat.

Rory stood up and began pacing back and forth on the rock. 'Okay, so you sort out the map, and I'll drag the boat out of the garage, pump it up and check for holes. I'll bring my puncture kit too.' Rory looked up at the trees. 'Yep, that should be it. How about you bring something to eat? And a bottle of water. Maybe two bottles, just in case.'

Rory sprang onto the muddy start of the path home. 'Tomorrow morning then, early. Don't forget to print out the map. That's important.' He began running up the hill. His movements were jerky with excitement and he was visibly trembling as he turned back to Fin. 'Getting married in New Zealand. Classic! It's about time for a big mission.' He disappeared up the path.

Fin waited. He sensed he wasn't supposed to follow Rory because they already had their tasks.

Rory appeared again, half squatting between shrubs. 'You coming? Or are you just going to sit there like a squashed crab?'

Fin's stomach sank – *he knows*. The shame of his lie filled him with a panicky heaviness. He promised himself he'd never let Rory down again.

'Anyway, whatever you're doing down there, keep this New Zealand stuff on the quiet. People get jumpy about big missions.'

Fin found it hard to believe that Rory was serious, but he remembered what Josie had said about talking to Great-Granddaddy – *some things are real even when you know they aren't*. So, until Rory changed his mind, Fin was determined to play his part.

~

He ended up having to ask Gran for the password to get into her computer. Josie didn't know it. Gran typed it in for him but wouldn't tell him what it was.

'A map? What on earth do you want a map for? And of what terrain precisely?'

'Just of Australia. Australia and New Zealand actually. I'm learning where things are. You know, for practice.' Fin knew she'd be suspicious, but he also knew Gran loved nothing more than 'practice'.

The map came out black and white, and it was less detailed than he'd hoped. He could see that New Zealand was directly east of Sydney, and it didn't look that far on paper. Fin suspected that the 'mission' was more of a game for Rory, like he was daring Fin to back down. He felt sick at the thought that they might try. But he was the one who'd accidentally suggested they get married, and Rory had been so nice.

He remembered the sizzle of fear and whispering that had spread through the playground the day a surfer was taken by a shark off Ballina. One of the older boys had shown his teeth and snarled, 'Dinnertime,' and this had prompted a group discussion of the most dangerous time to swim. Eventually they agreed it was early morning, that's when sharks feed.

CHAPTER SEVEN

Fin sat in Lindy's room studying the map. He ran his eyes around the coastline and tried to relate the bumps and dents to places he knew – Sydney, Coffs Harbour, Ballina. He could hear Gran talking in a continuous stream at Josie, saying no-one knew where Lindy was, and she couldn't run off leaving him there without telling them. She repeated words like 'irresponsible' and 'parental' and 'duty'. But he knew that defending his mum would make things worse. Eventually, Fin heard Josie climb up to her bedroom while Gran kept talking at her from the bottom of the stairs.

Lindy returned in the late afternoon, and Fin launched himself into her arms. She was pink and sweaty, and she smelled a bit like a doctor's office. She brushed Fin aside and went straight into a long shower upstairs.

When dinner was ready, Gran sat with her knife and fork in her clenched fists and waited for Lindy.

Josie said, 'I think we can start at least.'

She and Fin began chewing through their food – rissoles and veggies.

When Lindy came down the stairs, she looked calmly at Gran and said, 'Bon appétit.'

Gran stared at Lindy. 'I raised you to a higher standard than this.'

Lindy sat down. 'You first. It's only right that you should have the first dose of any ingredients.'

'Now what are you talking about?' Gran took a mouthful of rissole and pointedly chewed it with her mouth closed. She and Lindy didn't speak again all dinner, but the atmosphere at the table was so full of anger that it felt like they were screaming at each other. Josie tried to lift the mood with comments about the food and the weather; it didn't work.

As night fell, Fin found Lindy in her bed with the sheet wrapped tight around her. He'd decided he had to tell her about New Zealand. He almost hoped she would stop him, or that she might want to join them to escape from Gran.

'Mum?'

'Not now, little man. I'm all worn out.'

~

Rory hadn't said a particular time, so Fin only half slept as he waited for the sound of early-morning buses and for the light of dawn to creep around the curtains. He heard Lindy rising and falling in and out of a deep sleep. There were moments when she whimpered and ground her teeth before her breathing settled back into a slow whistle.

He knew he had to be the first one out of bed or Josie would be smoking on the patio. He made two tomato-sauce sandwiches and wrapped them in foil. Josie was right, there were no pickles. He climbed down over the rocks and gave the sandwiches an extra squeeze for tightness before tucking them under a little overhang. The sun was barely over the ridgeline but he could already feel its warm light on the back of his head.

Each hot second of the morning seemed to last longer than it should. He dawdled in the backyard tossing his golf ball from hand to hand and sat with Josie when she came out to smoke. He'd decided it was too late to tell anyone about the boat trip. They'd have too many questions, and Rory had said he had to keep it secret.

Josie didn't talk much. At one point, he heard Gran making herself a cup of tea and muttering, 'The early bird gets the worm.'

Josie sighed and spoke without looking at Fin. 'She's definitely not all bad. But your gran sure knows how to scratch at people.'

Fin didn't know what to say. Whenever anyone criticised his mum or Gran, they always said '*your* mum' or '*your* gran', like he was somehow responsible.

Fin poked his head into Rory's tunnel through the bush. He began to worry that they may not be able to find east, or just south of east, if the sun got too high in the sky. He watched a young magpie with its new, mottled chest feathers poking around in the grass. It looked like the bird had got there too late and the worms had already gone deeper underground.

'Golden Boy.' Rory's head was poking through the bush. He spoke in a loud whisper, as though Josie wouldn't be able to hear him that way. He beckoned Fin with a dramatic wave of both hands.

Fin hurried over and lay on his belly facing Rory. There were purple shadows under Rory's eyes.

Rory whispered, 'We're going to have to put the En Zed mission on the backburner for today.'

Fin felt his whole body relax.

Rory continued. 'It turns out I've got to see another jolly doctor. But we're a definite for tomorrow. I've checked the boat and she's A-one. Pumped up perfect and no holes. I listened in the morning and the wireless says there's going to be a bit of wind around but no rain. Anyway, I'll catch you up later. I don't know how long this doctor thing is going to take or if they've got to do more tests. Pop said I couldn't eat this morning, but I managed to sneak a couple of pickles. None the wiser.'

'Okay.' Fin wondered if the sandwiches would be safe under the rock ledge until then.

'I'll check you later.' Then Rory added as an afterthought, 'How'd you go with the map?'

'All done.'

'I don't know why he hates it so much. I reckon the internet's all right.' Rory looked down at the golf ball in Fin's hand and gave a thumbs up as he retreated.

Fin's day had become very empty. There was only the prospect of watching endless cricket or daytime TV. He walked back to where Josie was filling in a crossword with a short pencil.

'He's an eccentric fellow, your friend.'

Fin didn't know what eccentric meant.

'How about a touch of fruit salad? Just the thing, I reckon. Your friend won't be joining us for a nibble?'

'No.'

Lindy stayed in bed all morning and got up around lunchtime. She took a long time in the shower, and when Fin went in to say hello, she was sitting under the stream of water, shaving her legs.

'Shannon's coming at two.' She continued with her legs as she spoke. 'We are about to be in business, young man. In business.' It seemed like she repeated the words because she liked the sound of them. Lindy's busy moods often ended in crying, but it was also when she was most fun. Her green eyes would light up as she talked about whatever she was planning.

Fin again thought of telling her about New Zealand, but he decided it could wait until after Lindy's meeting. He knew Gran was saying things and working on ways to 'improve' her, so he didn't want to give her anything else to worry about.

'I've been waiting for something like this. I'm no good down the ladder. It feels so much righter to be my own boss.' She placed the little plastic razor on the floor and stood up to rinse off.

Fin now felt shy if Lindy saw him naked. At school they had said adults aren't supposed to. But she had never hidden her body from him.

She turned off the tap and began squeezing the water out of her hair. 'I've always considered myself a businesswoman, in a way. Chuck me the towel, would you?'

Fin passed her a thin towel.

'Out of my way, Finny. I've got some important getting ready to do.'

Gran and Lindy had another stiff, almost wordless exchange, and Gran announced to the house that she was going out. She grabbed her handbag from the hook by the door, and there was a loud thud as she left. Lindy pushed the couch back and busied herself setting up a meeting table. She'd bought a new blue-paper notepad and a packet of different coloured highlighters. Fin stayed close, stretched out on the carpet watching a shopping talk show as Lindy placed things on the table and then rearranged them. He loved being near her when she was looking forward to something.

She kept checking the time on the microwave, and at 2.15 pm she began to worry that Shannon wouldn't turn up. 'I can't believe it. After everything yesterday.' She sat with her head in her hands looking down at her empty notepad.

The sudden shifts in Lindy's mood were as clear to Fin as the bends in a familiar road. He'd spent almost every minute with her, and he knew her like he knew his own teeth – from the inside. She would be devastated if the woman didn't come. The last time he'd seen her so hopeful was when she'd applied to study speech pathology on the Gold Coast.

She hadn't finished high school, so she had to include a long letter about being a single mother with her application. She read it to Fin to make sure he was okay with what she'd written about him. And when the envelope with the enrolment forms arrived, they bought a bottle of wine, a bag of oversized marshmallows and the local newspaper, so she could check job ads for how much speech pathologists got paid.

She came home with a new notebook, a folder and a 'more studenty' bag. She met a surfing guy, Michael, who came to stay at Gustav's a few times. Then she decided to leave university after a few months because one of the professors hated her, and the money she was spending on petrol wasn't worth it. It was one of Lindy's bluest times. She'd have really long showers, and Fin found some whole pieces of toast on the couch.

There were three sharp knocks on the door. Lindy sprang to her feet, smoothed her hair and spread her lips wide. 'Is there anything in my teeth?'

'Looks good, Mum.'

She hurried to the front door and Fin moved into the kitchen to make himself a tomato-sauce sandwich. He peeked back into the living room to see who had arrived.

The woman, Shannon, was a slim, bright-blonde-haired lady carrying a cardboard box. She was wearing black pants and a white shirt, with a dark blue jacket over the top.

Lindy called to him. 'Finny!'

He hurried out and stood beside her.

'This is my son, Griffin. I told you about him.'

'Nice to meet you.' Shannon shifted the box awkwardly onto her hip and reached out to shake Fin's hand. He felt the soft, oily texture of her palm, like she'd just put cream on. Her face was covered in a thick layer of make-up that creased around the corners of her mouth.

Fin went back to the kitchen and looked through the little glass panels in the back door to where Josie was sitting on her patio. He finished making his sandwich quietly so he could hear what Shannon was saying.

The meeting was about 'expenses' and 'returns', and they spent most of it scrolling through things on Shannon's iPad. Fin stayed in the kitchen to eat and thought about Rory going to the doctor and maybe having a medical test. It was probably a neck test because he had those spots.

Shannon explained how the vitamin business worked. Each new business member paid their start-up amount for their vitamins and the 'recruiter' got to keep some of the money. She said that, at the start, you had to work hard selling vitamins and building 'hype'. The hype was the important part because it was how you attracted recruits. And once you had a few recruits, you could make money without doing anything because each recruit had to pay their recruiter some money every month.

Shannon said, 'So you were able to raise the capital for the start-up?

Fin felt his stomach tighten. He'd assumed Shannon had already agreed to lend Lindy the money. He felt sorry and a little ashamed that his mum would have to ask for a loan after Shannon had already been through the explanation. Fin wished he had the money to give her, maybe from being a speech pathologist or something. He peeked around the doorframe to check that Lindy was all right.

'Yes, of course.' Lindy removed an envelope she had tucked under her thigh and counted aloud, laying $50 notes on the table until she got to twelve hundred dollars. Then she tucked the money back into the envelope and handed it to Shannon.

'Just before we finalise that, there's a bit of paperwork to attend to. As you do.' Shannon said the word 'paperwork' with a chuckle. She produced a large stack of paper with tags hanging out the sides. 'I've marked where to sign. By all means have your lawyer look over it prior. That's, if you like?'

Lindy hesitated, as if she didn't expect to have to sign anything. 'All good.' She flicked through each page marked with a yellow tag and signed with her new pen.

'Pleasure doing business with you.' Shannon tucked the papers and the envelope into her bag.

Lindy giggled as she stood up. 'Pleasure doing business.'

'There's an information sheet for each of the products in the box. Not word for word, but you need to memorise them. Our clients are sophisticated consumers, and they often have questions. Thanks a *lot*, Google.' She let out a short, rattling laugh as she gathered her things and moved towards the door. 'You've got my details. I'll arrange to get you the rest of the product asap. I'm so glad this worked out.'

'Me too.'

Shannon opened the door and turned to shake Lindy's hand. 'Welcome to the next chapter of your life!'

'Oh, I feel like I'm going to cry. Thank you. Thank you so much.' Lindy placed her hand on her heart as she closed the door.

Fin ran into the living room. 'Where'd you get all that money, Mum?'

'You know me, little man. I'm resourceful.'

Fin knew, no matter how much he pestered her, she wouldn't tell him. He was happy for her, but hearing Shannon say 'next chapter of your life' made it even clearer that they weren't going back to Gustav's. There wouldn't be many sophisticated consumers in Old Bin.

CHAPTER EIGHT

As they rounded the first bend, Fin saw the sparkling surface of the river open up to the left and right. Rory was paddling at the front, steering them away from the banks. The sky was bright and Fin began to worry that the sun was already getting too high to guide them to New Zealand. He knew it was bad for your eyes to look at the sun, but he kept stealing glimpses as it broke the line of trees on the hill. Even if they took longer than expected to reach the sea, he was pretty sure he could remember where it had been when it was near the horizon.

The water was rippling through the flimsy plastic skin of the bottom of the boat. They'd left their shoes on Crab Rock and it felt as though the river was stroking his feet. Although the bottom was thin, the main part of the boat was pumped up so firmly that it only sagged slightly as he leant out for each stroke with his little paddle.

Fin had the map and the sandwiches wrapped up tight in a plastic bag at the back of the boat. Rory had two bottles of water and a can of diet lemonade. If he had been joking about trying to make it to New Zealand, or trying to test Fin, he gave no indication of it now. He was calm and focused on the task ahead.

The banks either side were steep here, silver-green with gum trees. The trunks changed direction in knobbly turns and the branches twisted around each other as if they were fighting. The boat rounded another rocky bend and the river opened up even more. In the distance, Fin could see the pylons of a high road bridge stretching down into the water.

'Boats ahead.' Rory used his paddle to point at two dinghies with fishing rods sticking out of them. His outstretched paddle sent a trickle of water down his arm and into the boat. The singing of the cicadas on either side of the river seemed to suddenly increase. Rory looked back. Fin nodded – *I'm still okay.*

The heavy black powerlines that ran between the high ridges, across the huge expanse of the river, were now directly above them. On the far side they were fastened to a concrete structure dug into the top of the hill. It had four huge columns on it like a shopping-centre car park that had been pulled out of the ground and turned upside down. It reminded Fin of the German buildings he'd seen in the old photos at Gustav's. Lindy had told him they were built chunky like that so people can't shoot holes in the walls. The curving black of the powerlines reminded him of the goat-head-shaped metal structures that held up the powerlines near Gustav's. And he wondered, if he kept sight of the wires, and walked and walked, whether he'd eventually make it back there.

The wind carried them closer to the tall pylons of the bridge. Fin pulled his paddle in and let Rory guide them into the widest gap between the blocks of concrete supporting the three centre legs of the bridge. The surface of the water seemed to shiver just as the wind hit them, pushing the boat left towards the concrete. The front swung around. Rory strained to drag them away from a collision. 'Be ready to fend us. Get your paddle up. Don't lean out far or we'll tip.'

Fin held his paddle out at shoulder height. He watched the muscles in Rory's skinny arms flex and slither as he pulled against the water. The wind seemed to push harder still. The back of the boat was now on a collision course with the concrete. Fin could see that each side was encrusted with the pearly-white of splintered oyster shells. He could also see that, rather than going straight down, the concrete supports flared out under the waterline, so they were now only a metre or so away from the shells.

Rory shouted, 'You! You! You!'

Fin drove the thin edge of his paddle hard against the corner of the concrete island. He felt the boat continue unchanged beneath him, and he was nearly pushed over the other side. He gripped tighter. The oar shaft flexed like it was about to snap.

76

Rory kept shouting, 'You! You! You! You!'

Fin imagined the jagged edges of the shells, then hissing bubbles bursting out into the water as the boat was cut open and turned into flimsy plastic beneath them. He imagined the blood on his knees and his hands as he tried to pull himself up the oyster shells. And it was almost as if he could see the trail of his blood ribboning down the river to the noses of the sharks that would come hunting them.

He pushed harder and heard a sandy, crackling sound as the paddle stretched. He felt the boat lurch suddenly and there was a gentle lifting as the wind crept under the right side of the boat. Rory leant back to balance them. Fin used all his strength to push.

The boat shifted forward. The paddle straightened and they were flung past the bridge onto the rippling surface of the river beyond. Fin pulled his paddle into the boat. He could feel his heart pumping in his neck and he was breathing hard.

Rory laughed. 'Whoo! That was a close one.' He mimed wiping the sweat off his brow. 'That was all you. You saved us!'

The boat continued along the river with the wind behind it and they didn't need to paddle. Although he was the younger of the two of them, and Rory was stronger, Fin had been strong enough when it mattered. Whatever they were doing, it felt like the sort of thing married people do.

They both leant back against the squishy sides of the boat and let the wind carry them. Fin could feel the heat of the plastic warming his T-shirt. It was a reminder that the sun was getting too high now to be useful for navigation.

They started paddling again and passed a boat ramp and a crowded marina. Fin felt the muscles in his shoulders fatiguing, and the neck of his T-shirt was soaked with sweat. As they rounded the next bend, the river presented them with a choice of two branches.

'Which way is it? Got your map?' Rory swung around and took the opportunity to rest for a moment with his paddle across his lap.

'I can have a look. But all this is so tiny on there.' Fin pulled his paddle inside the boat and retrieved the map from the plastic bag. 'Nup. There's nothing. This just shows Sydney as right on the edge of Australia.'

'So what do you reckon? Left or right?'

Each time Fin needed to work out his left from his right, he had to think back to when he'd first learnt. He was about four, and Gran had taken him to see the Christmas displays at a department store. As they were riding up the escalator to where Santa was having photos, Fin had asked, 'How do you know which way is right?'

Gran's little handbag had swung off her forearm as she pointed. 'You just know. That way is right.'

It wasn't until later in the day that she explained that right and left changed depending on which way you were facing. Thinking back to the two of them on that escalator was still the only way he could tell. 'I don't know. I've been keeping an eye on the sun and I reckon east is more that way.' Fin pointed.

'Good. Me too. That seems to be the way the water wants to go.'

They steered the boat past a huddle of white yachts tied to moorings near the point. Fin heard the ropes tink, tink, tinking against their masts as little waves gently rocked the boats. The sound felt safe and familiar. He remembered it from the caravan park, when his dad was there.

Rory hadn't spoken for a long time when he looked back and said, 'I could already murder one of those sandwiches and we haven't even cleared the heads.'

'You can have one if you want. I made two but there's no pickle.'

'They'll keep. I'd like to feel like we're getting somewhere first. We might need them later.' Rory's eyes rested on Fin longer than they needed to. 'How you holding up, Golden Boy?'

'Fine. I'm fine.'

The quiet way Rory kept checking on him was a reminder that Rory would always be a bit older. And no matter how long they knew each other, Fin would never catch up. He felt glad that he'd been able to tell Rory about boys not being allowed to marry. And then he thought about how Josie had said that, although she had been younger than Great-Granddaddy when he was alive, she was the older one now.

The sun burnt the boys from above. Fin could feel thin skin flaking off his bottom lip, but he didn't want to be the first one to reach for a drink. As Rory had said, they might need it later. There were more boats now, and the ridges and slopes of the hills leading down to the water were lined with big houses with white walls and clay-coloured tiles on their roofs.

A yacht moved across their path and a young man in sunglasses with his shirt off and muscles showing gave them a shrugging thumbs up to check that they were okay. The boys responded by lifting their thumbs high into the sky and the yacht moved past, leaving a rippling trail. Rory and Fin paused to watch each of the little bow waves slip under the thin plastic of their boat.

The river opened out into a bay and there was another, lower road bridge on the far side. Fin watched a bus passing over and he could hear the distant revving of its engine as it pushed hard up the steep hill.

'That's the ticket, I reckon. We head for that.' Rory pointed at the bridge.

'Yeah, looks right.' Fin was happy for Rory to do the navigating.

They paddled for the bridge. The hill on the left rose steeply from the worn sandstone of the shoreline. The houses were a mix of brown brick and white paint with balconies and tinted glass. As the boat drew closer to the bridge, Fin saw a line of yachts and white cruisers at another marina, and he could hear the rhythm of cars and trucks rolling over the joins in the road. There was a yellow warning sign low down – *NARROW*

CHANNEL KEEP RIGHT. The thumping and rolling of car and truck tyres above echoed in a pulsing roar, and they were careful to steer well clear of the centre pylons as they moved into the shadow of the bridge.

The brightness of the day stabbed at Fin's eyes as they came out into the light and, as they passed another line-up of yachts, some tiny sailing boats appeared from between a row of black pylons. Each of the boats had a bright blue and yellow sail and a white hull no bigger than Rory's inflatable. They were being led out by a man in a runabout. He was wearing a black cap and black reflective sunglasses. When he saw Rory and Fin he raised himself up for a better look. He sat back down and revved his boat towards them.

Rory craned his neck over his shoulder. 'Let me do the talking.'

Fin nodded, relieved. He felt that his family might understand, because they sort of knew Rory, but he had no idea what explanation he would give a stranger.

As the boat motored towards them, a sudden gust of wind rippled over the surface of the water and a desperate, high-pitched scream rang out. Fin looked and saw that one of the little sailboats had tipped over, and a boy was treading water with his black cap down over his eyes. Another boy was pinned under the sail and was pushing up to free himself.

The man and his boat were close now, but he gunned the engine and turned around sharply. He stopped and cupped his hands around his mouth to shout, 'You cool?'

Fin immediately threw his arm into the air in an exaggerated thumbs up, and Rory did the same. The man zipped back to the capsized boat.

Rory screwed up the whole side of his face in a wink. 'That was a close one.'

They passed the marina. On the left, there was a beach lined with tall pine trees and Fin could smell grilling sausages. It was a delicious contrast to the smell of salt water and boat fuel. Fin felt it in his stomach and began to think that his two-day-old tomato-sauce sandwiches might not be enough for the journey. It also reminded him that all he'd had to eat was a couple of scoops of Josie's fruit salad before she'd waved him off to play with Rory. He'd made a point of hugging her tightly, and she'd said, 'Careful. There's not a lot of squeezing left in these crumbly old bones.' He'd loosened his grip and she'd kissed his head through his spiky hair.

They continued paddling and, suddenly, in a gap between two hills, there was a flat line of blue where the ocean met the sky. Both boys pulled their paddles into the boat and sat looking out. The way forward was clear. They let themselves be carried by the wind.

Rory turned himself around to face Fin. His cheeks and the tip of his nose were pink with sunburn. They should have worn something more substantial than T-shirts and boardshorts. Although they were still inside the mouth of the harbour, it felt like they were a very long way from the shore. For the first time since they'd left the sheltered river near Crab Rock, Fin felt shapes moving through the plastic skin beneath them. All they'd encountered until now was the wake of boats, but these rolling rises and valleys had the unmistakable rhythm of ocean waves.

Two seagulls dived one after the other at the front of the boat. And suddenly, a whole flock converged on the same patch of rough water ahead. They were squawking and calling. More gulls dived towards them, encircling the boat, and they were packed so tightly that birds needed to hurry out of the way as Fin put his paddle in for another stroke.

Fin leant over the side, peering into the water. The surface began splashing and spitting upwards on its own, the same way puddles seem to boil when it hails. But there were no storm clouds, only a few distant puffs of white out to sea.

Fin shouted over the squawking and splashing. 'What is it?'

'I don't know. But it's bad.' Rory leant over to look down into the water.

The word 'bad' seemed to hang in the air. Fin tried to judge which shore would be closer if they had to swim. A slippery shape distorted the plastic bottom of the boat.

Rory looked back and, for the first time, Fin saw genuine fear in his eyes, almost like he might cry.

Rory shouted over the noise. 'Bait ball!'

Fin suddenly understood what was happening. A giant twisting school of fish was rolling like a quivering ball beneath the boat. The bait ball was so big that there was no way they could reach out beyond it with their paddles. Fin plunged his paddle back into the water and the plastic handle vibrated and tugged in his hands as thousands of tiny fish moved past. Rory was whacking and scooping seagulls as he tried to pull them clear. Fin paddled hard, but he was confused by Rory's urgency. How could a few little fish and seagulls hurt them?

The surface of the water seemed to swell and, a couple of paddle lengths from the side of the boat, a long shadow appeared.

'Shark!' The word erupted out of Fin like a sob.

Rory didn't look. He just kept paddling.

The tip of its rubbery dorsal fin broke the surface of the water as it cut into the bait ball and dived beneath the boat. Then it was back on the right side, only an arm's length away.

'Shark!' This time it was Rory.

Fin spun his head around to see that there were two more sharks on the other side of the boat.

There was no point paddling now. The sharks could outswim them in a second. The boys moved to the centre of the boat and sat back-to-back with their paddles pulled in. Fin felt the vibration of Rory's voice through his back.

'If it happens, go for the eyes.'

The plastic skin beneath them writhed and jumped as the bait ball split and reunited each time a shark torpedoed through. There were also other bigger fish, about half the size of the sharks, flinging themselves out of the water. They had a yellow fork in their tails. These fish were coming at the bait ball from below, piercing their way through until they broke the surface and slapped back down into the water, crashing into shouting seagulls as they fell.

The air was thick with birds, swooping and dodging to avoid each other.

'Here it comes!' Rory screamed each word separately.

Fin swivelled his head to see a shark, the biggest one so far, swimming fast towards the front of the boat. Its stumpy fin and the broad grey of the top of its head broke the water. It was aiming straight at them. Rory raised his paddle to strike and Fin imagined the two of them kicking to stay above the water after the shark had torn the boat away, their legs dangling into the bait ball.

The shark lunged at the boat with its beaten, scarred head. Rory let out a belly-deep growl and drove the paddle down hard. The shark seemed stunned by the blow. Rory speared the paddle at it again, this time stabbing at its eye. The shark rolled in the water and dived. The boat was intact. The paddle slipped from Rory's grip and fell onto a seagull in the water.

Rory slumped back into the boat. He squeezed in beside Fin with his eyes closed. 'You'll have to do the next one. My paddle's...'

Fin was blinded by a hissing spray of water. There was the sound of plastic tearing and the boat felt as if it was filling with water. Fin reached out through the blurry brightness of his vision and felt the writhing slipperiness of shark skin.

Rory began shouting, 'Get it out! Get it out! Golden Boy, get it out!'

And, as his vision cleared, Fin could see they were still afloat. But a giant fish had leapt in with them. It had yellowy spines running down towards its tail that were fanning out and then narrowing. Rory lay down and rolled tight against the side while the fish slapped its heavy body against the floor.

Fin let his paddle fall beside him and reached out. The fish was longer than his arm, but it had flipped itself around so that its forked tail was within reach. He remembered the slippery feel of the stealer's tail when he'd rescued it from the mud. This fish was ten times bigger. He snatched at it and wrapped one hand, then the other around its tail, and with a heaving motion, he swung it like a sack. The fish jerked and slipped out of his grip. It bounced off the inflated side of the boat and flip-flopped in a curving arc until it landed right across Rory's face.

'Aaargh!' Rory sat up in a frantic lunge, thrusting at the fish. Fin watched again as the giant fish flew sideways out of the boat and slapped into the crowd of seagulls.

Fin paddled hard; he had to keep swapping from side to side to stop them circling. The noisy fog of birds overhead began to clear and the surface of the black-green water settled. Again, he felt the rising and falling of sea waves beneath them. He looked ahead and could see the edge of Rory's paddle just breaking the water. He hooked it, raising it up just high enough to quickly snatch without touching the water.

The noise and chaos of the bait ball was off to their right now, and some small motorboats began moving towards it from the distant shore. Again, the wind pushed their little inflatable towards the opening in the heads – towards the sea.

Fin lay both the paddles down beside him and reached to where he had tucked his plastic bag. Rory was lying on his back with his arms crossed and his head curled forward, he'd had his eyes closed since he'd pushed the fish out. Fin checked for birds as he unwrapped one of the sandwiches and placed it carefully on Rory's chest. It rose and fell with each of his puffing breaths. Fin tucked the other sandwich away with the map and began a slow paddle towards the sea. He was careful not to dribble water onto Rory as he switched from side to side to keep them straight.

The crashing mob of seagulls was now further behind them, as if the bait ball was trying to move into the shallower safety of the bay. Fin saw a fat man in a black T-shirt and cap casting his fishing rod from a boat towards the birds. He imagined one of the seagulls swooping and screeching against the line after swallowing the hidden hook.

The sun was almost overhead. Fin could see houses and blocks of flats on the headland to the left, and a rusted green and yellow ferry leaving a fragmenting trail behind as it cut through the water. He looked to check on Rory; a single bite had been taken out of the sandwich.

'Nice work there, Golden. You saved us again. I was all out of juice by the time that kingy jumped in.'

It sounded like the right name for a fish that big – *kingy*. The yellow spines along the top looked a bit like a crown.

'Sorry I chucked him on you. His tail was as slippery as a…
It was slippery, anyway.'

'You did what you had to, Golden.' Rory gave him a
subdued thumbs up. 'Not a bad sandwich either. I like the
amount of sauce.' Rory took a big bite and filled his mouth
with bread. In another two bites he'd finished it all. He slowly
sat up and pointed towards the open sea. 'That way?'

'Yep. That way. The sun's high now, but that's where it
came up.'

Fin lifted Rory's paddle and tentatively offered it to him,
almost as a question.

'We've made it this far.' Rory took the paddle and turned to
begin paddling. His shoulders and the back of his neck were
bright pink, and Fin looked to see that his own arms were
equally burnt. Neither of them had thought to bring suncream,
and Rory had even set out without his usual neck-flap cap.

The steady rising and falling of the water increased and
occasionally there was a light tapping as the front of the boat
slapped onto the far side of a wave. It was too far to swim to
shore on either side now. There was a small white lighthouse
to their left, no taller than a normal house. Fin closed his
eyes to lock its position in his memory. It might be useful if
they had to find their way back in the dark. On their right,
a ragged sandstone headland pushed out towards the ocean.
There was a rhythmic fizz of waves against its lower rocks,
and it looked like there would be no way up the cliffs, even if
they could swim that far.

A little blue yacht appeared from behind the headland. Its sails were swollen with wind and it was leaning to one side. Fin could see the figures of a man and a woman on the deck. The woman was wearing a yellow life jacket. She rose to her feet and began waving her arms at them. Her mouth was wide open, as if she was calling out, but there was no sound. All Fin could hear was the steady wind in his ears and the gentle slapping as they went over each wave. He flung his arm in the air in an enthusiastic thumbs up, but he knew they were not okay. There was a sickening knot in his belly now. It would be lunchtime soon and Josie, at least, would notice he was gone.

They stroked their paddles in unison and Rory led the switching of sides, conducting the change with a tilt of his shoulders. As they cleared the headland, the harbour opened up to their right. Fin could see the tall spike of Sydney Tower and the surrounding skyscrapers huddled close like kids cosying up to the tallest boy. Although the depth of the blackish water was intimidating, the postcard look of the city made everything seem nearer and safer.

To their left and right, the surface was littered with the glinting white and silver of boats. But this section of rising and falling blue-black was empty. It was like no boat lingered in this last place before the sea. Rory pulled his paddle in and swivelled around to face Fin. 'Is this...?' Rory stopped abruptly. 'Wow. You're sunburnt, Golden Boy. You're like... You're like a sunset.'

Fin also pulled his paddle into the boat and felt the cool trickling of water on his bare legs. 'You're burnt too. Like a post box or something.'

'Come on, let's keep things professional.'

Fin didn't really know what professional meant, but based on the way Lindy used it, he thought it was something like nice clothes. 'Yep.'

'Anyway, is this, you know, doable?'

'What do you mean?' Fin imagined the possibility of them fixing their eyes on the little lighthouse and paddling back, and then all the way to the mudflat.

'I mean, it seems to be taking a long time. I mean, I don't want to tread on your toes or anything, you're the navigator and you've got that beaut map. But I guess I'm saying… Anyway, the sun's pretty high now.' Rory seemed to give up, like his tongue had run out of petrol. Fin would have given anything to know what Rory wanted him to say.

Rory seemed to find his words again. 'I meant, which way is New Zealand?'

Fin lifted his finger off his paddle and pointed out to the distant blue line where the water met the sky. 'That way.'

'Straight ahead?'

'Yep. I still remember where the sun came up. I closed my eyes when we got started so it's sort of drawn on the insides of my eyelids.'

'So we just go for it?'

Again, Fin wished there was a way of stopping time for a moment. He would crawl over and peer inside Rory's head to look for the correct words. Rory lifted his eyebrows to indicate that Fin was taking too long to answer, and the boat rose and fell with a bigger than usual wave.

'One way or another.' Fin wasn't sure what he was saying until he'd already said it.

Rory's whole face smiled back at him, although no part of it moved. Somehow, Fin had found the words to make Rory happy.

'New Zealand it is then.' He took up his paddle and cut into the water.

Again, Fin began switching from side to side with the wordless guidance of Rory's shoulders.

Suddenly, a wave bigger than all the waves before rose up in front of them. It seemed impossible that it could be so different from the others, like it had come from deeper in the ocean. They both froze, helpless to do anything as the front of the boat lifted. The wave was so steep, it was crested with a line of foamy spill. They rose up and up, steeper and steeper until the front of the boat struck out into the air. As the huge wave moved beneath them, the whole boat seemed to fall from the sky, and Fin felt his bum lifting up off the bottom.

Fin and Rory paddled to try to keep straight. As they slapped back onto the water, it felt like the boat wanted to turn sideways and roll down the back. There was the sound of loud splashing behind them. Fin looked up, expecting to see another big wave.

A giant white motor cruiser bore down on them, just about to hit. Fin pulled his paddle into the boat and hugged his knees. There was no point trying to out-paddle a motorboat. As he watched, he felt his arms shaking with the strain of squeezing so tight. But, just before the two boats collided, the bow of the motor cruiser swung around, and Fin read the blue letters on the hull – *POLICE*.

CHAPTER NINE

The police boat seemed to hold perfectly still in the water as two policemen in dark blue jumpsuits folded down a drawbridge from the back. Rory did a face-scrunching double-blink, which meant – *let me do the talking*. Fin felt his chest rising and falling in short, puffing breaths, and he wondered if they were doing something really wrong, if they were committing a crime.

The boat motored casually beside them as though it was held steady by a big hand under the water. One of the policemen clipped the buckle of a harness across his chest and another fed out rope as the first one walked onto the drawbridge. The policemen looked at the two boys without smiling. There was the low hum of the engines and the intermittent peppering of gravelly words from a police radio. No-one spoke. Fin wanted to give them the thumbs up, or call out, maybe something like 'ahoy!', but he knew that Rory wouldn't like it. Fin remembered hearing something about the 'right to remain silent', and he wondered if that was what the police were doing.

The policeman in the harness twisted around and grabbed Fin under the arms. He lifted him and set him down on the drawbridge. Fin wasn't sure if he'd just been arrested, but he felt his belly relax now that he had something solid under his bare feet. He held on tight to his paddle to make sure he didn't drop it over the side.

The policeman kneeled and pulled the boat alongside. Rory wrapped his hand around the policeman's ankle, climbed out and lay down on the drawbridge looking up at the sky. Still no-one spoke, they just knew what to do. It seemed like this sort of thing happens all the time.

The policeman pinched the plastic skin of Rory's boat and lifted it out of the water. 'Are you two all right?' He had light brown skin and a high, almost boyish voice.

Rory looked back at Fin. 'Yep.'

'Yep.'

The policeman in the harness handed Rory's boat back to the other policeman, who secured it to the side under elastic straps.

Fin climbed up and saw there were four of them on board, three men and a woman. They were all quiet and serious. The first policeman lifted the drawbridge, the engines growled, and the police boat swung towards the city. The policewoman had a round face with light freckles on her nose and white-blonde hair in a ponytail. She knelt down and looked them all over without looking into their eyes.

The first policeman spoke as he unclipped his harness. 'You boys are lucky we got the call. It's crazy sharky today.'

They took Rory and Fin to different parts of the boat to ask them questions. Fin knew he was supposed to let Rory do the talking, but there was no way he could refuse to speak. It seemed, on this boat, only the police had the right to remain silent. The policewoman sat him down on a plastic bench and asked him how they got there and where they were going. Fin tried to play it down and said they were just paddling in the river and weren't doing anything.

'River? What river?'

'I don't know the name of it. It's the muddy one behind my gran's house. It's really flat.'

'What's your gran's name?'

Fin realised that he'd never been sure of Gran's real name. 'I'm not sure. We just call her Gran.'

The policewoman said her name was Constable Kovich, but Fin was allowed to call her Kaylee if he wanted. She said she wanted Gran's address, but Fin didn't know it. He said they were just staying there for Christmas and then they were going back to Gustav's up at Old Binnalong. She wrote *Old Binnalong* in her notebook. He knew Rory would be mad at him for talking to her.

Kaylee held up a pump bottle of suncream. 'Are you allergic to this?'

'I'm not allergic to anything.' Fin said it proudly, as if it meant he was strong. They weren't allowed to bring peanut butter to school because one of the boys was allergic.

'Well, put it on. All over you.' She squirted a big pump into Fin's hand. 'You boys are fried.'

He rubbed the cream into his legs and arms. The policewoman kept talking and giving him more suncream and asking questions about his mum and about Old Bin, and about Gran and Josie, and about his dad. Fin explained that he hadn't seen his dad for a long time. He didn't mean for it to sound like it was a sore point, but she seemed to think it was important and said, 'Right,' as she wrote in her notebook.

As the boat motored further into the harbour, the policewoman handed him a bottle of water and asked again, maybe for the third or fourth time, what he and Rory were doing out there and why there wasn't an adult with them. 'Do your gran and your mum know where you are?'

The bottled water was icy cold, and Fin felt every centimetre of its journey from his tongue to his belly. 'No, they don't know where we are. They wouldn't have…' Fin felt his story beginning to slip. 'We were just minding our own business or whatever.'

Kaylee spoke in a gentle, friendly way, almost whispering. 'They wouldn't have? They wouldn't have what? Let you do it?'

'Hey, let's keep this professional.' Fin hoped this would be enough to get her to back off.

'Of course.' Kaylee also seemed to think this was a good idea.

They sat silently and looked out at the houses and unit blocks lining the harbour. Smaller boats moved out of the way of the big police boat.

Fin tried to sound casual, like he didn't mind one way or another, 'So, where are you taking us? I mean, are we going to jail?'

'Jail? Were you boys doing something wrong?' Kaylee continued looking out at the passing shore.

'No, no. Well, I didn't think it was wrong.' Fin was overcome with a heavy feeling that the story was going to come out one way or another. He could see now that the police had separated them deliberately.

Fin looked down at his legs. They were shiny with suncream. 'I don't think it was wrong, anyway.'

'What do you mean? Was there someone else in the boat?' A hint of panic showed in Kaylee's eyes.

'No. Just us.'

She relaxed. 'Well, come on. Just tell me what you boys were doing. I'll help you to sort it out, but I'm starting to get worried now. What's the big secret?' She turned her head so she could look right into his eyes.

'Well, it's just...' Fin looked around, hoping for help. But all he could see was Rory's pink legs sticking out with his feet against the side of the boat. 'It's just we can't do it here so...' He shrugged as if to say – *you know how it is.*

'You can't do what, Griffin?'

'You know, get married.'

'Get married?' Kaylee's face seemed to light up.

'Yeah, you know. Boys can't marry boys here, that's why.'
It felt good to be telling the truth.

'That's why what?'

'That's why we were going there. You know, to New
Zealand.'

'Oh, New Zealand?' She seemed surprised but under-
standing. 'New Zealand's a long way.'

'Anyway.'

The policeman who'd pulled them from the water came to
speak to Kaylee.

He said, 'I managed to get a phone number. It wasn't easy,
though.'

'Yeah.' She nodded exaggeratedly. 'You and I should chat.'

They stepped into the cabin under where the captain was
steering the boat. Fin wanted to rush over to Rory to apologise
for telling them, but Rory wasn't moving.

The police stayed inside for a long time, and they all
seemed more relaxed now. They spoke in careful whispers,
but Fin overheard bits and pieces.

The first policeman seemed to do most of the talking.
'I've tried the number but there's no answer. The kid says his
grandpa never answers the phone.'

The boat passed under the Harbour Bridge and turned
into a bay near the smiling face of Luna Park. The coloured

carriages of the Ferris wheel cast a moving shadow on the concrete and the water. Fin heard a slapping rattle and looked to see Kaylee picking up a little fishing rod that had fallen onto the deck. She looked back with annoyance at the first policeman. 'You know you can't bring this bloody thing on board, Tommy.' She held the fishing rod out towards him.

'Oh, come on, Kaylee. I thought I might get my mum a couple of juicy kingies for tea. She's an old lady, Kaylee. You don't want to take away her dinner, do you? It's good for arthritis.'

Kaylee turned away from him.

Tommy continued, speaking to the back of her head. 'Anyway, I thought I might catch a kingy, or at least some bonito. I never expected we'd catch a couple of eight-year-old gays.'

Kaylee spun around. 'Tommy! Will you please not be yourself? Just for ten minutes? Just stop being yourself, Tommy. Stop it.'

Tommy ducked as if he was expecting her to throw something at him.

She turned back towards Fin and mouthed, 'Sorry.'

Fin gave her a little thumbs up.

The police boat stopped and sat drifting near a line of yachts on moorings, and the four police officers stood together to discuss what to do with the boys. The captain had a brown beard and the other one was a skinny guy with glasses. He looked much younger than the rest.

Tommy spoke in a quiet voice. 'The kid's given me an address.'

'What about the other one?' The captain seemed irritated.

Kaylee said, 'He doesn't know. He's from the North Coast and he doesn't know anyone's phone number. He's staying with his grandmother next to the other one.'

The captain shook his head. 'Oh, come on. Where are these people?'

Tommy seemed eager to give the captain some good news. 'I've buzzed the sarge up there and he reckons he knows the families. I don't know how you want to handle it, but this guy's not going to answer the phone and, if we take them back to the island, someone will have to watch them for the rest of the day until we can find some cake-eaters to come get them.'

'Not our problem.'

Tommy quickly continued. 'I was thinking one of the Gladdies might come down and get them from Huntleys.'

The captain went back to the steering wheel. 'Steve would have to come down if I'm going to hand them over... Give them a buzz and see.'

The captain climbed back into the wheelhouse and the boat began moving. Kaylee told Fin they were going to drop them so they could wait on the mainland rather than on the police island.

The boat pulled up at a wharf with a big sign that read – *HUNTLEYS POINT*. A chubby policeman and a policewoman were standing on the wharf. The policeman's hat looked too small for his big head. They told the boys to squeeze all the air out of Rory's boat, and then they drove them up the hill to the police station. They sat in the waiting room with their bundled-up boat and paddles. Rory remained adamantly silent.

The policewoman came out to check on them a couple of times and gave them little cups of water. She said they still hadn't been able to reach Rory's pop.

Rory whispered to Fin, 'Did you tell?'

'Had to.'

Rory's face dropped, like all the air had been sucked out of him. He spoke in a barely audible whisper. 'Mum says you never talk to police. Never. No matter what they promise.'

Fin felt like crying.

Rory shook his head and melodramatically drained the last of the water in his cup. 'Jeez. We're done for.'

Eventually, the policewoman came out and said they couldn't contact Rory's grandpa, but someone was coming to drive them home. By the time the two policewomen arrived to collect them, the trees around the police station were casting long shadows over the car park. They bundled the deflated boat and the paddles into the boot of the police car and the boys sat in the back.

The telegraph poles set a steady visual rhythm in the fading light, and he thought about how all powerlines must be connected to one another. He imagined the electricity here zipping all the way along the wires to the ridge at Old Bin.

The car pulled up outside Rory's house and one of the policewomen said, 'Good. The lights are on.'

The other one turned to Fin and said, 'And you're next door, right?'

Fin nodded.

'Let's get you home then.'

One of them took Rory to his house with his bundled-up boat and paddles, and the other one walked Fin to Gran's front door.

Rory said, 'See you in a sec,' and gave Fin the thumbs up before he walked off.

Fin almost cried with relief; it seemed that Rory might forgive him for talking to the police.

The policewoman knocked on the door and Gran answered. Her eyes looked like she'd been crying. 'Griffin? Dear Lord. What have you done, dear?'

'Hi, Gran.'

Fin could hear Lindy screaming from inside the house. 'I just can't take this anymore!' She was really shouting and separating each word.

The policewoman began speaking to Gran in a deliberate, formal way, 'Hello, Missus...'

'Ms Alverton. It's Mzzz.' Gran enjoyed correcting people, even police.

'Yes, Mzzz Alverton. Young Griffin here was picked up on the harbour. He was *on water.*'

Lindy screamed again from inside. 'You can't hide from me! I'll find you.'

'Mum!' Fin called out to Lindy. Gran must've done something to her.

The policewoman continued, but she began leaning to one side so she could see past Gran, into the house. 'It seems his playmate and he found their way out onto the harbour. It was significantly perilous...'

There was a loud grunt and a crashing noise inside. It sounded like Lindy had thrown something onto the floor.

'Mum!' Fin really shouted this time.

The policewoman continued. 'Is everything all right, Mzzz...?'

Lindy appeared in the hallway behind Gran. As soon as she saw the policewoman, she hurried towards Fin, elbowing Gran out of the way. She pulled Fin into the house and wrapped her arms tightly around his head.

The policewoman looked at Lindy with a steady gaze. 'Hello, Mzzz...?'

Lindy was wearing her business clothes – professional clothes. She brought her face close to Gran's so their noses were almost touching. She spoke in a loud whisper. 'How dare you?'

'Whatever are you talking about, dear?' Gran giggled.

Lindy turned her attention to the policewoman. 'I don't know what she told you, but...'

The policewoman interrupted. 'I know you both must have been very worried...'

Lindy's whole body was quivering, and her heart was thumping so hard that Fin could feel the impossible speed of it in his forehead. She hadn't been like this since the snake at Old Bin.

Lindy spoke fast, 'Whatever she's told you, whatever it is, she's poison. She's a poisoner! It's all lies. Nothing but lies. Lies!'

The policewoman was slow and precise with her words, 'Are you the mother of Griffin, ma'am?'

'Of course I am! Oh no. She hasn't said something like that, has she?'

'I'm not sure what you mean?' The policewoman took a big, slow step backwards.

'This wicked woman is a danger to us all. She's poisoned me. Poisoned my food! Griffin will be next. Nothing's ever enough. She's the danger to children here!' Lindy began a series of sharp pushes against Gran's arm until Gran had to step outside next to the policewoman. As soon as Gran was clear of the door, Lindy slammed it so hard that the squares of stained glass rattled after it closed.

Lindy pushed Fin into the house. 'Run, little man, run!'

Fin felt tears pooling in his eyes. This was all his fault. 'Mum? What is it, Mum?'

'They're going to take you away again, baby. They're going to take you away from me. That bitch has reported me again. They'll take you if they catch you. Run, little man.' She was pushing him through the living room towards the kitchen and the back door.

'Mum, you don't understand.'

'Not now, Griffin. Just go.'

Fin smelled the happy scent of Josie's cigarette smoke and ran towards the back door.

'Belinda?' It was the voice of the policewoman calling from the front.

Josie was standing beside her chair at the back. She was puffing hard, as if she was trying to get her breath back while she smoked. Her face was red and her forehead was slick with sweat. 'There you are. I've been climbing up and down to billyo trying to find you.'

Lindy was suddenly standing in the back doorway.

Josie looked up at her. 'What's happened?'

'She's ratted me out to the child-protection people again. They're here to take him.' There was a frantic rasp to Lindy's voice.

'Belinda. We need to talk a minute.' The policewoman was in the living room now.

Josie's mouth dropped open in disgust and she threw her cigarette down. 'Oh, Antonella.'

Fin thought – *Antonella. That's right. That's Gran's name.*

Lindy screamed in a high-pitched wail, turned and ran through the kitchen, straight at the policewoman. 'I won't let you take him! Run, Finny. Run now!'

The policewoman put her hands up and caught Lindy by her wrists. 'Belinda! Step back!'

'Mum, it's not…' But Fin knew it was pointless to try to fix this now.

The momentum of Lindy's run sent the policewoman toppling backwards over the couch. Lindy went over with her. They landed on the coffee table and kept rolling. The policewoman's boot cracked the screen of Gran's TV.

'Armed police officer!' The other policewoman was shouting through the front doorway.

Lindy sprang to her feet and ran towards the stairs. The other policewoman entered the living room with her hand on her gun holster. The first policewoman was getting to her feet in front of the broken TV.

Fin chased his mum up the stairs. 'Mum, they were bringing me back! Mum!'

Lindy was halfway out the open window when Fin reached their bedroom. 'Sorry, little man.'

Fin knew she'd be ruined if she fell from that height.

'Belinda!'

Fin turned to see the two policewomen at the top of the stairs. One was talking into a police radio. Although it was all happening so fast, Fin noticed every detail. The little smear of blood at the corner of the first policewoman's mouth, the cracked glass of her wristwatch, the white scuff marks on the chunky toe of her police boot. When he turned back to look at Lindy, he could see the galah-pink of the twilight sky through the open window.

She was gone.

CHAPTER TEN

Fin felt like he hadn't slept all night. He had forced his breathing into the slow rhythm of sleep until Gran had climbed out of Lindy's bed and tiptoed back to her own room. Then he'd moved onto the wobbly familiarity of the pump-up. He could have got up and crept downstairs in the night, but he didn't want to see something he shouldn't.

When the morning light began to transform the room, he listened for the reassuring whooshing of cars, but none came. Only the distant toot of a train and the soothing hush of light rain on glass. As the reality of standing and walking approached, the pain in every part of his burnt and peeling skin seemed to intensify. So he waited, changing from side to side to ease the pain of his sunburn.

The sheet was sweaty and bundled up under his legs. He could feel the sticky surface of the pump-up peeling off pieces of skin as he sat up. The usual excitement of

Christmas morning was stained by what had happened. He rose carefully, pulled a T-shirt over his head and shoulders, and placed his hand on the doorknob. But he looked back at the curtains to confirm the sun was rising before he opened it.

He felt the old timber in the stairs stretching under his feet as he crept down. The house was dark, apart from the slow blinking of the coloured Christmas tree lights in the living room. Gran had taped newspaper over the broken TV screen. The story on the page had a photo of a spongy-faced man with thin wisps of gold and silver hair. The way Gran had stuck him on made it look like he was paused on the screen. She said they had to tidy everything up because someone from the government was coming to talk to Fin and inspect the house to make sure it was safe for him to live with her. She'd asked him to help her try to move the TV out to the street, but it was too heavy.

Before he allowed himself to look under the tree, he tentatively opened the front door to check. The two carrots he'd placed on the front doorstep had been chewed to the bum end, and the can of beer had been opened. He lifted the can and looked inside to see if any was left. It was still about a third full. There were slimy snail trails around the edge of the can and on the top. He wiped it clean with his T-shirt and poured the warm fizzy liquid into his mouth. As he forced himself to swallow it down, he wondered how so many adults could be so wrong about something; it was horrible.

There was a thin, almost constant drip running from the roof above, and he looked up to see where the gutter had been bent out of shape. He put down the can and, now more certain of what he would find, went to check under the Christmas tree. The biggest of the presents had his name on it: *To Griffin Alverton, From Santa.*

Fin lifted the box, held it to his ear and shook. Nothing.

'Merry Christmas, Golden Boy.' Josie had started using Rory's nickname for him. She had her shiny black sports pants and pink jumper on, even though it was already muggy-hot in the house. 'Did he…?' Josie lifted her eyebrows in excitement.

Fin nodded and placed the present back under the tree. He knew they'd have to wait for Gran before they could open anything.

Josie wrapped her arms around him. 'Merry, merry Christmas, Mr Boy. Or maybe it should be Mr Golden?'

'Oh, Josie. You don't have to call me mister anything. We've known each other forever.'

Once Gran was up, she and Josie sat side by side on the couch. Gran was already dressed for going out, with a busy-patterned dress and her hair done. One by one, Fin placed parcels on the laps of the two old ladies and put his presents on the coffee table. He left any with *Lindy* on them under the tree.

Once he'd distributed everything, Gran began unpicking the sticky tape so she could reuse the paper. Fin tore the wrapping from the biggest box first. It was a *Star Wars* melamine breakfast set. Through the clear plastic on the front, he could see a bowl and a big spoon with a picture of R2-D2 on it. He didn't know what 'melamine' was, but it sounded expensive. Despite everything, Santa hadn't let him down.

The next parcel had his name on it but didn't say who it was from. He opened it and knew straight away. It was a smooth wooden box. Lindy had painted the outside of it with a swirling green and silver pattern and, in black long and loopy writing – *May the Force Be with You*. He almost cried when he saw what she had written. Lindy always made sure there was something special about her presents, something that existed only for him. He opened the box to find a little brown card inside – *Here's a box to keep your treasures in, My Treasure*. He felt his chest and shoulders flood with the warm feeling of his mum. Josie reached out and pulled him into a hug.

~

After Lindy had gone out the upstairs window, one of the policewomen had pushed past Fin. The other one hurried down the stairs. The one at the window seemed to hesitate before looking.

Fin was calling and calling, 'Mum! Mum! Mum!'

But the policewoman hadn't let him look until she'd leant right out to check. He could hear sirens in the distance. Then the policewoman pulled herself back into the room, and he heard the other one's voice crackle through the police radio. 'The suspect is on the roof.'

Fin ran down the stairs behind the policewoman and when they got out the front, the policewoman called out, 'Belinda! Just stay where you are. It's all good. It's all good. We're going to be able to sort all this.'

Gran appeared behind him and they both looked up to see Lindy standing right on the pointed peak of the roof.

She had her arms out, balancing like a tightrope walker. 'She'll poison him too! He'll be next.'

Gran seemed to shout and whisper at the same time. 'Sweet Jesus.'

The second policewomen said, 'Better get him to a neighbour's.'

And Gran shepherded him over to Rory's front yard.

'Mum!'

Gran had grabbed his head and twisted it away firmly so he couldn't look.

Lindy called down to him, 'It's okay, baby. I won't let them take you.'

'They were bringing me back!' He was crying now, and his throat was stingy and dry as he shouted to her.

Rory and Pop were standing on their front step looking up at Lindy. Gran and Pop exchanged a few stiff words, and Fin heard him say, 'You can't say I didn't warn you,' under his breath.

Gran asked if Fin could wait inside the house and Pop stood aside to let him walk through the open doorway. Pop stayed outside looking up at Lindy.

Rory followed Fin inside, and they squatted down on the worn-out carpet in the front room. Fin was trying hard to stop crying, but it wasn't working.

Rory was almost crying too. 'Is this all about New Zealand?' Rory's burnt skin made his eyes look an even lighter brown.

'I think so.'

As the sirens came close, one of the police officers started talking on a loudspeaker. Rory opened a side window so he and Fin could watch. The front lawns of other houses had groups of people talking and looking up. Lindy kept shouting that she would never let them take her boy again, and she wasn't coming down until she had a lawyer and some papers to make sure. And then she'd go quiet for a while, sitting on the ridge of the roof. At one point, one of the firemen had leant a ladder up against the gutter. He called out that he'd hold it steady if she wanted to climb down.

Lindy stood and screamed, 'Get it away! Get it away!' She said, if they wouldn't get her a lawyer and the papers, they'd have to come up and get her. And then she said, if they tried that, she'd climb into the big gum tree next to Gran's; the fireman took the ladder away.

The voice on the loudspeaker would try to tell her every now and then that everything was all right. They kept calling her 'Belinda', and it made it seem like this was happening to someone else's mum. Fin and Rory huddled side by side at the window and didn't speak.

A bigger fire truck arrived with extra equipment and ladders. These firemen seemed much more serious about getting her down. The voice on the loudspeaker stopped and Lindy began prowling back and forth along the ridge of the roof. She didn't need to hold her arms out now.

Another man's voice started over the loudspeaker. He had a gentler tone. 'The best thing for everyone, especially you and your boy, is for you to climb back down. Nothing's happened yet. Everything can be undone. No-one's crossed any lines yet. It seems like there's just been a misunderstanding.'

This new voice seemed to make Lindy suddenly angry. She walked towards the voice, shouting, 'I'm not coming down! I'll stay up here forever if I have to. It's all lies! It's that evil woman again.'

A violent scream erupted from Fin. 'Mum!'

She stopped suddenly, about a metre from the gutter, and looked over at Rory's house.

'Mum!'

And then she slipped.

She flopped down hard on her side and reached back, trying to grab onto anything to stop her fall. Her legs went over the edge. There was no sound. She managed to dig her forearm into the gutter. Her whole body swung back and forward off the edge, and then she dropped again. She grabbed the edge of the gutter with the fingertips of one hand and hung there for a moment. And then she swung herself to the side and was able to reach up with the other hand.

Everyone watching seemed to breathe out at the same time. The original fireman, the one with the ladder, hurried towards her, angling the ladder up.

Lindy screamed in a mixture of frustration and pain.

There was a loud cracking sound. One after the other – crack, crack – like gunshots. And at first, Fin had thought the police were shooting at her.

The guttering sagged and the metal roared as it began to pull away from the old roof. One by one – crack, crack, crack – as each screw tore loose, Lindy sank down lower. And then the gutter broke away completely and the downpipe was all that was supporting her. It began pulling out of the wall in jolting increments until the downpipe came away and levered like a vaulting pole, heaving Lindy and the broken sections of old guttering out into the front garden. Fin watched her body swinging back and forth until the toppling downpipe crashed her down into Josie's nasturtiums.

There was silence again.

Then Lindy sprang to her feet and ran in the direction of Rory's. Fin ran out to meet her. Just as she was about to reach him, the two female police officers tackled her onto the lawn. One of them looked up at Pop from the ground and shouted, 'Get him inside!'

Pop forcefully turned him around and walked him into the kitchen. Fin could hear his mum screaming for him.

They sat at the kitchen table and Pop poured him a diet lemonade.

Rory was the only one who spoke. 'She looked like a jolly ninja when she went over.'

~

Fin pulled himself free of Josie's arms and closed the box, leaving Lindy's Christmas card inside. He shuddered and managed to control his tears as he placed it on the floor and began tearing the wrapping paper away from his next present. This one was clearly labelled: *To Griffin, Lots of love, Gran.* The torn paper revealed a softcover book. It smelled like glue and looked more like a schoolbook than a present – *Mensa Kids: Train Your Brain Puzzle Book.* It had a picture of two kids reading on its cover. *Get Your Child Ready for an IQ Test and a Gifted-Child Qualification.*

When Fin looked up, Gran's eyes were open wide and she was almost bouncing with excitement. 'I got it online.' She took the book from him and began flicking through it. 'I thought we could do some together.'

'Okay.' He looked around at Josie for some help with how he should react.

Josie was staring at her tea and seemed determined not to look up. Fin had heard Gran talk about Mensa before; it was a club for smart people that she was in.

The last present with his name on it was from Josie: *To Fin, Love always, Josie.* He peeled away the paper to reveal a Lego *Star Wars* Imperial Assault Hovertank.

'Oh, Josie. Thank you.' He only had mismatched Lego at Gustav's; he leant in to hug her.

'I got you another one too, but this one was sort of extra and didn't bear wrapping.' She lifted a brown paper shopping bag from beside the couch. Inside, there was a bright orange hat with a wide brim and a big pump bottle of suncream.

'For next time,' Josie whispered.

Gran stood up. 'There'd better not be a next time, that's all I can say. There's been more than enough drama in this household for one lifetime.' She drained her cup of tea. 'I'm embarking on a strictly drama-free diet from now on and you two would do well to join me in it.'

Fin and Josie sat close beside each other on the couch. Fin noticed that the brim of his hat had *Golden Boy* written in thin black permanent pen.

Gran continued. 'Anyway, we've got a lot of getting ready to do, packing the food. And, dear me, Jocelyn, you can't wear that. They'll think you're one of the patients. They'll never let you back out.'

Josie loudly sipped her tea and Gran went into the kitchen.

~

They were going to visit Lindy in hospital. Gran said the doctors hadn't wanted them to visit so soon, but they were making an exception because it was Christmas Day.

Fin began assembling his hovertank on the living room floor while Gran finished making the sauce and carving the turkey. Then she packed it all into plastic containers and stacked them in her bright blue esky. When they were ready to go, he pulled his new hat on, and Gran and Josie lifted the esky into the boot of Gran's little silver car. He would have liked to go and wish Rory a merry Christmas, but he knew Pop wouldn't welcome a visitor on Christmas Day.

Gran drove slowly, with occasional surprising bursts of speed. They turned into a narrow street, and Fin looked through the reflection of his face and his bright orange hat. There was an old wire fence with bushes growing up against it and, beyond that, a graveyard. He held his breath. Lindy always stopped breathing when they drove past graveyards. Fin assumed it was because she was worried she might breathe in a ghost. And now she was locked in a hospital next to a graveyard.

Everything was wet from the morning drizzle, but the sun had come out and Fin could smell the saltiness of rain steaming off concrete. Gran parked in a covered car park. She and Josie shared the weight of the esky, and they had to stop a couple of times to rest on the way. They took the lift up to the second floor and their surroundings seemed to age as soon as the doors opened. The walls were pale green and everything else was plasticky white. A young nurse greeted them; her hair was mousy blonde, like Lindy's, and she had a pouty way of talking. She leant down to speak to Fin and he could see right up her nose.

'Merry Christmas.' She reached out to shake his hand.

Gran reminded the nurse that they had reserved the 'family room', and the nurse told Gran and Josie they had to put their handbags in a little metal locker. Then she gestured at the esky and said, 'You've not got any glass or metal in there, do you? Any cutlery?'

Gran seemed almost ashamed. 'All plastic, as instructed.'

The nurse didn't move and kept looking at the esky. Eventually, it became clear that she meant they had to show her. When Gran lifted the lid, Fin was pleased to see his new bowl sitting on the top of the plastic boxes and plates.

'Thank you.' The nurse stepped towards a big door that beeped and clicked. She held it open and Gran and Josie had to crabwalk through with the esky between them.

The nurse took them into a big room with a ping-pong table in the middle, a TV mounted high on the wall, and some old couches and plastic chairs around. One young man was standing at the ping-pong table and looking down. His mouth hung half-open and he was perfectly still. There was a wide man in a security guard uniform sitting with his back to the TV, playing with his phone. He looked a bit like Tommy, the water policeman.

The nurse slid open a glass door and led them into a room with a table and plastic chairs. There was a small window with a clock above it, and two low armchairs. Gran and Josie heaved the esky onto the table and Gran began unpacking boxes, plastic cutlery and plates.

'I'll have Belinda join you shortly.' The nurse stepped out and gave the door an extra push to make it click.

Gran almost had the whole Christmas lunch set up when Lindy arrived. The nurse opened the door for her and then made sure it clicked behind her.

'Mum.' Fin launched himself at her.

'Little man.' Lindy seemed completely normal. She hugged him long and kissed the top of his head. She was dressed in her home clothes, grey tracksuit pants and her Rolling Stones T-shirt. She'd even brushed her hair.

Lindy let her shoulders drop. 'Hi, Mum.' She gave Gran a big hug.

'Merry Christmas, dear.' Gran squeezed her tight.

Josie kissed her on the cheek. 'Merry Christmas, Lindy.'

They sat down to lunch. Lindy pulled her chair close to Fin's and she kept leaning against him and looking at him as they ate Gran's turkey with her special cranberry sauce. Josie had made potato salad and beans. She'd also brought a chocolate orange and Italian nougat, and she put it all out at the start. Fin ate chunks of turkey from his *Star Wars* bowl between bites of dessert. Everyone made an effort to eat as much as they could; Gran had packed too much turkey.

They all behaved as if everything was normal, and Lindy was on a one-person hotel holiday rather than in hospital.

'Well, I guess there's only fifteen minutes to go.' Lindy nibbled a bit of chocolate.

Gran knocked twice on the table. 'My, how time flies. It's so good to see you looking well.'

'Yes, um. I am, um...' Lindy seemed to want to say something.

Josie rose from her chair. 'Why don't we let you two catch up?'

Gran nodded. 'Yes. Oh, darling. It's so good to see you like this.'

Josie moved towards the door.

'Yes, we'll use the facilities. The facilities.' Gran followed Josie. They had to pull at the handle a few times before there was a loud click and the door opened.

Lindy took Fin's hand and led him over to the armchairs by the window. She looked at each corner of the room like she was checking they were really alone.

'So, are you all right?' She seemed to be searching his eyes.

'Yes, Mum.' He could feel tears rising. 'I'm all right. Crazy sunburnt, but you can see that.'

'I like your hat.' She pulled it off his head and looked all through it, checking each part of the brim and inside. 'Golden Boy, that's nice.'

'How long until they unlock you out of here?'

'No need to worry about me. I'm safe in here. It's you we need to worry about. She can't get at me in here, but you're still there and I can't protect you now.' Lindy was speaking calmly.

'What do you mean, Mum? Why do I need to be protected? Deirdre's not here. She's up at Old Bin. The police were bringing me back, anyway.'

There was a gentle, all-knowing clarity in the way Lindy spoke. 'Little man, it's not Deirdre. She was just a bit player. Just the start of it. She's got you now. It's Gran. It's always been Gran.'

'What do you mean it's Gran? What's she going to do to me?'

'Finny, we don't have much time. I can explain everything later. But anyway, it's poison, slow-acting stuff. Eventually, you're dead, except for the outside. And she's got you.'

'But, Mum. What can I do? If you're in here, I mean. What can I do? Will they let me stay in here with you?'

'Shhh.' She held her finger up to his lips and looked at the ceiling, then placed his hat on his head. 'You can't. But I told your father. He said he'll drive straight to get you.'

Fin felt like he'd been punched. My father? How had she contacted him? And, if she knew where he was, why hadn't she called him before?

'It's okay, little man. He'll come. He said he'll drive straight to Gran's. He knows where it is. But you have to promise you won't tell anyone before he comes. Finny, you have to promise.'

Fin had so many questions.

'Griffin, you have to promise.'

'I promise.'

'I know you probably don't remember him. You were so...' She looked out through the little window on the door and saw Gran and Josie making their way back through the common room. 'He has to come. They took my phone away, but I managed to borrow one to call him.'

The door clicked and Gran pulled it open.

Lindy continued in a hurried whisper, 'I told him to carry an umbrella so you know it's him, not one of Gran's imposters. No matter what he says, *do not* go with him if he doesn't have an umbrella. It's the only way you can be sure it's not one of her people.' Lindy stood up and turned. Her voice was different, more tense. 'How were the facilities?'

'Not exactly The Ritz.' Gran made a point of wiping her hands with a tissue she pulled from her pocket.

'Not exactly The Ritz.' Lindy repeated Gran's phrase. 'But I suppose The Ritz isn't a place you get the sort of help I need.'

'Yes, dear.' Gran began putting the lids back on plastic tubs. 'Precisely.' Gran seemed happy that Lindy was in hospital.

Josie looked down at Fin, worried, and then she looked up at Lindy 'Do you need us to bring you anything in here, darling?'

'I have everything I need. And I know you'll take wonderful care of Griffin. You both will.'

Josie held her hand out to Fin and pulled him into a quick hug.

Gran finished packing up the esky. 'Merry Christmas, dear.'

'You too, Mum. You too.'

Fin fell forward into Lindy's arms and squeezed his eyes tight to stop tears coming out.

'Soon, little man. Soon.'

He stayed there until the door unclicked. Then Gran and Josie lifted the esky, and he followed them back out to the car.

~

Josie opened a bottle of champagne as soon as they got home. She poured Fin a pineapple juice and the three of them sat on the couch trying not to look at the broken TV. Gran complained about the rain and said that any tradesman who came to fix the gutters at this time of year would be an 'extortionist'.

Gran and Josie said things like 'wasn't she looking well' and 'won't be long now'. There were long silences, and each one seemed to increase the pressure in the room; the big house felt so empty. Eventually, they drifted off to their separate areas. Josie smoked more cigarettes than usual and stayed outside with her fan blowing the smoke away. Gran went to sit at her computer.

Fin crawled into the tunnel through the bush to look for Rory. It was still drizzly hot, and the cooling sprinkle of rain felt nice on the backs of his legs. The boggy moisture of the ground was soaking into his T-shirt, but he didn't care; he just wanted Rory. He watched the flyscreen door at the back of Pop's house. It would be so simple to go up and bang on it or shout out. But there had been no sight or sound of Rory since Lindy fell. This was the third day now, and it meant something was wrong.

'You'll be getting some of that cream on before there's any more adventuring, mister.' Josie was calling out, but Fin could tell her voice was muffled by a cigarette between her lips. 'Where's your friend, anyway?'

Fin shuffled backwards into the drizzle and went to Josie. She indicated the chair he should take, away from the trail of smoke puffing out of the fan.

'Nice seeing your mum?' Josie lit the cigarette.

Fin didn't answer.

She continued. 'As good as can be anyway. Under the circumstances.'

All Fin could think about was the idea that, somewhere out there, his dad was moving towards him.

Fin shifted left and right to settle himself solidly in the chair. 'Do you know my dad?'

'Yes, I know your dad. I knew him before.' Josie's face transformed into a sad, blinking smile.

Fin felt sure that, if he was quiet for long enough, Josie would keep talking. After Lindy had been able to contact his dad so easily, even from the hospital without her phone, it was clear they all knew a lot more than he'd realised. He had wanted to understand, but every time he'd asked, or tried to find something out, Lindy cried. And she stayed crying, sometimes for hours. So he'd stopped asking.

Josie took a sip of her Christmas champagne. 'I don't know how much you remember of all that. Or if you remember. You were only little.'

'I remember the caravan. What do you mean all that?'

'All that, all that, Golden Boy. I know you're trying to sort through this pickle. I love you dearly, but I don't know. I'm sorry. It's not my job to tell you about your own father.'

Fin waited, hoping she might say more, and then asked, 'What does he look like?'

'Well, he looks a bit like you, I suppose.'

This felt badly wrong, like someone he didn't know had just stolen a piece of his face. He'd accepted that, in a way, your blood always belonged to someone else first. But it seemed unfair that you didn't get to have your own face. If he'd just been out there looking however he looked all this time, why hadn't his dad come for him until now, just when it seemed like it was getting all wrecked? He'd never even telephoned.

Fin wanted to be back at Gustav's. If he could get back there, he'd stay there by himself eating garden stuff until Lindy got out and made her way home; she'd know where to find him. But it would also mean no Rory.

'What do you mean like me? Which bits? My nose or something?'

'Well, I'm not sure. Your eyes mostly. And maybe your nose a bit.' She looked at him more closely. 'Yes, you've definitely got them. He had a good set of eyes. Resemblances are funny though. Not easy to get a finger on. They tend to make more sense in the long run. You'll look more like him as you get older. Or not. You'll get to see for yourself eventually, one way or another.'

Fin wanted to tell her that his dad was coming. He trusted Josie, but he'd promised. And it might get back to Gran somehow. If she found out, she'd stop it, and she'd maybe even lock him away so his dad couldn't get to him.

He imagined the blood moving around inside him, and a man's shoes walking along the path out the front, near where Lindy had crashed into the nasturtiums. He felt glad about the drizzly rain because his dad wouldn't look strange carrying an umbrella, but it also meant an imposter might have one.

Fin felt his heart beating faster. 'How long have you lived here with Gran?'

'Well, it's been twenty-seven years now since your great-granddaddy passed. So, that long.'

'And has Gran ever tried to get you? Or do anything to you or whatever?' He tried to make it sound like a normal question, like it wasn't too serious.

'Don't you worry about me, Mr Golden. I couldn't have lasted this long without a few tricks up my sleeve.' Josie looked at her bare arms. She'd taken off her jumper, and she was wearing a blouse with little yellow and white flowers and no sleeves. 'A few in my pockets, at least.'

'You mean like an antidote?'

She giggled and took another quick sip of champagne. 'I don't think there's any antidote for your gran. Nothing powerful enough anyway. One thing your gran's always known is…exactly what she's doing. There's no antidote for that.'

'You mean in the food?'

'Your gran? I do my level best to keep that woman out of the kitchen. Except for Christmas turkey, of course.' Josie drained the last of her glass and tapped her finger on it twice. Her gold wedding ring made a tinkling sound. 'Would you?'

Fin took the glass and retrieved the bottle from the kitchen. It was heavier and the liquid was bubblier than he expected, but he managed to fill the glass right to the top.

Josie's eyes widened when she saw it. 'You might have to carry me to bed after this one.'

'Josie?'

Her eyes made it clear she didn't want to talk about Gran.

'Anyway, could you tell me something? Just a bit more about what he looks like or something?' Fin tried not to show how sad he felt.

'Yes, of course. I'll tell you what I remember. But my old head's getting faded, and it feels like a long time ago now. He had one of those faces, a bit like you. The cheekbones show through. A face like he was famous, like he was in the movies. And his hair, back then anyway, his hair was wavy and long. All the way down to his shoulders and midnight black. You've never seen anything like it.'

'Yeah?'

'Griffin?' Gran's voice called out from the living room and her footsteps came towards them through the kitchen. 'How about we get stuck into your book now? I think you're really in for something.'

Gran looked at Josie's champagne glass and screwed up her face in disapproval. She made a point of adjusting the angle of Josie's smoking fan so it was pointed more directly away from the kitchen door.

Josie took a big sip of champagne. 'Another time.'

'Come on, then. The patio has held your attention long enough.' Gran took Fin's hand and led him into the house.

CHAPTER ELEVEN

It felt wrong to wake up in Lindy's bed without her, but Gran had packed the pump-up away because it might 'develop a leak'. She'd told him he wasn't allowed to go down to the river anymore, after what happened with the police. And now that the TV was broken, he couldn't even watch the daytime soap operas that came on between the shopping talk shows.

By late morning he'd worked his way around the same circuit a few times – the front lawn to look for his dad, Josie's patio and Rory's tunnel through the bush. He'd tried to stay away from Gran in case she made him do more IQ test practice. But eventually he decided to ask if he could have a turn on her computer. He'd already re-read his only *Star Wars* book twice, and anything was better than another slow circuit of the house.

She said he had to tell her 'precisely' what he wanted to look at. 'I've no intention of allowing you to infect my computer with a virus.'

He said the first thing he could think of. 'I want to look at maps.'

She made sure he couldn't see her fingers as she typed her password in to unlock the computer and stayed behind him, watching what he was doing.

He found a map website and typed in *Old Binnalong*. It came up straight away. His school was marked on the map, and he recognised some of the street names. He zoomed out further and saw where the bus stopped near the corner of their dirt road, and then he kept going and could see Ballina and the coast, and then he could see the whole of Australia, with Papua New Guinea at the top.

Lindy had said that his dad was driving straight to Gran's to get him. So Fin tried to work out the furthest place he could be coming from. He ran his eyes around the coast and decided that Perth was about as far away from Sydney as you could get without a boat or a plane.

Gran leant in from behind. 'Papua New Guinea? You can cross that off your list right now. Why on earth are you researching that?'

'I was just looking. See Perth there?'

'Yes, I see Perth, Griffin.'

'How long do you think it would take to drive from there to Sydney?'

'I don't know why anyone in their right mind would want to do that. Unless such a one had not been informed of the invention of the aeroplane.' She giggled as she leant in to look

130

closer. 'But if you had to… I'd say three days. Four at the most. Why do you want to know that?'

He closed down the map website and stood up from the computer. 'No reason.'

He walked out the front to check for his dad again and tried see through the bushes into Rory and Pop's windows. The curtains were closed, and the faint sound of talk radio was the only indication anyone was in there. He flopped down on the grass and closed his eyes. He heard the far-off rumbling of the city and the twinkling of small birds. It had only been two weeks since he and Lindy had caught the bus down from Old Bin, but he could more or less tell the time by the changing voices of the daily birds. It was like each part of the day had its own singers. And he knew that the mottled brown and yellowness of these songs meant lunchtime.

He again remembered what Lindy had said – *I told your father. He said he'll drive straight to get you. He'll drive to Gran's. He knows where it is.* And each passing second promised the sound of a man's footsteps on the path, a man with an umbrella. He settled into the pinky-blackness of his closed eyelids, rolled his head side to side on the rough grass and thought about how Josie had described his dad – long black hair, like a movie star. Fin realised that he'd never even seen a photo of him. It didn't make sense; Lindy could have shown him old photos on her phone.

There was a light thud on the ground nearby, heavier than a pair of bird feet. Fin half opened his eyes to soften the shock of the full brightness of the day. A golf ball lay beside him on the grass. He read the looping brand name – *Titleist*. He grabbed the ball and sprang to his feet as his chest was flooded with a warm Rory-ness.

Fin scanned the bushes for Rory's pale eyes, but there was no sign of him.

Rory's voice rasped in a loud whisper. 'Golden Boy.'

Fin's heart leapt again. The sound seemed to be coming from the road.

'Golden Boy.' Rory popped his head up from behind Josie's nasturtiums. He was lying flat behind the mound of tangled flowers and soil that Lindy had made when she crashed down.

Fin felt the sting of his sunburnt face stretching into a smile. 'Hey.'

Rory stayed lying down like a soldier. He gestured for Fin to join him in the dirt.

'What is it?' Fin whispered as he crawled between the nasturtiums and the wonky guttering the firemen had laid on the roadside.

Rory pointed to a bush in the corner of Gran's lawn and wriggled towards it on his hands and knees. Fin followed him into the dark space inside.

'Who are you waiting for?' Rory looked to make sure no-one had seen them.

'Not anyone.'

'You've got a pretty funny way of not waiting for anyone. You've been staring out all morning.'

'You saw me?' Fin began tossing the golf ball from hand to hand. If he knew Fin was there, why hadn't he said anything?

'We've got to keep this on the QT.'

Fin frowned to show he didn't understand.

Rory continued in his loud whisper. 'On the quiet. Anyway, you're really not waiting for anyone?'

Fin felt sick at the thought of lying to Rory again. 'You can't tell anyone.'

'Come on, Golden Boy. Do I look like a jibber-jabber?'

'You have to promise. It's serious.' He knew it would make him feel worse about it if Rory knew he was waiting for his dad, but his dad never came.

'Yeah. I promise, I promise. What's the big secret anyway? Who is this joker?'

'It's not a joker. It's maybe my dad.'

'What do you mean your dad? If it's just your dad, why have you got to go all undercover about it on the lawn and all this hanging about? Does he even have a phone? Why don't you just call him up and get his ETA?'

'Yes, he's got a phone.'

'So?'

'You can't tell my gran. She'll do something. My mum's in hospital.'

'She's lucky it's only the hospital and not in the cemetery after trying to run from the cops like that. It was like the Olympics.' Rory realised he was talking too loud and began whispering again. 'So, all that was about New Zealand?'

'I think so.' Fin didn't want to let the subject change without explaining properly to Rory. 'I mean, my dad's coming to get me. You know, to take me away with him.'

'Well, that doesn't sound too bad. Probably for the best, anyway. That's what I wanted to tell you. You and me aren't supposed to be chums anymore. Pop says I can't. He reckons your family are bad luck, and I'll end up in jail or something. He said your mum getting nabbed by the cops is just the half of it.' He paused and seemed unsure if he should go on. 'Anyway, I'm not even supposed to be telling you, but I would have felt like a right louse disappearing without giving you the heads up. Especially after you asked me to marry you and all that.'

Fin squeezed the golf ball so tightly that it felt like his knuckles might pop through his skin.

Rory looked away. 'You know, it might be for the best, sort of.'

This made no sense. Only a few days before, Rory was willing to fight off sharks so they could stay together.

Fin searched Rory's eyes for a solution. 'But what does that actually mean?'

'I guess it means, sort of, you and me. You and me are just kind of neighbours now.' Rory's mouth struggled to find the shape of each word.

'But it's not right. Why can he tell you who your friends are? What if you don't like the ones he chooses? They could be all kinds of people.'

'Come on. You're shooting off a lot of details there. It's not like this is my idea. And I'm the one who got us in this bush, anyway. So it's not like...' Rory's stern look made it clear he wouldn't tolerate any criticism of Pop. 'Anyway, it's not my idea.'

'But what about later? Tomorrow? You know?' Fin couldn't believe that feelings like this could just be put away.

Rory was getting impatient. It seemed like he'd decided that he wasn't going to get sad, but Fin was pushing him that way. 'Hey, let's not get this backwards. All morning you've been shifting around the grass ready to rush off with your no-phone dad.' Rory stopped dead. 'Sorry, I shouldn't have called him that. I don't really know about his phone situation. Anyway, out here looking for your dad to take you away and you haven't given me so much as a bo-peep about it.'

'But I can't come to your house. You said about your pop and visitors.'

'Well, I guess you've got me there.'

Both boys sat looking out through the gaps in the leaves, as though this would be the perfect moment for Fin's dad to appear. Fin rolled the golf ball in circles around the palm of his hand and wished Rory's little boat had made it.

Rory twisted awkwardly to put his arm around Fin's shoulder. 'So anyway, Pop will be getting shirty. So...' Rory held his face still and close.

Fin could feel Rory's breath on his skin; he was so close that Fin could have licked him if he'd stuck his tongue out.

Rory's expression changed to one of apologetic shame, and Fin knew it meant he wanted his golf ball back.

'Sorry, it's a Titleist.'

Fin placed it carefully in Rory's hand.

Rory moved onto all fours to climb out of the bush. 'Drop us a postcard if you do end up somewhere. Number fourteen – one four.' Then Rory was gone.

Fin managed to hold himself still for a full minute before he cried. He needed his mum. He needed to be with her, back at Gustav's with a record on. No snakes or Deirdre or any of this. He needed home.

He checked that Rory wasn't watching and he cried some more. Then he crawled out of the bush and stepped onto the road. He looked up at the powerlines and wondered how long it would take if he just started walking.

~

He had become used to the morning smell of cigarette smoke as he passed through the kitchen towards the back door, but Josie wasn't on her patio. The sun was low and gold-grey, and the sunrise birds were still going. He dragged Josie's fan out from beside the wall and angled it away from his chair. He clicked the switch and the plastic blades whirred into life; everything would be set up for when she came down.

He heard the click of the kettle and caught a glimpse of Gran's morning face through the kitchen window. He stayed as still as he could in the hope that she wouldn't notice him. The teaspoon clinked against the cup as she stirred her tea, but she didn't step outside.

He continued waiting, but Josie didn't come. And, as the sun began to climb higher and the sticky daytime air slid up the valley, he decided he'd take a banana and a glass of water up to her. But once he reached her bedroom door, it felt wrong to wake her if she was resting. So he ate the banana and drank the water on the carpet outside her door.

The morning passed slowly. He re-read the first two chapters of his *Star Wars* book and practised rolling his golf ball through a little tunnel he made out of cookbooks stacked up on the carpet. He knew that Gran hadn't been in to check on Josie because he'd heard her making phone call after phone call in the front room. She was talking really fast, sometimes shouting as she told different people that her wheelie bin had been switched by one of the neighbours. She said she was certain it had happened because she could 'recognise her own by the smell', and she didn't want to 'make allegations', but she could 'identify the culprit if it was necessary for a swift resolution'.

When it was getting close to lunchtime, he decided he had to check on Josie, even if she was sleeping. The idea of it made his skin feel suddenly wet. But Lindy had said the poison Gran used was slow-acting. So, if that's what was wrong, he might still be able to help her. He collected her cigarettes from the kitchen windowsill and opened her bedroom door.

She was on her side facing the door with the doona pulled right up against her chin. Her eyes opened slowly as he stepped inside. 'You spying on me?'

'I thought you'd be dying for one by now.' Fin held up her cigarettes.

She shook her head as she sat up. 'In more ways than you know, Golden Boy.' She took the cigarettes, opened the window beside her bed and patted a place for him to sit. Then she retrieved an ashtray from a drawer, lit a cigarette, and made a point of blowing the smoke out the window.

'Are you all right, Josie? I don't mean...' Fin was determined to ask. 'But is it Gran, you know?'

'Antonella?'

He rushed the words out, 'Do you think it could be her poison or whatever?'

'Poison? Your grandmother's going to have to try harder than poison if she wants to get rid of me.' She took another long draw on the cigarette. 'No. Not poison. Only a headache and bone tired. I expect it'll just be a twenty-four-hour thing.'

He felt such a sense of relief that the excitement and fear about his dad coming bubbled up. He needed to tell her, particularly if there was a chance that she might want to come with them to get away from Gran.

'Josie?'

'Yes, Griffin.' She coughed lightly as she said his name.

'Well, anyway, I was with Mum…' As soon as he said 'Mum', he knew he couldn't say it. He'd promised.

'Yes, it was nice to see your mum, wasn't it?' Josie put out her cigarette, half-smoked. 'It would have been nicer if it hadn't been in hospital, but they were kind to let us in for Christmas.'

'Well, anyway… I've sort of forgotten what I was going to say.' He made a point of looking her in the eyes so it would sound more convincing.

'Sort of?'

'Yep. Sort of.'

'Well, if you sort of remember, you know where to find me.'

He leant across to hug her, but the way he was sitting made it awkward, and they ended up just resting their heads together.

Josie leant back so she could look at him. 'You know I'll always have an eye out for you, don't you? Whatever happens with your mum, wherever she is, or your gran or anyone. I'll always make sure you've got a hug and a big bowl full of whatever you need.' She reached around to pull him closer. 'While ever there's breath in these lungs, I've always got you. And I'm not going anywhere.'

'Thanks, Josie. Yeah, and Mum will be out soon.'

'And don't worry. I can handle your gran. I'm tough, even if I don't look it. And nowhere's that far in a taxi. Wherever you end up, I'll come if you need me.'

Fin stayed leaning against her until she nudged him off the bed and said she was going to rest a bit longer.

As it started getting dark, Gran said she was heating up some frozen soup. But Fin told her that he'd already eaten a sandwich for dinner. And that night, in the dark of his mum's old bedroom, he could hear his heart beating when he closed his eyes. It felt like it was exercising to get stronger.

Gran unclicked the door and climbed in behind him, pressing her boobs into his back and breathing into his hair. Her smell was different at night. She put something on her skin that had a scent in it like a bathroom. Fin made sure his breathing stayed even so she thought he was asleep, but he also wanted to wriggle just enough to keep her awake.

As he lay there with Gran's snuffly breath against him, he remembered the moment in the bush beside the road – the closeness of Rory's face – and imagined that now, it was Rory snuggled into him. It seemed so unfair that Rory might disappear from his life because Pop thought Lindy was bad luck, or thought they'd get into trouble or something. And, even so, couldn't Rory just say no or sneak out? Fin tried to cling onto the toastiness of Rory, but it began to slip away. He knew that dark and empty feeling, like you might end up in real trouble; it was what had stopped Fin going down to the river since Gran had made her rule. It seemed impossible that Rory might end up in jail, like Pop said, but he also knew they had already come close when Fin had told the policewoman the real reason they were going to New Zealand. He hated it, but he understood that Rory couldn't risk upsetting Pop.

He wriggled and breathed loudly until Gran snuffled awake and crept out of the room.

CHAPTER TWELVE

Gran was hunched forward, pecking at her computer. She was hitting the keys so hard that the keyboard rattled against the desk. Fin smelled cigarette smoke and hurried out to find Josie on her patio. He flopped into the chair beside her and adjusted the angle of the fan. 'You better?'

'Fit as a fiddle.'

She made fruit salad and dished out three bowls. Gran didn't look up from her computer as Fin put hers down on the desk beside her. Over her shoulder, he read the words *Notice of commencement of legal action for trespass and public nuisance.* The page was blank below that, except for the words:

Dear Mr Coleman,
RE: GARBAGE BIN EXCHANGED WITHOUT CONSENT

Fin and Josie ate their fruit salad on the patio, and he practised handstands on the back lawn. Josie clapped each time he stayed up and she seemed better, but he noticed that she didn't smoke as many cigarettes as usual. The clouds cleared, so Josie made him wear his hat and smeared suncream on his peeling skin. They stayed out there most of the morning. He kept listening for the front door, but he'd begun to accept that the man with the umbrella was not coming. It had been three days and, even if he was driving from Perth, he should have arrived by now.

The high-pitched squawking of Gran's mobile phone broke the silence in the house, and Fin heard Gran answer.

'Alverton residence.' There was a moment of silence. 'Oh, darling. Yes, yes, of course.'

Fin's heart leapt and he ran inside.

'We're all fine here. Yes, and young Griffin's fine too. He and I have been having a wonderful time working our way through the book I gave him for Christmas. In that respect at least, he takes after his grandmother.' She looked up and saw Fin, lowered her voice and walked into the front room. She closed the door behind her.

He tilted his face upward to try to catch his tears with his lower eyelids. He wanted to ignore Gran's rule and escape down to the river, but he also didn't want to go too far in case Lindy asked to talk to him. He paced around until he found himself in the walk-in pantry beside the kitchen. This was one of the only places in the house, other than the patio, that felt like it belonged to Josie. Gran only cooked at Christmas.

The shelves went all the way up to the ceiling and their white paint had worn through to bare wood where jars and packets had been moved in and out. Fin tasted a single warm tear as it trickled into the corner of his mouth. One of the shelves had a line of old teacups that hung from little brass hooks. He imagined tapping the first one and the chain reaction that would follow. He noticed that last two hooks had no cups, they seemed to be waiting, ready for cups that were already broken.

He breathed slow. If his mum wanted to speak to him, he didn't want to sound upset.

'Griffin!' Gran used her sweeter, calling-out voice.

He took another deep breath. 'Yes, Gran.'

She was standing in the kitchen with her old mobile phone. 'Your mother. What on earth are you poking about in there for?'

Fin took the phone and tried to get away from Gran, but she followed him into the living room.

'Hello?' Fin could hear shouting in the background.

'Finny? Oh hello, little man.' The line went quiet.

He could tell Lindy was trying not to cry. 'Hello?'

'You okay? Everything okay there?'

'Yes, Mum. Nothing bad's happened. Josie's here too.'

'Yes, Josie. Of course, thank God.' Lindy stopped and there was a long pause.

Fin heard more shouting and then the banging of doors in the background.

'And your grandmother, of course.' Lindy's tone shifted suddenly. 'It's a godsend she's taking care of you.'

'Mum, are you all right there?'

'Yes, Griffin. Yes, I'm all right. The doctors here are getting me the help I need. Don't you worry. I'm more than safe here.'

'When are we going home?' He craved the clear air of Gustav's.

'Home?' It sounded like she didn't understand what the word meant. 'There's been a few questions here. At this stage, anyway, I'll be a few weeks at most. I've told Shannon. I haven't been too clear, of course. And she's going to hold down the fort with the business side of things.'

Fin found himself shouting, 'A few weeks?' He couldn't hold the tears in now. In a few weeks, school would have started at Old Bin. 'What do you mean a few weeks? What's wrong with you?'

'Now, little man. I know it's hard for you too. Mummy's... Anyway, Mummy's safe here, at least.' Lindy's voice was getting croaky.

'But, Mum...'

She interrupted him. 'I know. I know.' The tone of her voice was sadly familiar. It had a frustrated edge to it, like he made her life more complicated.

Gran stepped in front of Fin and gave a disapproving shake of her head.

Lindy continued, more quietly, as if it might prevent the hospital people from listening in. 'Have there been any... visitors?'

Fin moved towards the kitchen. 'No, Mum. No visitors.'

'Oh.' She resumed in her more formal tone. 'Well, I guess...by now... I guess that's that, then.'

Gran came even closer so she could listen in.

Fin stepped into the pantry to get away from her, but she followed him in. He said, 'Yes, that's that.'

'Don't keep your mother, dear.' Gran reached out for the phone.

'Gran says... She says I've got to go.' He spoke slowly, stretching out the space between each word.

'Okay, little man. Okay, we'll talk soon. You be good.'

'Yes, Mum.' He handed the phone back, turned away and stepped right up to the pantry shelves so he could cry without Gran watching. He imagined he heard footsteps out the front.

Gran walked away to finish the call with Lindy and then returned and stood in the doorway to the pantry to watch what he was doing.

Fin struggled to get words out. 'When are they going to let her out?'

'Not until she's ready. And anyway, they won't release her unless it's into my legal care. Not after all that. They'll make sure the formalities are seen to with a guardianship so there isn't a repeat. That way, I'll be making the decisions for you both.'

The idea that Gran could decide everything for them when she got out did not sound good. 'So when?'

'Griffin, I'm a lot of things, but I'm not a doctor.' Gran seemed strangely happy about it. 'And while we're on the subject of things I'm not, I'm not a telephone technician. I've no idea how to change the sound of this awful thing.' She held the phone out towards him. 'But continuing with that frightful phone ringer just won't do. It's an embarrassment. It came with the unit, but it barely sounds like a telephone at all. You'll need to change it for me.'

Fin stepped out of the pantry, blinking away tears, and took the phone. 'What's your passcode? It's locked.'

Gran took the phone from him. 'I'll put it in for you.' She turned away and then handed the phone back unlocked.

~

Josie turned on her fan, raised a cigarette to her lips, and put it back in the packet without lighting it. 'Where's your little friend, the opinionated one? He hasn't poked himself through in a while.'

Fin sat down beside her and switched the fan off. 'He's not opinionated.'

'He's made his opinions on fruit salad pretty clear.' Josie reached for the cigarette packet again; she pulled her hand away with a sigh. 'Don't get it into your head that I don't like opinions, mister. Truth be told, I like nothing better.'

Fin wasn't sure if being opinionated was a bad thing, but it sounded like it. 'He's got opinions. Just he's not opinionated, that's all.'

'Well, then I like him all the better. May he last long.'

Fin repeated the phrase in his mind – *may he last long* – and they both looked at the tunnel through the bush.

Josie continued. 'Actually, your friend and his opinions are a sign of thawing relations. And I like nothing better than thawing relations. Barely a word has passed between us and Mr Coleman for fifteen years until you boys. New generation.'

He thought to tell Josie that he and Rory weren't allowed to play together anymore, but he didn't want to disappoint her. It also might get back to Pop somehow.

'Yeah. I guess he hasn't been around.' Fin tried to sound casual. 'His mum's not here so he goes to see her.'

'Yes. I know. I remember Angela. Two peas in a pod she was with your mum. Proper chums. Angela had opinions, and they were good ones too. I'm sure she's still got them, but...' She paused and looked right into his eyes.

'But what, Josie?'

'But things sometimes get terribly muddled and, Golden Boy, back then anyway, there were all sorts of problems about it in the end. For silly reasons.'

Fin felt like she might keep going if he stayed quiet.

'Anyway, your friend and his opinions are a good sign. And I suspect we'll bring him around on the subject of fruit salad over time.'

Fin could feel the story of Lindy and Rory's mum slipping away. 'What do you mean by muddled?'

'Oh, Golden Boy. I don't want to go raking through old leaves. Enough to say that some risky things happened and a whole lot of blame got lumped on people who didn't deserve it.' She paused for a moment before deciding to go on. 'Your father most of all. He was the one who got the worst of it. He wasn't always good, but he was best of us back then.' She grabbed a cigarette and lit it. 'Could you switch my fan on for me?'

Fin angled it to point away before he switched it on. 'Yeah?'

'I know you don't know much about him, your dad. Or anything of this. But you should know that he loved your mother…and you. And he meant every bit of it. And when things got…muddled, he got blamed for the lot. He didn't argue, though. He did it to protect your mother, and he didn't care what happened to him because of it.' She took a thoughtful draw on her cigarette. 'Some people,' she pointed to the kitchen with her thumb, 'have forgotten that. But there's never only one side to a story. You know her.'

'Is that why, you know, he went away? Because of the muddle with Rory's mum?'

'Griffin…' Josie leant forward as if to whisper a secret.

Gran was suddenly standing at the kitchen door holding Fin's old sneakers. 'In this household, we do not leave hazards on stairs, young man. One fall down those stairs and I'd be finished. No good to anyone. Neck broken on the landing tiles!' She tossed his shoes out into the middle of the lawn. 'Not in this house.'

Fin and Josie looked at the shoes; Gran had thrown them surprisingly far.

Josie spoke, shaking her head. 'Antonella.'

'Enough said. Action, not conversation, I say. I'm making a pot of tea. What about for you, young man? Lemon and honey?'

'Yes, please.'

Gran went back into the kitchen and began making tea. She seemed to be unusually noisy, banging cups and speaking the steps out loud to herself.

Josie looked at Fin with an expression of weary resolve. She spoke very quietly but exaggerated the movement of her lips to ensure Fin could understand her. 'You're a good boy.'

After what Lindy had told him about poison, and what Josie had said about keeping her out of the kitchen, Fin didn't like the idea of Gran making tea. He'd said yes without thinking.

'Josie, are you okay? I mean, are you okay with Gran doing this?' He pointed to the kitchen.

'What choice do I have?'

'We could get out of here. You and me, until Mum gets out. We could get a taxi somewhere.' Fin was speaking quickly, taking advantage of the sound of the boiling kettle to hide what he was saying.

'I wouldn't give her the satisfaction.' She puckered her lips and leant forward for a kiss.

Fin stepped closer and she kissed him on the forehead.

'One thing I'm not going to do, mister, is waste my life complaining about living. Nor should you, particularly you. You've got adventure in you. Your gran's right about one thing, it's action that matters. Your great-granddaddy was like that. There's too much waiting and complaining in this world.'

Gran appeared and loudly banged down a saucer piled with biscuits. She put Josie's tea in front of her. 'I thought I'd join you in the wind. That is, as long as you can hold off puffing on those horrible things for a modicum?'

'As you wish.' Josie's shoulders dropped.

Gran went back into the kitchen and returned with another cup of tea and Fin's lemon and honey. She grabbed a biscuit. 'Go on then.'

Fin brought a biscuit to his lips and pretended to take a bite. He concealed the rest of the biscuit in his hand and scratched off a corner on the side of his chair.

Gran raised her teacup in a toasting motion. 'Happy festive season to you both.'

'Merry Christmas. Many happy returns.' Josie took a sip.

Fin raised his cup to his lips and mimed taking a sip, but he didn't let any of the lemony liquid into his mouth. It had a strong, spicy scent, a bit like Turkish delight.

They sat together and Gran did most of the talking. She said that she had 'commenced proceedings' because Mr Coleman had switched their garbage bins without her permission. In response, the council had said they would issue the whole street with new garbage bins, but they were a new kind that were 'inadequately small'. She said that she'd 'obtained advice' and sent some more letters, and she was now certain that the 'matter was in hand'.

Josie nodded along, but she mainly looked at Fin as Gran spoke. Fin wondered what Gran wanted to put in such a big garbage bin.

When her tea was finished, Gran clacked her empty cup on the table. 'Well, I'd better get back to it. I've got a mountain.' She went inside, leaving her empty cup behind.

Fin walked out on the lawn to pour out his lemon and honey. Then he crunched his biscuit between his fingers and let the crumbs fall around his feet. When he turned back, Josie was draining her teacup. He thought of calling out to stop her, but it was too late.

He sat back down, and Josie took a bite from a biscuit.

'You'll be all right, mister. Your mum will be back to her opinionated self in no time.'

Fin opened his mouth to object, but Josie gave him a smile and a wink.

'I think I've done enough sitting for one day. I've never been so tired in all my life as these last few days.' She stood slowly. 'Rest my eyes.'

She gave him a reassuring, warm smile, but then her face was strange. Her right cheek went flabby and she began pushing the last bit of chewed-up biscuit out onto her wobbling chin. There was fear in her eyes and her mouth was dribbly and out of control.

'Josie?' Fin took a step towards her and managed to catch her in the chest with his shoulder as she collapsed forward. 'Josie!'

She was silent. Dead weight. Her legs were giving way. He knew he wasn't strong enough to lift her back up, so he swivelled around and dug his back under her. He couldn't prevent her from slipping, so he went down with her weight, tilting forward until he was hunched over on the ground with her on his back. She was lifeless on top of him.

'Gran! Gran!' There was no response. He shouted louder this time. 'Gran! There's something wrong with Josie.'

Gran didn't come.

'Rory!'

She was dead, floppy heavy. And it was taking all his strength to hold her. He knew he couldn't move or get up without dropping her onto the bricks.

'Rory! Help!'

He could feel each of the bones in his spine straining against the weight. His ribs stretched out with each breath. Gran wasn't coming to help. Now he knew it was poison. He shouted again, 'Josie!' He could feel the slimy warmth of her saliva making its way down the right side of his neck.

He planned how he could get her off without cracking her head onto the bricks. He'd have to try to crawl over to the grass and then gently roll her off. Then he could call an ambulance from Gran's phone. But he knew she wouldn't let him, not until the poison had finished doing its work. And even if he could get the phone off her, she'd been careful to hide the passcode from him. He moved his arm forward, but she was resting so unevenly that she nearly slipped off onto the bricks.

He reached his hand out in an attempt to crawl, but the slightest shift in the angle of his back started her slipping. Her whole body was doughy, and it was only the smallest area of balance that was keeping her on.

'Rory!'

A little black picnic ant crawled underneath him. It was making its way over the mighty dips and rises in the bricks with a crumb from Fin's biscuit on its back. He spoke quietly, trying to preserve the strength in each breath, 'Careful, little ant. That biscuit's no good.'

There was a dull thud and two big couch cushions were suddenly beside him on the ground.

Gran wedged them in close. 'I'll try to steady her as you roll over.'

Fin felt his muscles almost give way with relief. He tilted Josie to the right and she began to slide off him, flopping onto the cushions. Gran steadied Josie's shoulders and neck and, as soon as she was lying down, Gran straightened up her head. Then she hurried into the house with her phone pressed to her ear.

Fin looked more closely at Josie. Her eyes were open, but she didn't seem to be inside. There was gooey, biscuity saliva all over her cheek. He put his hand on her chest to check. He thought he could feel her ribs moving, but he couldn't be sure. He felt again, but she was dead still. He stretched the front of his T-shirt out and wiped the spit and biscuit mush off her face. She wouldn't want anyone to see her like that.

'I'll get you fixed up, Josie. You just make sure you start breathing again.' Then he added as an afterthought, 'May you last long.'

Fin heard the crunching of leaves in the garden and spun around. Rory was on all fours, his head poking out of the tunnel through the bush. Fin and Rory's eyes locked together. It felt to Fin like he was close, almost as though they were sitting nose-to-nose. Rory didn't speak or get up to come towards them, but he held his thumb up and kissed his thumbnail, like he was blowing a good-luck kiss.

Gran reappeared and began pulling at Josie's shoulder. 'The ambulance is on its way. They said we've got to roll her onto her side.'

Fin pushed; he had to keep hold to make sure she didn't roll right over. He looked again, but Rory was gone.

Two ambulancemen arrived. They pulled out her false teeth and put them in a see-through bag as they asked Fin questions about what happened. Then they strapped her onto a stretcher and carried her out to the ambulance.

Fin went back to the warmth of Josie's patio. He tightened his stomach and tried to cry but the feeling was stuck inside him and tears wouldn't come. He was too scared. It was clear to him now that his mum had been right. Gran had started with Josie to get her out of the way. He would be next.

'Come on then.' Gran was calling from the front door.

Fin hurried through the living room. Gran was dressed up. He went to follow her out, but the sick fear that filled him made him feel off balance, and he felt himself falling forward, like Josie had fallen. He caught himself with a long stride, and Gran turned to look when she heard him stomp on the landing tiles near the front door. She looked tired but also happy, like she'd finally got what she wanted. Fin knew that everything Lindy had said about Gran was true.

'You won't be going anywhere without shoes. Not today!'

He hurried out past Josie's fan and the couch cushions to collect his shoes from where Gran had thrown them on the back lawn.

~

The nurse said they couldn't see her yet; the doctors were still working. So he and Gran sat against the wall below the TV in the only two empty chairs. There was a baby asleep in its father's arms, but all the other people were tired-looking and old. Gran went back and forth to the nurse's counter to demand a 'diagnosis', and then she stepped away to make a phone call. Fin's back and shoulders were aching, so he pulled his knees up and twisted around to rest against the back of the hard plastic chair.

Gran returned from her phone call. 'Griffin, get your knees down.'

Fin didn't move. He'd just managed to find a position where his shoulders weren't hurting.

'Griffin!'

He swung his feet back onto the floor.

'If nothing else, this whole thing is a lesson in the importance of doing what I say. Otherwise…' Gran paused and looked at him closely.

Fin finished the sentence in his head – *otherwise, I'll poison you too*. And for a moment, he felt glad that his and Rory's boat trip meant Lindy was safely in hospital, at least for now.

Gran pulled out the Mensa book. He said his arms were sore and he didn't feel like he'd do well in any tests.

'How about we just knock off a page or two?' She held the pencil up to check its sharpness.

He felt so worn out and sad that the pencil slipped through his fingers. Gran took it from him so he could just say the answers while she wrote. Fin watched as the tendons in her hand bulged and slid side to side. Her knuckles looked like paper that had been unfolded so many times it was starting to fall apart. He imagined the skin pulling tight as she pinched and sprinkled the poison into Josie's cup of tea.

Eventually, a young doctor with perfectly straight hair came to say that Josie had stabilised. She said they still didn't know what was wrong, but they were investigating. Fin noticed that Gran squeezed her elbows against her sides when the doctor said 'investigating', and she immediately stood up and pulled the doctor away to have a conversation where Fin couldn't hear.

They drove home as it was getting dark. The air inside the house was sticky and dead silent. Gran had bought him a sandwich at the hospital, but he'd torn it up and hidden it in his pocket, so he was feeling weak with hunger. Gran went straight into the front room and closed the door.

He used one of Josie's sharp knives to cut up a chunky fruit salad and ate it on the couch while he looked at the pink face of the newspaper man stuck to the TV. He slurped water straight from the bathroom tap before he went to bed and, for the first time since Lindy went to hospital, Gran didn't come in for her cuddle.

~

Fin was shocked awake. It took a moment before the patchy paint reminded him that he was in Lindy's room at Gran's. He was already sitting up, and all was silent except for the song of a lonely night bird. The pieces of his dream were all around him in the dark – the shattering windscreen glass flung forward and the outline of a tree with all its branches cut off halfway along. The dream was so fresh that he knew he would return to the place with the shards of glass and the cut-off tree if he lay back down. So he walked quietly into the bathroom and patted cold water on his neck until any chance of restarting the dream was gone.

And then, through the gap in the bathroom window, he heard a shoe step onto the front path. He listened close – nothing. He trod as lightly as he could as he went down. The tiles near the front door were cool under his feet, and he gripped the latch tight as he unclicked the lock. He stepped out into the night and was careful not to let the door close behind him. He heard movement in the leaves above and the billowy flap of a bat taking flight, but there was no-one there.

It had been four days now since Lindy had told him that his dad would come straight to get him. But four days was long enough to drive from the furthest possible place in Australia. He sat down on the step and felt the weight of it come down on him – no-one was coming. His only option was to escape. He could leave now, heading north and following the powerlines. But someone might notice him in the dark. He'd have to wait until morning.

CHAPTER THIRTEEN

The sun was already glowing around the curtains when Fin woke up again. He pulled his shoes on and tucked his golf ball into his pocket. He'd made up his mind to leave, but he couldn't go without telling Rory.

The dew was still heavy on the grass as he crawled into Rory's tunnel through the bush to wait. Everything about Pop's house was solid and motionless; even the all-day mumble of the talk radio was gone. He knew that once Rory heard what Gran had done, he would do anything to help and, together, they could make it all the way to Gustav's.

He began counting his breaths, as though that would make time go faster. He slowed down as he approached a hundred, hoping the door would fly open and Rory would appear. He reached a hundred and one, then a hundred and two, and stopped counting. He thought about the rune tiles his mum had tried to hide from him the day he killed the crab – ᚺ, *you can't go back*, and ϒ, *the life-and-death rune* – and he knew now that the runes had told Lindy what was coming. But the giant fuss about New Zealand had got her locked up in hospital.

He retrieved his golf ball from his pocket, squeezed it hard and imagined it could grant him a wish – *Josie would be all right, and I'd be back up at Gustav's with Mum.* But then he remembered the stress and fear of the last days there, after Deirdre and the snake. And quickly, as though he could mentally scribble it out and write a new wish over the top – *Josie would be all right and my dad would come.*

He squeezed his golf ball again to lock in the wish, and he heard a quiet crunching of leaves to his right. Crunch, crunch, crunch, stop. Crunch, crunch, crunch, stop. It sounded like a little bird hopping and searching through the leaves. The sound seemed to be very close, but he still couldn't see anything. He looked back at Rory's house – nothing. Again, crunch, crunch, crunch, stop. He could just make out the rounded ears and little eyes of a bush mouse. It was only a few centimetres from him. He could have reached out and grabbed it if he'd been quiet and quick enough.

The mouse sniffed and looked straight at Fin, then it looked side to side. Fin realised he was in its way. He thought about wriggling backwards to clear the mouse's path, but he was worried it might be the moment Rory emerged. He stayed where he was with his eyes fixed on the mouse. Each time it took a few creeping steps, its little body would stretch out, and then it would retract into a perfect, furry ball. The mouse looked at him, took another step and looked again. Then it seemed to make up its mind. Its little body stretched out and it began to run.

There was a sudden movement to his right. It was like the ground beneath the leaf litter had erupted, and the old leaves had exploded upwards. The mouse instantly launched itself in a flailing leap. Fin only saw the brown head and the shiny eyes of the snake when it recoiled to make its second strike.

The mouse continued running while it was in the air and Fin smelled the familiar woodpile smell of urine and fur as its little body slapped into his cheek and its tail whipped across his lips. The snake's prey was now wriggling against Fin's face.

The snake's black eyes were fixed on the mouse. Fin tried to roll left to pull his face back from the tiny body of the mouse, but he was held in place by the stiff branches of the bush. He was trapped there.

He prepared himself for a brown-snake bite on his face. And it seemed like the time it took to draw each breath had stretched. He felt the jittery pressure of the mouse's feet against his face as the snake launched its second strike. But, rather than retreating, the mouse leapt towards the snake's open jaws with its little paws reaching out and its mouth wide open. It caught the snake by surprise in mid-air, wrapped its little arms around the top of the snake's body and sunk its teeth into the flesh just below the head. The snake snapped away from the mouse, and its whole muscular length seemed to leave the ground like a cracking whip. The mouse was flung away through the bush and Fin saw a flapping wound like a tiny mouth in the side of the snake's neck. He heard the crunching of leaves as the mouse ran away through the bush.

Fin dug his hands into the damp earth and propelled himself backwards with a sudden push. He flopped down hard onto the spongy grass of the back lawn, and as soon as his stomach hit the ground, he sprang to his feet and began to run. He lifted his eyes towards the kitchen door. Gran was standing on the brick patio with her hand inside a bag of sliced bread. She was dressed for going out.

'We're leaving.' She handed him the bag of bread and went inside.

Fin looked back at the tunnel through the bush. His golf ball was still in there.

~

Gran started an argument with a woman's voice coming from a speaker on the boom gate at the hospital car park. Gran said she needed to be assured that the machine had 'acknowledged the validity' of her three-day parking ticket and that she wasn't going to be 'extorted' for an extra payment. Nothing the woman said would satisfy Gran and she only gave up once the woman provided her name, job title, and an email address for written complaints. By this stage, there were cars queued up behind them and the drivers had begun honking and calling out through their open windows.

Gran and Fin walked through the hospital foyer, past the people drinking coffee and eating toast in the cafeteria, and Fin saw fruit salad piled high behind the glass on the counter. They stepped into a lift crowded with old people and nurses, and Gran made a point of telling him loudly that she'd 'pulled strings' to ensure that Josie had a private room. Fin was suspicious about why Gran thought this was a good thing. He thought Josie probably would have been better off sharing with someone. Apart from the company, it would be safer to have a witness if Gran tried anything.

They approached the nurses' station and Gran announced her arrival. 'Antonella Alverton.'

Once the nurse worked out that this was Gran's name rather than Josie's, she directed them to a room in the corner. Gran barged in and Fin followed cautiously. Josie was in a bed, lying perfectly flat on the mattress without a pillow under her head. She had a breathing mask on and a drip going into her hand. The mask was making a gasping, sighing sound and Josie seemed to pause for too long between each breath.

'She hasn't regained consciousness.' Gran pulled the Mensa book out of her bag and placed it on a high table in the corner. 'She can't see, but they say she might be able to hear.' Gran retrieved a pen from her handbag and held it up to show him. 'But I don't know that there's much point us talking to her. What would we say?'

Fin approached the side of the bed. 'Hello, Josie.'

She looked narrower than she had the day before, as though there was less of her inside her skin.

'Anyway, I'll go and demand a prognosis. I may be some time.' Gran tugged the bottom of her shirt to straighten it. 'You could wait your whole life for answers in this place.'

Fin stayed standing by Josie's bed as Gran marched out of the room.

'Hello, Josie. Hello.' He wanted to reach and touch her, but he was afraid some of the poison might get on him. 'They have a big fruit salad downstairs. A huge one. I would have brought you a scoop, but I don't have money.'

Josie's breathing mask kept puffing and hissing. She was so still that it seemed impossible she might get better. Fin laid his hand on the blanket over Josie's leg and began gently stroking. There was only one thing he needed to know. And although Josie couldn't talk, he thought there might be some way she could signal.

'Josie, did Gran do this to you? You know, did she put poison in your cup of tea? Is that what the doctor is investigating?'

Josie didn't move.

'Sorry, Josie. I know you can't talk, but I kind of really need to know. I'm by myself with her now.' He started to cry. 'I'm sorry, Josie. But if it's true, I mean, if Gran used poison on you, if that's what the doctors think, just wiggle your leg a bit. Just wiggle a bit if she's the one who did it. I'll feel it if you wiggle. Once is enough.' He stroked her leg through the blanket again to remind her where his hand was. 'Please, Josie. Anything, just one wiggle.'

Suddenly, her leg stiffened and her eyes sprung open. They were wide and straining out of her head, like she was filled with rage.

'Josie?'

Her head pulled sideways into a terrible, scowling yawn. It looked like her mouth was trying to pull itself off the side of her face. She flung her arms straight up above her chest with her hands shaped into two straining claws.

'Josie!' Fin was shouting now and crying at the same time.

Her body jolted and squirmed as if waves of furious electricity were zapping through her. He grabbed her arm to try to reassure her. Her eyes widened further, and she stared right at him with a look of terrible, hate-filled rage.

'Help! Help!' He ran to the door. 'Help! She needs a doctor!'

Two female nurses hurried towards him and he ran back to Josie's bedside. Her eyes were still fixed on him.

'Josie, it's me.'

One of the nurses placed her hand firmly on Josie's shoulder to stop her rolling out of bed. A growling burp erupted from Josie and a splash of yellow vomit filled up the breathing mask. It had a horrible smell like rotten fruit.

'Get the boy out! Get the boy out!' The nurse holding Josie was yelling to the nurse on the other side of the bed.

'Josie!' Fin was really crying now.

The other nurse put a hand on his shoulder and ushered him out of the room.

Fin called out her name one more time – 'Josie!' – and before the nurse closed the door, he turned, raised his thumb and kissed it, like he was blowing a good-luck kiss.

As soon as he was in the corridor, he ran. Each part of his body moved in an unstoppable, coordinated motion. It felt like he was flying and he only needed to maintain contact with the ground so he could steer. He ran out towards the lifts and saw a green exit sign. He pushed on the door and began skipping and leaping down the echoing concrete stairs. All he could think about was emerging beneath the open sky at the bottom. The same sky that stretched all the way to Gustav's.

He pushed hard on big doors and the sticky humidity of the air outside flooded into the cold concrete of the stairwell. He was in a laneway behind the hospital, and there was a loading dock filled with overflowing laundry bags. He ran behind a few short brick buildings. Could his mum be somewhere here? He ran faster and scanned the shapes and colours of each building for anything familiar. But they all seemed newer and cleaner than where they were keeping Lindy. If he could find the cemetery, he'd be able to follow its old fence to Lindy's building.

His side ached from a stitch, and his shins hurt from running on hard ground. He began to slow and, eventually, he found himself approaching the white picket fence of an empty cricket field. He gave up running and sat down heavily on the sloping hill overlooking the grass. If he was really going to escape, he couldn't do it like this. He was going to have to plan properly.

He thought about ways, other than walking, he could get back to Gustav's by himself. He didn't have any money, and it had felt like a very long way on the bus. He knew he could steal the money from Gran's purse and find the number of the bus company, but Gran wouldn't give him the code to unlock her phone.

The best plan he could think of was to just start walking north, following the powerlines. But he knew Gran would have the police out looking for him. He could stick to the coast, stay off the roads. It would be harder going, and there would be more of a chance of getting lost, but he'd be safe from police cars until it was time to turn west towards the hills. And, if Rory would come, they could fish along the way for food.

The grass of the cricket field seemed to grow clearer before his eyes and, as though he was seeing things clearly for the first time, he knew Lindy was right. Gran planned to poison them and now Josie had confirmed it. His mum couldn't help him and his dad wasn't coming. If he was going to survive, he needed to save himself. And, if he wanted Rory's help, he was going to have to knock on Pop's door.

'Griffin?'

Fin turned to see a bearded security guard in a grey uniform.

'Yes.'

The security guard mumbled into his radio, then said, 'Come with me, please.'

~

Gran refused to speak to him in the car on the way home. She said she was 'too distressed'. When the security guard had led him back to her, she made a point of bending over to look him straight in the eye and telling him that he'd given her a 'heart attack'. She'd also said, 'It's as though you don't appreciate how many competing needs I've got on my plate at the moment. Caring for your mother and Josie, as well as for the likes of you.' She didn't say anything about what had happened with Josie. She went straight to her computer when they got home.

It was too dangerous for him to stay now. He had to go. But if there was any chance that Rory might come, he'd have to knock on Pop's door. He knew Gran wouldn't stop typing until she'd drafted the letter about the parking-station woman, so he'd have a bit of time. He put on a long-sleeve T-shirt and tied his light-blue hoodie around his waist; Rory might say they could leave right away.

Just as he reached the top of the stairs, Gran appeared in the doorway to the front room and turned to come up. He hurried back into Lindy's room and slid in behind the open door; he could see through the gap between the hinges.

He watched as she reached the top of the stairs. He found himself holding his breath as she approached. He was frozen.

She didn't know he was there. She had a small, pointy bottle in her hand, innocent-looking, like it could have been medicine. But he knew what it was.

She drew closer, within about a metre now. She looked sad and tired, with an almost regretful expression on her face, like she was resigned to poisoning him but wouldn't enjoy it. She reached out to push the door. And stopped. Fin was terrified she would see him. He closed his eyes. He could hear her breathing. She stood there, like she was deciding something. Then Fin heard her feet on the carpet, and he opened his eyes to see her disappearing into the bathroom.

As quietly as he could, he hurried down the stairs, out through the front door, and he ran through the front garden and knocked hard on Rory's front door and waited. Pop swung the door open. He was dressed in a polo shirt and shorts; the skin of his white legs was mottled with pink and brown blotches. His eyes widened and his head wobbled on top of his neck like it was balancing there. His body was drifting from side to side above his legs like he was on the deck of a boat.

'Yes?'

Fin made a point of speaking loud and clear. 'Hello, Pop. I'd like to talk to Rory, please.'

Pop paused for a moment and then turned and led the way down the corridor. Fin stepped in, closed the door and followed behind. The darkness was almost total. Pop ran his hand along the wall as he walked, before turning through a doorway.

Sunlight glowed around the edges of the pull-down blinds above the kitchen sink. He'd been so focused on Lindy last time that he hadn't noticed the walls were painted the same pale green as the benchtop and the kitchen table. The faded yellow of the cupboard doors showed the uneven smudges made by years of hands reaching for the handles.

Pop kept his back turned. 'Milk and sugar?'

'Yes, thank you.' Fin lifted the chair so it didn't scrape on the lino before he sat down.

The silence seemed louder with the rattling of the kettle, but each time Fin went to speak, words wouldn't come. Gran had once told him not to put his elbows on the table, so he kept his arms by his sides.

Pop turned with two mugs. He placed one in front of Fin and sat in the chair opposite.

'It's madness out there. I'm barely on the threshold before I'm jolly soaking from it. In this heat. Don't know how the boy does it.'

'It's very hot, the sun.'

'He'll come to his senses shortly and run up from the river. Won't be long.' Pop slurped his tea as if he was trying to bubble it full of air. 'Your mother pull through?'

'Yes. She's in hospital, but she's all right.'

'Good for her.' He took another slurp of tea.

Now that he knew Rory was down in the bush, he hoped Pop would let him leave. But he also knew he couldn't ask to leave until he'd finished his cup of tea.

Fin put his lips to the edge of the mug and slurped. The heat of the liquid shocked the thin skin behind his top teeth. It was the first time he'd drunk tea.

Pop seemed to look at him for comment.

'It's nice-tasting tea.'

He relaxed back in his chair. 'Your father keeping busy?'

Fin's hands shook as he took another slurp. 'Yes, he's keeping busy.'

'We didn't always see eye to eye. Your dad, I mean. But he's no slouch. A stand-up bloke and always trying to patch things up between people. As if there's a jolly point sometimes.' Pop sat up straight each time he took a sip.

Fin slurped some more tea.

'We all know your mother can have her moments.' He winked. 'But your father wouldn't hear a bad word about her. And always minded our Angela, the boy's mother. But he's a straight shooter when it counts, your father. Send him a cheerio from me, won't you? A straight shooter.'

'Yes. I will.'

Pop had another slurp of tea. 'And I'll bet you're that too. A straight shooter?'

Fin was trying to finish his tea as quickly as possible, but it was too hot. 'I'm sorry. I'm not really sure what that means.'

'Not too fancy with the truth. You tell the truth, do you?'

'Yes, I do.'

'Well, you would. Belinda landed the better of them, that's for sure. The boy's father's been AWOL mostly since the start.

And even less with the expenses. Wouldn't even know how to put his hand in his pocket, if you ask me.'

Fin's mouth was prickly with heat; he guessed there were two big slurps left in the mug.

'Our Angela went through higher education. Graduated now. Fully qualified. Your grandmother might like to know that.'

'Yes.' Fin could feel the sweat on his neck and his heart was beating like he'd just run up a hill. He judged that he could finish the tea in one big mouthful. He tilted the mug and slurped.

Fin felt the hot liquid overfilling his mouth and some trickled into his throat. He screwed up his face to stop it, but a violent cough erupted from him and sent tea spraying out across the table. Fin heard the sound of the back flyscreen door opening and slapping closed. Pop stood quickly to stop the tea running into his lap and seemed to lose his balance. He tried to grab the bench as he came crashing down onto the lino.

Rory appeared in the doorway and screamed, 'What did you do?' It was an accusation rather than a question. He stared at Fin as he knelt to help his grandfather.

'But...' Fin could feel tears welling in his eyes.

Rory retrieved a silver flask from the old man's back pocket. He unscrewed the cap and pressed the neck of it to Pop's lips.

'I told you not to come here. You're bad luck! He's got a hip replacement.' Rory's face was contorted in violent rage.

'I'm sorry. I didn't mean… It was the tea.'

'Go!' Rory snarled the word through his teeth.

Fin stood and ran. He felt tea trickling down his legs. He swung the front door open, crossed the lawn and kept running up the street. He was determined to set out for Gustav's now. But, without Rory, he wasn't sure if he could make it. The police would probably find him and bring him back. And worse, the ambulance would deliver Lindy to Gran when the doctors let her out and she would be trapped in Gran's 'legal care', and she'd have no chance now Josie was gone. He couldn't take that risk.

He thumped the knuckles of his clenched fist into the side of his head. ϒ – had come, and Rory's voice seemed to echo inside his head – *you're bad luck*. It was the only time he had seen Gran make Josie a cup of tea. He had known not to drink the lemon and honey, but he didn't stop Josie. He'd just watched while she drank down the poison. Why had he accepted the tea from Pop? His stomach tightened, but there was no point crying now. If he had any chance of surviving, whatever the cost, whatever happened to him, he had to stop Gran. There was no way he could make it all the way to Gustav's on his own. It was too late for Josie, but he had to do something, *anything*, to protect his mum.

He kept running until he found a scruffy path between two big houses; it led down into the bush. The mud-crabby smell of the riverbed told him that the tide was low. He followed a narrow path along the mudflat until he reached

Crab Rock, and he paused on the smooth surface. There was no smell of fire, but he could sense that Rory had been there. It was almost as though he could feel the places Rory had touched the stone.

He climbed around to look in the little overhang where Rory stored his crab equipment. It was all tucked back so that no-one would see it. He reached in and felt a coil of fishing line, pulled it out and placed it to the side. Although he didn't know how to fish, he knew it might be useful if he ended up alone.

He reached in again. This time his hand landed on the smooth handle of the tomahawk, and he drew it out slowly. He wrapped his other hand around it and lifted it high, then he brought it down in a fast practice swing. He lifted it again and swung a heavy slice through the air. He knew now, if it came to it, one blow from this little axe would be enough. He and Lindy would finally be safe.

He tucked the coil of fishing line into his pocket and carried the tomahawk up the path towards Gran's. Before he reached the back lawn, he stomped his feet to scare away any snakes and slid the tomahawk under the rock ledge, the same placed he'd hidden the sandwiches for New Zealand.

He passed Josie's fan and the table; her empty teacup was still there. He stepped quietly into the kitchen. There was a sandwich on a plate on the bench, it had been cut once diagonally. He lifted the top slice of bread and buttery pieces of tomato flopped onto the cheese inside. There was no sign of Gran. He was careful not to touch the insides to make sure he didn't get any of the poison on his fingers.

The trap she had set had not caught him this time, but the longer he stayed, the more chances she'd have to get the poison into him and he'd be like Josie. He imagined the flat hospital bed and the plasticky pressure of the puffing mask. It felt like there was only one way this could end. He again thought of running, just to see how far he got. But then he thought of Lindy once she was released, stuck alone here with Gran and, instead of him in the puffing mask and the hospital bed, it would be her.

He crept through the house and looked into the front room. Gran's head was outlined by the glow of her computer screen. He imagined the weight of the little axe in his hand and knew that sitting at the computer with her back turned would be the perfect moment. The thought was horrible, but there was also a cold feeling of certainty about what he had to do.

As she lifted a sandwich to her lips, she noticed his reflection in the front window and spun around. She made a point of chewing and swallowing her bite of sandwich before speaking. 'Don't hover, dear. I made one for you. In the kitchen.'

'Yes, Gran.'

He hid the sandwich under some other stuff in the bin and grabbed a banana and an apple from Josie's fruit bowl. He was going to have to time this perfectly. There were a lot of things that could go wrong.

~

As Fin lay in bed that night, the thought that he might never see his mum again curled around him like a rope. The solution, a single blow to Gran's head, had seemed simple. But it wasn't. Even though she was a murderer, she was still a person, and he hadn't even been able to chop the crab properly without Rory.

More than anything he wanted to run home to Gustav's and, if he could keep sight of the powerlines, he might just make it. But he also knew that if he escaped, Lindy would still be trapped here and Gran would never let her go. He had to do something to stop her; he had to fight back. There was no way he could just chop her with an axe. Whatever he did, it needed to look like an accident.

He heard the stairs creak under Gran's feet. He rolled over to face away from the door and kept his breathing deep and regular. The door opened and the light at the top of the stairs showed through his eyelids. He heard her step into the room. His heart was beating so hard he could feel it in his neck. For all he knew, she had a knife or something to strangle him with, and he realised that she probably thought he was poisoned from the sandwich. He wished he'd kept the tomahawk with him.

The sheet lifted up. He stayed perfectly still and could smell her soapy scent. He felt the mattress sag as she climbed in and slid one of her soft arms under his neck. She cuddled into his back, and the thought of listening to German records at Gustav's kept him calm enough.

After about twenty minutes, Gran's breathing changed to the humid rasping of sleep. He was determined to stay awake.

~

He woke in the sweaty dark. Gran was gone. The fading colours of a dream hung in the room for a moment. He tried to hold on to it and remember. He'd been up on the ridge at Gustav's, under the big goat-head powerlines. Rory was there and they'd both been listening to the hum of the wires and looking back over the house and the agistment cows.

He climbed out of bed and took each step individually so that any squeaks would sound like isolated noises in the night and not like someone walking. Outside, he felt the cool grass on his feet, then the roughness of the stone, then the smooth wood of the handle as he retrieved the tomahawk. He carried it back into the house and tucked it in the space between his mattress and the wall. He made sure to point the blade down so he couldn't roll on it in the night.

CHAPTER FOURTEEN

When he woke up, he could hear the calls of magpies and the sound of cars out on the road, which meant he had slept in later than usual. He was thirsty and his stomach had already begun aching for food. He reached down to check the tomahawk. It was gone. He spun around, expecting to see Gran holding it by his bed. He felt again for the little axe. The door swung open and Gran entered, carrying a tray with toast and a mug on it.

'It felt like that sort of morning to me. I made you hot chocolate.' Gran spoke in a casual way, as if there was nothing remarkable about her breakfast tray. But they both knew she hadn't brought any food or drink up since Lindy was locked up.

Fin scanned her face for any sign that she had found the tomahawk. She set the tray down on the bedside table. There was a calm, almost defiant look in her eyes as she continued staring at him.

Fin realised what she was waiting for. 'Thank you, Gran.'

'You're welcome.' She turned and left the room.

Fin waited until he heard her at the bottom of the stairs before he looked under the bed. The whole space was crammed with vitamin boxes. He tried to shift the bed away from the wall, but the boxes were wedged in behind the heavy bed frame and their combined weight was like a solid block under the bed. He looked again from above but the side of the bedframe was pushed hard up against the wall. The only explanation that made sense was that Gran must have watched him get it, and she had crept in to take it while he was sleeping.

He ripped up the toast, and he had to flush the toilet four times before the brown milkiness of the hot chocolate and all the crumbs went down.

Gran forced him to stick at Mensa practice longer than usual. She seemed to feel he owed it to her after she had made him breakfast. She marked his tests and said his results were 'going backwards'. He hadn't been able to concentrate because he was so hungry, and he'd been paying attention to every detail of her body language. As soon as she let him go, he headed out to the back lawn. Was it possible that he'd imagined getting the tomahawk last night? He stomped his feet to clear snakes, then he reached in and felt the morning-cool stone where the little axe had been. He stuck his head in as deep as he could into the shadowy place below the little ledge.

'Griffin!'

The sound of Gran's sweeter calling-out voice was so close that she must have been on the back lawn. When he stood up, he saw that she was only a metre or two away.

He looked into her eyes for any sign. 'Yes, Gran?'

'I've told you you're not to go down there. I won't have you running off again.'

He pulled himself over the ledge and, once they were inside the kitchen, she retrieved a bunch of keys from the pocket of her jeans and locked the back door from the inside.

'I've got a mountain to get through.' She took a knife from the drawer and an apple from the fruit bowl before she went back into the front room.

Fin looked out through the little glass panels on the back door and wondered why anyone would make a lock you can't open from the inside.

He spent the morning searching for ideas, but it seemed pointless because he didn't really know what he was looking for. There were plenty of ways he could cause an accident that would hurt her – fire, hot oil, a heavy box falling on her or even a bookcase – but that wouldn't do the job. She'd just be more determined to kill him than ever, and now she had the tomahawk.

He kept returning to the stairs. She'd said it herself – *in this household, we do not leave hazards on the stairs. One fall down those stairs and I'd be finished.* The problem was, if he put any 'hazards' there, she'd see them for sure. He could try to push her, but he thought the police would be able to tell the difference between someone who'd fallen down stairs and someone who was pushed. He needed something that would trip her over but she wouldn't see. The best thing he could come up with was one of the thin wineglasses. He could always clean it up before the police came, but there was no guarantee it would work. The reality of what he had to do rose up in him again, the horrible consequences of this planning. But how else could he protect his mum from what had happened to Josie?

And then the idea struck him, the invisible weapon that might just save Lindy – *fishing line.* If he could rig Rory's line across the stairs, there's no way Gran would see it, and he was sure it would be enough to trip her over.

He walked slowly up the stairs with his eyes flicking left and right. Tying it to the banister would be easy, but the other side was just skirting board and flat wall. He thought of tying a big loop to the banister and laying it on the stairs, but that might just tangle her foot up. If he was going to be sure it would work, it would need to be fastened at both ends.

He searched the kitchen cupboards and drawers for anything he could use. Gran had left the door of the front room open, and he could hear her typing. Each time he heard her keyboard stop rattling, he would rush to the living room floor and sit beside his half-assembled hovertank. After about an hour of looking, he flopped down on the couch. He could hear Gran on the phone again; she was using her important voice.

'His callous practice of hacking off the branches at the fence line is one thing, but it's extended to an incursion onto my property. He's now lopping the branches off right at the trunk, which would be impossible from his side of the fence.'

Fin heard the lunchtime birds starting, and it felt like they were calling him to come outside. He thought about checking the front door to see if he could get out, but it was too risky. Gran might see him and then she'd lock that too.

'I don't care whether it's better for the tree to remove them close to the trunk. I care that it evidences an incursion onto my property. My daughter planted that tree as a child, and I will not permit it to fall prey to an alcoholic vandal.' There was only a brief pause before she continued. 'In that case, please provide your full name and staff identification number. And be under no illusion, my complaint about the disrespect you have shown, and the fact you have casually dismissed my concerns will be writ large to the highest level.'

Fin heard the sound of her keyboard rattling on her desk.

He'd searched Lindy's room and everywhere he could downstairs, but he'd been too scared to look in the other bedrooms. Gran had followed him out to the rock ledge, and she might follow him upstairs, but he had to try.

He kept listening for the sound of Gran's keyboard as he climbed the stairs and crossed to Josie's door. He gripped the old metal doorknob, twisted and leant forward. But the door didn't open. He turned the knob the other way, but still the door didn't move. He looked closer and saw there was a scratched old keyhole; the door was locked. He knew Josie wouldn't have locked her bedroom door before she came down to the patio that last time. So Gran must have locked it. He looked around at the doors on Lindy's and Gran's bedrooms and saw they also had keyholes. It meant it would only take one click while he was sleeping and he wouldn't be able to get out.

He'd searched everywhere else, and now that Gran had found the tomahawk, he had to do something. It meant there was only one more room to look in. He listened again for the keyboard before he passed the bathroom and reached out for the handle of Gran's bedroom door. He heard the springs stretching in the latch as he slowly twisted; the door swung open.

All the curtains were closed and the bright sunlight was almost completely blocked out, but he wasn't going to risk turning on the light. He listened again for the sound of Gran's rattling keyboard before he took a step inside and carefully closed the door behind him. He flicked his eyes quickly around the room. It had been years since he'd been invited in for a story on her bed but the room still looked the same. On the wall to the left there was a large painting of a tree; it had wavy branches, like coral rising up to the top and flowers growing around the trunk. Gran's bed was made, and there were two flower-pattern cushions on it. They were stuffed so full that they looked like they were going to burst. There was a little wooden desk below the front window with two dark-wood cabinets either side. The cabinets had clear glass doors so you could see the painted figurines inside, mostly of elephants and flamingos.

He tried the little desk drawer; it was locked. He looked inside the cabinets for anything he could use to fasten the fishing line to the skirting board. He moved over to the shelves beside her bed. There was a line-up of notebooks and a stack of cassette tapes, like the few German ones they had up at Gustav's. Each tape had 'Belinda' written on it with a date. And dangling from the lowest shelf was what looked like a ponytail of blonde hair. It was fastened with a hair clip that was resting on the shelf, and it hung down so that it was nearly touching Gran's pillow. He reached out to touch it. And, as soon as his fingers brushed the hair, he knew it was Lindy's. It was like Gran had chopped off a piece of her to keep it trapped.

He pulled his hand away suddenly and the ponytail flopped onto the floor. As he bent down to retrieve it, he heard the quiet but unmistakable sound of Gran coming up the stairs. He flung himself onto Gran's bed and bounced over to the other side. He sprang towards the door, but it was too late, her footsteps were already passing the bathroom. He saw the doorknob turn as he flattened himself against the wall beside the door. He hoped it would swing open to hide him.

Gran only opened the door far enough to step inside. Fin froze. The half-open door offered no cover, and she was close enough that he could have reached out and touched her back. She walked over to the desk by the window, retrieved the bunch of keys from her pocket, unlocked the drawer and pulled out some papers and long envelopes. She hunched with her head hung forward as she sorted through them on the desk. Fin knew that as soon as she found what she was looking for, she'd turn around and see him. He thought of crossing back towards the bed and flattening himself against the carpet. But she might hear him moving closer. He had to get around the door and out.

Gran set one of the envelopes to the side, gathered up the rest of the papers and put them back in the drawer. He had to go now. She pulled her keys out of her pocket, and Fin used the sound of the jangling metal to mask his two steps forward. She inserted the key into the drawer lock. He took a step sideways, keeping his eyes locked on the back of her head. This was his chance. But suddenly, she looked to her right and stopped. Fin knew there was no point running. She had sensed him now. He braced himself and imagined her reaching for the little axe.

She moved towards the shelves beside her bed and, as she bent over to pick up Lindy's ponytail, Fin took a step to his left and jumped backwards through the doorway. After another two steps, he made it to Lindy's room and flung himself onto her bed, lying on his back with his hands behind his head.

He heard Gran's bedroom door close and the sound of her keys again before the click of the lock. He felt a surge of blood up his neck as he thought how, if he'd managed to hide down beside her bed, he would now be locked in.

'Griffin?' She used her calling-out voice.

He spoke the words too fast. 'Yes, Gran.'

She appeared in the doorway holding a brown envelope. 'Get your shoes off the bed.'

He swung his feet off the side so he was sitting up and listened as Gran went back downstairs.

He felt the ache and heard the hungry gurgling of his stomach. He thought about Josie's fruit salad, and about the last time he had seen her, wriggling with the truth of what Gran had done. He'd spent the morning searching for a way to secure the fishing line, but he was no closer than when he started. And he needed to eat.

He listened again for the sound of Gran's keyboard and made his way downstairs. Without Josie to refill it, the fruit bowl was getting low, but there was a banana left and a little pear, enough for a small fruit salad. Once he'd chopped up the fruit and filled a little bowl, he tucked in a spoon and went to open the back door so he could eat on Josie's patio. But the door was locked. He stepped back towards the kitchen bench and then took a few more steps into the pantry. It wasn't the patio, but it felt like one of Josie's places.

He put his bowl on the shelf below the line of teacups hung on hooks from the shelf above. He ran his eyes along the line of dangling cups and, again, noticed the two empty

187

cup hooks at the end of the line. As soon as he saw them, he knew he had found what he was looking for.

~

At about two o'clock, Gran called out to him from downstairs. He tucked the cup hook and a coil of fishing line into the toe of his worn old sneakers. He'd measured exactly how much fishing line he needed to make it across the stairs, and then he'd cut it longer to allow for the knots at either end. He'd also found a spot on the skirting board behind Lindy's bedroom door where he could practise screwing the hook in out of sight. He'd learnt that he had to push really hard and turn slowly until the screw bit into the wood. But, after that, he just had to twist until it was all the way in.

It would take less than a minute but he'd do it in two stages. After Gran had gone to bed, he'd screw in the hook and then, when he was sure she hadn't heard him, he'd come back to fasten the fishing line across the top of the stairs. Once she'd gone down, he'd unscrew the cup hook and put it back in its place in the pantry, and he'd run over to Pop and Rory's, bang on the door and say, 'Gran's fallen down. Call an ambulance.' He found himself mouthing the words in silent rehearsal. He knew that the more upset he could look the better.

He checked again to make sure the hook and fishing line were safely hidden in his shoe before he quietly walked downstairs. Gran was at her computer and there was another cheese and tomato sandwich waiting for him on the bench. He took it up to the bathroom, tore it into small pieces, wrapped them in toilet paper and flushed them down. He washed his hands thoroughly and then scooped up and drank as much water as he could to ease his hunger.

He went back to Lindy's room and thought about trying to heave the bedframe up so he could pull all the boxes out and see if the tomahawk had somehow managed to squeeze its way through the impossibly narrow gap. He hooked his fingers under the frame, and the bed lifted slightly but not high enough to remove a box. Even if he could manage to lift it with one hand and slide the boxes out with the other, there would be no way he could get all the boxes back under in time to hide what he was doing if Gran came to check.

He let the bed frame go and turned to look at himself in the mirror. He stood tall, the way he had stood on that first morning. His face was still patchy and peeling from sunburn, but it had begun to heal and didn't hurt anymore. His light brown hair had gained some length since his mum had clipped it all off and it was starting to lie down thin on his head. There were purply-brown smudges of tiredness on the skin under his eyes; it made his eyes look a darker green and deeper, like they extended further back into his head.

CHAPTER FIFTEEN

Gran cooked spaghetti with tinned tomato and grated cheese for dinner, but she didn't make Fin sit at the table. Instead, she sat with a tray on her lap and looked at the newspaper on the smashed TV. Fin stood at the kitchen bench, occasionally tapping his fork against the edge of the bowl before dropping bite-size pieces into a little plastic bag. He'd put toilet paper in the bottom to dampen the sound of the spaghetti falling in.

After Gran finished dinner, she placed her bowl and tray next to the sink and said, 'Time for bed, dear. Happy New Year.'

Fin's heart thumped as she leant towards him. She kissed the top of his head, turned away and walked towards the stairs.

'Night, Gran.'

He waited until she was gone and then went to the kitchen to scrape his food into the bin. He scrunched up some paper towel and put it on top so she wouldn't see. He looked through the glass panels on the back door and saw Josie's teacup still sitting on the table outside. He managed to keep his face still as the tears ran onto his lips. Her smoking fan was still there too. Gran hadn't mentioned Josie for two days now. It was clear she wasn't going to need her fan again.

Fin lay on Lindy's bed as night came. He was fully dressed, with his sneakers on. Not long after sunset, he heard the thunder of New Year's Eve celebrations in the distance – the early show. A couple of years before, he'd gone with Lindy and Gran to see the fireworks over the harbour. Lindy had wanted to stay for the midnight show so Fin could experience the new year really coming in, but Gran had said the highway would be 'impossible'. So he and Lindy had waited up, sitting side by side on chairs on the back lawn to listen to the distant explosions. He remembered how Lindy had kissed him and said, 'Happy New Year, little man,' and how they had both been too tired to keep talking. As she had tucked him in that night, she said, 'Made it through another year.' At the time, Fin didn't think it sounded like much of an achievement, but now he understood what his mum had meant.

After the sounds of the early fireworks had faded, he realised it might look suspicious if he ran over to Rory's fully dressed. So he put on the old T-shirt and cotton shorts he wore as pyjamas and folded up his clothes, including his hoodie, and put them on top of his shoes. He tucked them right in the corner so he'd be able to find them in the dark if he had to.

He tiptoed to Gran's door and listened for the snuffling of sleep. Her bedroom was too quiet, so he hurried away in case this was the moment she chose for her night-time cuddle. Again, he waited. As well as the usual sounds of frogs and fruit bats, there was the rising and falling of party music in the valley. When it felt like long enough, he crept back out to listen at Gran's door. This time he heard the unmistakable slurpy rasping she made when she was fast asleep.

He retrieved the cup hook from behind his door. He moved to the top of the stairs and pressed the hook hard into the skirting board. The whole piece of timber rocked against the wall and crackled as though the paint was tearing. He paused. Listened. He checked again at Gran's door and could still hear her breathing slow and even.

He moved back to the top of the stairs and pushed hard on the hook, turning until he heard the woody straining of the screw biting. The timber squeaked. He imagined Gran appearing in the grey dark behind him, holding the tomahawk and calmly bringing it down. He continued twisting – one, two, three, four, five, six. As soon as the cup hook was set, he hurried to Lindy's room and climbed back into bed.

He listened for any sound of Gran. But apart from the distant mumble of parties and passing cars, it was silent. He decided it was best to wait to tie the fishing line until he was absolutely sure she hadn't heard him screwing in the hook.

She'd found the axe, so she'd know he was planning something. It was better to wait. The warm stickiness of the air was like a soothing soup to float away on. He felt his head drop forward into sleep, so he pinched hard on the tight skin of his thigh. The stinging burn in his leg charged his blood and he was awake again.

When he felt like he'd waited long enough, he retrieved the coil of fishing line and crept to Gran's bedroom door to listen. She would be confused about why the poison wasn't working on him, and she'd start looking for other ways. He imagined her standing on the other side of the door, ready to swing it open and strike him with the tomahawk. Again, the fear and desperate uncertainty that had consumed him earlier in the day rose up. It was enough to make his whole body spasm and he leapt backwards. But then he remembered what Lindy had said in the hospital – *she's got you now. It's Gran. It's always been Gran.* And he knew he had to do it. Lindy would be out soon, released into Gran's care. She wouldn't have a chance.

He leant towards the door and, again, heard the snuffling rhythm of sleep. He moved to the top of the stairs and wrapped the end of the fishing line around the banister, looping the line to secure it in a slip knot. He worked largely by feel, and he was careful not to let go. It was almost impossible to see the clear line in the dark. He knotted it and pulled the long end to slide the knot tight and secure it.

He moved to the other side and slipped it through the curve of the little hook. He pulled it tight and ran his hand along to check. It was perfect. He looked down the steep stairs at the tiled landing and the front door; he was now sure it would work. He began winding the line around itself. He couldn't let it slip.

There were three loud thumps on the front door and the doorbell rang. Fin knew it could only be the police knocking this late. They must have somehow found out what he was doing. He unwound the line from the hook in a clumsy panic and dug his fingers inside the loop around the banister. He heard Gran turning the handle on her bedroom door. He pulled hard, with the line cutting into his fingers, and he kept pulling until the line slipped through the knot and it was bunched up in his hand. He didn't have any pockets in his pyjama shorts, so he stuffed the twisted bundle of fishing line down the front of his underpants as Gran approached.

'Go to your room.' She flicked the light switch at the top of the stairs. The golden brassiness of the cup hook shone bright. If she had seen it, she didn't say anything. As she made her way down the stairs, there were three more loud thumps on the door. Gran stopped and looked back at Fin. 'Go to your room. Stay there.'

Fin was frozen at the top of the stairs. If the police had come for him, there was no point hiding in Lindy's room. Gran looked at herself in the little mirror on the dresser by the entrance. She straightened her hair and opened the door just wide enough to look out.

'Hello, Antonella.' It was a man's voice.

'Oh no.' Gran went to shove the door closed again, but it wouldn't go.

It looked like the man had jammed his foot in so she couldn't close the door. Gran took a step back, letting the door swing open. Fin could see the man in the doorway. He had black wavy hair to his shoulders. He was wearing black jeans with a few scar-like scratches and holes, black work boots and a black T-shirt that was stretchy around the neck. He had some greeny-grey tattoos on his upper arms.

'You can't come in.' Gran used her in-control voice, the one she used when she felt people weren't listening to her.

'I'm not here for a cup of tea, Antonella.' He lifted his head to call up the stairs. 'Griffin!'

'You're not fit!'

The man stepped towards her, but he didn't try to push past. He raised his voice louder to call out again. 'Griffin!'

Fin's brain was stuck in a gummy disbelief. This couldn't be real. It had to be one of Gran's tricks. She must have discovered his plan and arranged for an imposter to stop him.

The man lifted his eyes and caught sight of Fin at the top of the stairs. His expression changed instantly from a look of determination to fear. His shoulders relaxed. 'Griffin?'

'I told you to stay in your room!' Gran was really shouting.

Fin stayed where he was. He felt the fishing line bundled in his underpants and looked down at the little brass hook. Suddenly, the painted walls around him seemed to sharpen and become real again. There was a stunned silence between the three of them.

'Griffin?' the man called up again, gentler this time.

Fin made his way down the stairs carefully. He stayed close to Gran, tucked in behind her. This man looked sort of right. Josie had said he had long hair. Fin looked closer at his face. He had deep green eyes, a sharp jaw, and the skin on his face seemed to cling closely to the bones underneath. It made his nose look sharp. He had the beginnings of a little dark beard. But he did not have an umbrella.

The man leant down to speak to him. 'Griffin?' He was gentle and curious, like he wanted to be sure he was speaking to the right boy.

Fin nodded but stayed tucked in behind Gran.

'You're most of the way to a grown man.' He extended his hand to shake, but Fin stayed where he was. He wasn't going to shake hands or do anything.

'I'm Dylan. Your dad. We've met before...when... But you probably don't remember. You were little.' His eyes were getting shiny. He reached out to shake Fin's hand again, but Fin wouldn't take it.

Fin looked up at Gran. It was unlike her to stay so quiet. Fin wanted her to put on her important voice and sort this out. He knew his mum had chosen a signal for a reason, and he wasn't going to believe anyone who came to the door.

The man spoke again. 'Sorry I took so long. I was way out of town when your mum called.'

The casual way he said it felt like a punch in the stomach. Fin wanted to shout – *But why didn't you hurry more? Why didn't you get a taxi? It was urgent. I was stuck here and she's killing us all.*

The man reached out his hand to shake again, but Fin pulled further away behind Gran. She cuddled into him and seemed to relax. Fin was almost certain this was a trap, and this man was an imposter. Why had he come right now?

The man stood up suddenly. 'I almost forgot.' He stuffed his big hand into the back pocket of his jeans and retrieved a folded piece of paper. He knelt down, a little closer to Fin, and unfolded the paper to show him.

There in the centre, drawn in wobbly thick black ink, was an umbrella.

'The shop had run out of real ones.'

Fin leapt forward in an involuntary lunge. He wrapped his arms around Dylan and pushed his face into his strong shoulders. He smelled of cigarette smoke, carpet and sweat, exactly like a dad.

Gran shouted, 'What on earth is that! What is going on here?'

Dylan ignored her. He looked directly into Fin's eyes and spoke only to him. 'You'd better get some things together. Whatever you want. But don't be long.' He flicked his eyes at Gran. 'My guess is we won't have much of a head start.'

Fin understood that he meant Gran would call the police.

He ran up the stairs. Gran shouted behind him, 'Please don't do this, Griffin. Please.'

He changed into the proper clothes he had stashed against the wall – his grey tracksuit pants, blue T-shirt. Gran was still shouting downstairs, saying words like 'child services' and 'parental responsibility'.

He bundled up his hoodie and all the other clothes he could carry and headed downstairs.

'No, Griffin. No. You simply do not know what this man is capable of.' Gran was trembling now and her voice was weak.

Dylan said, 'Don't you have a bag or something?'

Fin shook his head. Gran had put his suitcase away somewhere and he wasn't going to ask for it now.

'Okay then.' Dylan opened his arms and grabbed the bundle of clothes. 'Anything else?'

'One sec.' Fin hurried past Dylan, turned down the little pathway beside the house and ran out into the backyard. He could feel the coil of fishing line rubbing in his undies. He knew this might be his last chance, so he just had to hope the brown snake was sleeping. The dimpled surface of his golf ball showed white in the dark. He reached into Rory's tunnel and snatched it from its nest of dried-out leaves. He ran back to Gran and Dylan at the front door.

Gran was really crying now. 'This is not right! You don't know what you're doing. The damage this will do…'

'I know enough about damage, Antonella. My son is not staying here.' Dylan spoke resolutely but without shouting.

Fin had only ever heard Lindy call him 'son'.

'But he doesn't know his way back.' Gran was pleading.

Dylan looked down at Fin. 'Right?'

Fin's whole body was shaking. He wasn't cold. 'Right.'

'Let's go.' Dylan turned away with his arms full of clothes.

'No, no, no. I won't allow it. I won't let you take my grandson.' She bent down to speak to Fin. 'Griffin, please don't do this. You don't know this man.'

Fin looked into her puffy eyes and then he turned away.

'Oh, darling, wait. Wait. Just one minute. Wait.' She grabbed her handbag from the hook above the dresser and began riffling through. 'Take this.' She reached out and handed him her driver's licence. 'Take it. At least you'll have the address. You'll know where your home is.'

As he and Dylan walked past the recovering nasturtiums towards the road, Fin tucked Gran's licence down the front of his underpants next to the fishing line. The night air seemed too quiet, like the dark was waiting for something. Dylan opened the back of his white station wagon and dumped the bundle of clothes in before he opened the front passenger door for Fin. The door had two round dents and a long scratch along it. Once Fin had climbed into the seat, Dylan crouched down to stretch the seatbelt across Fin's chest.

Dylan climbed in and started the engine. Fin looked up and saw Gran standing in her nightdress on the footpath only a metre or so from the car. He lifted his hand in a half wave as Dylan steered the car out into the empty dark. And Gran was gone.

The streetlights rose and faded in the window. Some of the houses were still lit up with New Year's Eve parties.

'You okay?' Dylan kept his eyes on the road. 'You need anything?'

A vision of the little brass hook appeared in Fin's mind; it wouldn't be long before she saw it and realised what he had planned.

'Where are we going?'

'I'm not exactly flush with cash at the moment. So I was thinking Darwin.'

The only thing Fin knew about Darwin was that it was right up on top of Australia.

Dylan continued. 'I've got a mate up there with a big old house and a tree full of mangoes. He's got all these other Chinese fruit trees too.' Dylan flicked a checking glance at Fin. 'I've got my boat parked there. And most of a dirt bike. We can stay as long as we like. At least until your mum gets out.'

Waiting somewhere eating mangoes and Chinese fruit until his mum got out of hospital seemed like the best idea in the world. Fin nodded. 'Okay.'

'Okay then.' Dylan seemed relieved, as though he had expected Fin to say no. 'Darwin it is.'

'How far is it?'

'I've never actually driven it from here. I'd say somewhere between a *really* and a *bloody* long way.' Dylan stroked the dashboard like he was patting a horse. 'But I reckon this old rooster's got enough get-up left to make it all the way.'

Fin leant back in his seat and checked that the seatbelt was tight across his chest. 'Okay.'

Dylan looked down again. 'It's good to see you, Griffin.'

'Mum usually calls me just Fin.'

'Just Fin it is then. Like a shark!'

They turned into a busier road full of New Year's Eve cars. He remembered Gran's words – *the highway will be impossible* – and he hoped they'd make it out of Sydney before the police tried to find them.

'Have you got a phone?' Fin kept his eyes on the road.

'Yeah, I've got a phone. But the screen got...smashed up. It works, but you can't dial four or one or seven. It can still answer though.' Dylan spoke more gently. 'Anyway, if you need to make a call – and you can, of course – we can find a phone box. But, I don't know, I'd maybe think twice about calling anyone unless you're dead certain you want them to know where you are. Up to you, but just saying.'

'Okay.'

Dylan let out a nervous chuckle as he spoke. 'Now, this is kind of silly. But the bloke I got the car off managed to jam a tape in the deck.' He pointed to the old car stereo. 'I've tried everything. But I can't budge it, even blocks the radio.'

'That's okay.'

'Well, I hope you like Slim Dusty.' Dylan clicked the button and the twanging sounds of country music burst out of the speakers. It was loud, and made talking impossible, but Dylan seemed to like it that way. It suited Fin not to talk for a while too.

They made another turn onto a wide freeway. The cars in the adjacent lane were rushing past and it felt like Dylan's car was struggling to keep up. Fin saw a big green road sign that read *Berowra 11 – Gosford 51 – Newcastle 142*. And he knew that, whatever happened, he was a few kilometres closer to Gustav's. He rolled his golf ball in the palm of his hand and promised himself he'd stay awake.

CHAPTER SIXTEEN

When Fin woke up, the car was slowing and there was the rushing sound of rough road under the tyres. He held still for a moment and only opened his eyes halfway. He saw a brown road sign that read *FOREST OF TRANQUILITY.*

Dylan pulled the car into a freeway rest stop. Through his half-open eyes, Fin could see a ute and a backpacker campervan, like the ones that parked along the coast road near Ballina. Dylan stopped and rolled backwards until they were shaded from the glow of the single streetlight. He turned off the engine and the headlights, and they were suddenly in the dark, alone together. It felt very quiet.

Dylan climbed out and there was the sound of peeing on the grass beside the car before he folded the back seats down flat, climbed into the driver's seat and tapped Fin on the shoulder. 'Griffin?'

Fin turned as though he was rousing from sleep.

Dylan spoke gently, bringing his face close. 'You climb over the back. I got you a sleeping bag, the new blue one. There's a pillow there too if you want.'

Fin unclicked his belt and climbed between the front seats. He pushed his pile of clothes to one side and stretched out. He unrolled the sleeping bag and cuddled into it. There was a sawdusty smell in the rough upholstery.

Dylan reached around to lock each of the doors and tilted the driver's seat back. 'I don't know about you but I could murder some chicken wings.'

Fin wished he hadn't said 'murder'. He imagined the police climbing the stairs at Gran's and the cup hook glinting in the low light.

~

When Fin woke again, the insides of the car windows were steamed up and drippy with their breath. The sun hadn't broken the tree line and the morning light was still brassy. It was already hot in the car, and it felt like the air was second-hand. Dylan's head was lying straight back in his seat and his breathing was thin and hissy.

Fin wound down the back window and a tumbling stream of cool air flowed over him. He could hear the crunching of magpies hopping and poking through the grass and fallen leaves outside. The sound reminded him of Gran's. He thought about the missing tomahawk and the little hook and shuddered at how close he had come.

He rolled over the shiny slipperiness of his new sleeping bag, clicked open the door and climbed out. Dylan continued sleeping, motionless and upright in the driver's seat. His skin was leathery, and he looked older than he had in the dark. Although he didn't have much money, he'd bought a sleeping bag for Fin; that was something.

There were cars and trucks parked all around them. A tired-looking man in crumpled clothes was trying to flatten his curly hair as he peed on the grass. Fin walked along the row of parked cars towards the freeway, and he felt the coil of fishing line and Gran's driver's licence rubbing in his underpants. The crunching of his shoes on the gravel changed to solid thuds on sealed road. He looked up at the long stretch of freeway and scanned the edges for powerlines to follow. But there were none.

He turned back and headed to the toilet block. He checked no-one was watching before reaching into his underpants, and then he tucked the coil of fishing line under some newspaper at the top of the bin. He thought about throwing Gran's driver's licence in with it, but he decided to keep it for now. Apart from anything, it was a link to his mum.

He peed in the silent toilet block and dawdled back to the car. As soon as he began edging the door open wider, Dylan woke with a start and held up his clenched fists to fight. Fin froze. He wasn't used to being around men and punches.

Dylan spoke as though his lips were giving shape to a sleepy sigh, 'Ah, only you.' He clicked the ignition key and pressed the button on the stereo. Slim Dusty sang:

She's the pride of all the railway men 'cross country where she flies...

'Nothing like a touch of Slim to start the day.' Dylan winked. 'I don't know about you, but I could eat the nuts off a duck!'

'Oh.' Fin felt like he had to say something more. 'Do ducks even have nuts?'

Dylan cupped his hands around his mouth and pretended to call out the window. 'Hey, duck! Drop your trousers. We've got a couple of weary travellers here in need of some information.'

Fin giggled.

'You sleep all right?'

'I like my sleeping bag.'

'Me too.'

Slim Dusty continued on the stereo:

...the western flowers are blooming and the air is just like wine...

It was midmorning when they pulled up in the main street of a little highway town.

'They must have a pair of duck's nuts for you around here somewhere. I generally prefer a duck's bum. Personally, I mean.'

Fin was aching with hunger. They scanned the empty shops for any sign of food, and Dylan pointed to an A-frame chalkboard up ahead – *BACON AND EGG ROLL*.

They sat at a table by the window. Dylan pulled some money out of his pocket and put it on the table. He said Fin could order whatever he wanted, so Fin ordered the big breakfast; he was determined to eat as much unpoisoned food as possible.

The café was run by a wavy-haired woman who was taking the orders and cooking everything herself. The only other customers were two tired-looking workmen. Fin went straight for the bacon as soon as it arrived. He ate with his hands, tearing up the toast and the hash brown. The flavour of everything was turbo-charged. It was only once the food began slowly reaching his stomach that his chest and belly relaxed.

He knew Dylan could just drive off and leave him somewhere, but at least he wasn't trying to poison him. And with every kilometre they travelled north together, he was closer to Gustav's. Fin tried to think of what Rory would say – *you have to be a realist.*

'You like a fry-up.'

Fin nodded without pausing to speak.

'Pleased to see you chowing that bacon. I thought you might be, you know, vegetarian.'

Fin continued eating without a break.

'Not that I've got anything against it or the like. Vegetarianism, I mean. Your mum and I went through a phase.'

Lindy had never told stories about Dylan. She'd only mentioned him by name a few times. And although Fin had known her his whole life, he knew very little about her life before. He had so many questions for Dylan, but the most important one was – *where have you been?*

Dylan continued. 'But I'll tell you what, even though breakfast is a bit cheaper, a vegetarian lifestyle doesn't come without a cost.' Dylan's eyes lit up. 'I mean, the human digestive system goes berko. And I'm not talking about a bit of chair air, I'm talking completely off the rectum scale.'

Fin had to swallow quickly to avoid spitting out his mushed-up food as he laughed.

'Yeah, your mum and I thought we'd try it, and it was going to be all clean living. But I'm telling you, vegetarianism is like rocket fuel for the human stink pipe!'

They were both giggling and shaking now. The workmen and the café owner looked around to see what was so funny.

'And when I say rocket fuel, that's probably even selling it short. More like lava. That's it. Lava, in my limited experience.' He held one finger up as if he was making an important announcement. 'An actual anal volcano!'

Fin had to brace himself against the table so he didn't topple out of his chair. Most of the kids in his class at Old Bin were vegetarian.

'And your new sleeping bag, forget that. Even with your brand-new, double-stitched bag with heat seal, you put a vegetarian in that and *boom!* Instant destruction.' Dylan looked around at the others in the café and lowered his voice. 'Anyway, glad to see you. And that you like bacon. You and I are going to get along.'

Dylan clicked the button on the stereo as soon as they were back in the car. They followed the road further north.

They had my future wrapped up in a parcel,
And no-one even thought of asking me...

With every kilometre they travelled, the landscape became flatter. The sun-scorched brown and yellow of the plains was interrupted by an occasional rust and concrete structure that looked as if it had been put there by aliens – round and grey with a rusted roof like a helmet and pipes coming out. Fin thought to ask what they were for, but he didn't want to seem like he didn't know things.

Dylan said the gas for the air conditioner had all leaked out; it just blew hot. They kept the back windows open as they drove, but the rushing air was too noisy to leave the front ones down for long.

They'd only been going for an hour or so when Dylan patted the dashboard again and said, 'Jackpot.' He pulled over beside a big old building with the words *TOP PUB* written in big letters on the side. On a blackboard next to the front door: *Pool Comp Tonight.*

'You wait here.' Dylan climbed out and disappeared inside the pub.

The hot air in the car was oppressive. Fin wound down the window but it didn't help much. There was no-one on the street and only an occasional passing car.

Dylan seemed to be taking a very long time, and Fin thought he was probably inside drinking beer. Eventually, the heat was too much, and Fin climbed out of the car. He plopped down on a worn-out wooden picnic bench at the front of the pub. It was shaded by the dark timber of the upstairs balcony. A little sign read – *No Kids After 8.30 pm.*

There was a scruffy park across the road; it had no play equipment, just picnic tables and two white statues of scared-looking lions. They were lying flat on their bellies and had their paws crossed. Their worried eyes stared at the pub across the road. It seemed wrong for lions to be so afraid.

The pub door swung open and Dylan appeared with a lit cigarette between his lips. He took a long draw and puffed the smoke out towards the balcony above. 'That's better.' He sat down at the table and held the cigarette low and away so the smoke wouldn't blow in Fin's face. He kept smoking and not speaking and looking across at the lion statues.

After he'd smoked every last bit of the cigarette, Dylan stubbed it out and said, 'I've got some good news and some bad news.'

A police car slowed as it passed. Fin's heart raced.

Dylan turned his face away from the road. 'There's a pool comp. The prize money is a hundred and fifty. And that should just about see us most of the way in terms of fuel. And bacon, of course. But anyway, that's the good news. The bad news is that the comp doesn't start until eight thirty, and it's not even midday now.'

Fin was relieved the bad news wasn't the police. 'So what does that mean?'

'It means we've got a way to get some money. A hundred and fifty. And we need it because that old rooster is nudging empty. But we have to hang around in this lifestyle destination for the rest of the day. And we've got no money. We can camp in the pub a bit. They've got water and aircon. But they won't let us stay all day if we don't buy anything. Don't worry, I've got some cash stashed in my boat in Darwin, so we'll be right once we get there.'

'But...' Fin began to speak but changed his mind. He imagined himself as having a similar expression to the worried lions across the road.

'But what?'

'But what if you don't win?'

Dylan's face broke into a huge smile. It was the first time Fin had noticed that one of his top teeth was missing, halfway down the right side.

Dylan lowered his chin and spoke in a serious tone. 'There aren't many things that are certain in this life, Shark Fin Boy.

But one thing I can assure you, and I mean this absolutely one hundred per cent.' He scrunched up his nose and nodded. 'I'll win.'

'Okay.' Fin suddenly felt surer they would make it to Darwin. 'Anyway, my friend calls me Golden Boy. My best friend...' Fin paused, unsure whether to go on. But he decided, if Dylan was going to be his dad, they were going to have to start telling each other things. 'His name's Rory. We even wanted to get married.'

'Married? You need your head examined. You don't need to get married. Just find someone you're going to hate in five years and give them your house!' Dylan winked and then realised this had been the wrong thing to say. 'Come on, I was only joking. He sounds like a mint guy. Rory, hey? And good on him about the name – Golden Boy – it suits you. He's next door to your gran and Josie?'

Fin nodded; it didn't seem like the right time to tell him about Josie.

'That Rory. I met him. He was a real skinny baby. Your mum and his mum were thick as thieves.'

Fin sensed an opportunity. 'It's only Rory and his pop there now. His mum's away, so I didn't see her. I only went in there once, and Pop says Mum's bad luck and makes people go to jail. What's that about?'

'About your mum and Angela? You'd best ask someone else.'

'But everyone says that. No-one tells me. And I can't go to Rory's because Pop hates me for something, and I don't know why. Everyone keeps lying to me.'

'I'm not lying, Golden. No-one hates you.'

'Then tell me.'

'You're right. Secrets never did anyone any good.'

The knowing way Dylan spoke made Fin suspect that he'd somehow guessed about the fishing line and his plan to kill Gran.

'Anyway, I like your real name too, Griffin Martin. That was my idea.'

His whole life, his family name had been Alverton, and it suddenly felt as though, each time he'd said it, it had been wrong. Dylan seemed to be searching Fin's eyes, perhaps looking to see whether he knew who had named him.

Fin said quietly, 'I like it too.'

Dylan swung around to face the road. He pointed to the lions and said, 'I wonder what they're so nervous about.'

∽

Dylan moved the car under a tree in a gravelly parking area behind the lion park. They filled a couple of plastic bottles with water and lay down on the grass under one of the trees. The water was warm, but it was water. They had no food.

They stayed under the tree as long as they could. At one point, Dylan dozed off and started snoring lightly. Fin tried to sleep too, but the place was strange and he was worried the police car would come back. They spent an hour or so in front of the stand fan in the beer garden, but Dylan was unsettled and kept moving, like he didn't want anyone to see them.

They returned to the car as soon as the cool southerly wind arrived. Dylan washed his face at the park tap and crouched by the side mirror to pull the knots out of his long hair. Fin found a spot in the back near the open door where the breeze flowed over him.

'Those lions guard things, you know? Usually houses. There must be something precious in this park if they need lions guarding it.' Dylan climbed into the front passenger seat and explained that he and his mum had lived in Hong Kong for a year when he was eleven, after his parents split up. Dylan said his mum worked in a club there. It was the only time he'd been out of Australia.

Every new thing Dylan told him made Fin feel surer it would work out. 'Why did they? Split up, I mean.'

'I think it was maybe Dad just loved himself more than he loved her. But all the big houses and buildings over there have lions guarding them.' Dylan stroked the dashboard again and leant over to look at the little radio clock. 'Right. It's nearly time and I'm going to have to sign up. I'm sorry about this, but we really need the money.'

Fin realised Dylan was planning to leave him in the car.

'It'll be a couple of hours at the most, maybe three. We really need the money and there's no kids at night.' Dylan was doing his best to sound reassuring. 'You can lock all the doors. It's New Year's Day and there won't be anyone around. Happy New Year, by the way.'

Fin struggled to raise his voice above a whisper. 'Happy New Year too.'

'Anyway, it's a kind of only-hope situation. We'll never make it to Darwin on the power of your farts alone.' He smiled with his eyebrows up and reached over to place his hand on Fin's shoulder.

'Okay.' Fin knew he was right. They needed money. And suddenly, his fear of being left alone in the car at night was replaced by the fear that Dylan might not win the pool competition.

'You've got lions here to guard you and... Actually, climb over.' He gestured for Fin to climb over into the driver's seat. 'So, if you want me, you just have to hit the horn. Three long honks and I'll come sprinting.' He moved his arms and elbows back and forth like he was running. 'But you'll have to click the ignition on first. Try it.'

Fin turned the key in the ignition and the engine started up.

'Now the horn.'

Fin pressed the horn and startled himself with the loudness of it.

'See? Hear it for miles. Do you want to have a little drive?'

Fin put his hands on the wheel.

215

Dylan slid the driver's seat forward. 'Yep. You can reach. Okay, that one's the brake. That's the important one. Don't press the other one for now. Ready?'

Dylan clicked the gearshift, and they moved slowly forward on the gravel. Fin had to sit up straight to see past the steering wheel and, when he pressed the brake, the car stopped.

'That's the idea.'

Fin steered the car around the car park until Dylan directed him back to their parking spot behind the trees.

'Mate, you're a natural.'

Fin liked that.

'Okay, you sit tight. Lock all the doors and try to get some sleep if you can. I'll be back shortly. And honk, you know. Anyway, maybe stay out of sight. Some people have a thing about kids being in cars.'

Dylan left and Fin locked all the doors. He lay flat in the back so no-one could see him as night fell.

The park was next to a train line and Fin heard the rattles and thumps of freight trains scraping their carriages along. At one point, a ginger cat sprung up onto the bonnet and peered in. Fin lunged forward, reaching for the horn, but he settled back. The highway streetlights cast an orange glow across the park. The only other car nearby was abandoned. It had streaks of rust and all its windows broken. He wished Rory was there. They would have had fun camping in a car. Only a few hours before, he'd been screwing in the cup hook; since then, everything had changed. He even had a new name – *Griffin Martin*.

So far, Dylan had been right; people had gone into the pub, but no-one had come into the park. He tucked his legs into his sleeping bag and looked up at the thin glass that was keeping the world out. The air in the car was warm and still. He imagined Dylan's steely-eyed focus on the pool ball in front of him, imagined the pressure building as the competition went on and the prize drew closer. He found himself praying – *please let him win*. They really needed the money.

Suddenly, Fin was awake. He had no idea how long he'd slept. The orange light and the shadows around the car were constant in the dark heat, but there was a new sound – the crunching of unsteady footsteps. The sound of his dad.

He lifted himself and peeked out the back window, careful not to raise himself up high enough to be seen. He could make out a figure coming towards him through the shadows, but something wasn't right. The figure seemed wider and shorter than Dylan, with short hair.

Fin lay down flat and looked up at the window. The footsteps became heavier and more uneven. Fin slid his legs free of his sleeping bag. The man stopped a couple of metres away, and Fin could see his wonky-shaped ears. He had stubble on his cheeks and was wearing a brown work shirt with the collar loose. He leant against one of the trees and sighed as he peed. Fin was silent, perfectly still.

The man approached the car. He was very close, almost sliding along the driver's side. Fin was looking right at him now and could see the weathered lines running down his cheeks. The man paused at the driver's door, and Fin heard the quiet, unmistakable sound of the door handle lifting. Fin felt a wave of panic. He'd escaped from Gran only to be murdered in a car.

The man stepped back and, for a moment, it seemed like he would move on. But then he retrieved something from his pocket and stepped towards the car again. There was a scrape and rattle. Fin leapt from where he was in the back and lunged for the ignition. He clicked the key and the engine revved to life. The man staggered back, and Fin pushed hard on the steering wheel. Three loud honks tore through the dark.

The man continued to back away. He was looking straight at Fin. He seemed unable to understand what was happening. Fin pressed again with three long honks. He looked across at the pub, expecting to see his dad in full sprint across the road. But the park and highway were both empty. The man looked down at the screwdriver in his hand and tucked it into his pocket. He lowered his head and began jogging away. Fin knew Dylan would be there any second. He thought how he'd have to warn him about the screwdriver if a fight started. He hoped his dad would run out with a pool cue still in his hand.

The man kept jogging and disappeared. Fin stopped the engine so as not to waste petrol. He scanned the patches of shadow and orangey light around him. He pulled his sleeping bag against him and its squishy familiarity helped. He pulled his shoes on in case he had to run.

After what seemed like hours, Dylan swung open the pub door, casually crossed the road, peered in and tapped on the passenger window. Fin unlocked the door and Dylan sat down heavily in the seat. He smelled like cigarettes.

'Did you win?'

Dylan pulled a crumpled bundle of twenty-dollar notes from his pocket and showed it to Fin. 'You bet. You can climb over in the back again if you want.'

Fin wanted to tell him about the man with the screwdriver, but there didn't seem much point now. He climbed between the seats and lay down.

Dylan sat in the passenger seat and tucked his knees up. 'That ought to see us right for petrol and bacon for a while.'

CHAPTER SEVENTEEN

Fin felt a gentle hand on his shoulder, rousing him from sleep. 'Mum.' He opened his eyes, expecting to see the familiar walls of his room at Gustav's. Instead, he saw Dylan leaning over with a sad look in his eyes. Fin jolted awake and flung his head around to look for the screwdriver man.

'Come on, Golden Boy. You've got to get your belt on.' Dylan smiled to himself. 'Golden Boy...'

They stopped at a little petrol station to fill up. Dylan flopped back into the driver's seat and said, 'Don't you love that feeling of a full tank? Like you can keep driving until you run out of road.'

'Yeah.' Fin thought how Lindy would have liked that. He also thought, when he was older and could get some money, he'd sneak out and buy Lindy a tank of petrol so she could have that feeling.

With each kilometre they travelled, the landscape became flatter and the horizon seemed to widen. There were occasional gatherings of pale trees, but it was mostly dried-up, scrubby paddocks with rusted-out houses. Dylan was quieter today, more focused on driving.

The flat land rose up into some low hills and Fin saw a beautifully familiar sight. Up ahead, stretching through a wide path cut through the trees, were powerlines on goat-head-shaped scaffolding running over the little hills and out of sight. There were two steadying cables bolted into the ground where they began; this was the start of the whole line. From here they only went one way. And Fin knew, if he kept walking, following the electricity through the bush, eventually he'd find his way back to Gustav's. There'd be enough to eat in the garden and, whatever happened, Darwin or no Darwin, he could stop there and wait. Lindy would come home eventually.

He'd thought about suggesting to Dylan that they just drive to Gustav's, but he knew Lindy might not be happy about it when she got out. They'd hardly ever had a visitor. And, for now, he wanted to keep Gustav's as his fallback if things didn't work out. He etched the details of the landscape into his memory, the pale trees, the rounded hills, the new black surface of the road. He closed his eyes, recalling them and making sure he wouldn't forget this place, the start of the line.

As the road continued, he saw a sign – *Quirindi: Nest in the Hills* – and repeated the phrase in his mind so he'd remember it. A twisting flock of little white-bellied birds flashed across the road in front of them. Dylan hit the brakes to stop them glancing off the windscreen.

'Whoa! That was a close one.'

Fin looked back and saw the birds darting through the trees and thought again – *nest in the hills.*

Dylan said, 'Now I know why they're called swallows. We nearly swallowed them.'

Fin laughed. 'Rory would love that.'

Dylan seemed to enjoy having an audience for his jokes. 'Sounds like you two are a riot.'

'Yeah. We've got a spot down near the water.' He thought for a moment before continuing. 'We have fires.'

'I'd like to see it sometime.'

Fin didn't think Dylan would ever be welcome at Gran's. 'Yeah.'

'I was a bit older than you but we used to fish down the back there. It was full of them, bonito and bream…and mud crabs. Even kingies. You would have loved it. But then we all started getting spots on us, and they said chemical stuff was leaking into the water from the closed-down factory further up.'

The road passed through a little town and they found a café in an arcade off the wide main street. Since they'd left the hill with the swallows, Fin had been thinking about Rory's spots and how he could warn him about the chemicals in the crabs. Dylan ordered two big breakfasts with extra bacon on one.

The bacon was slippery and good. Dylan took his time eating and kept sitting back in his chair. Fin thought how, if he'd been with Lindy, she'd be looking at her phone. Dylan had a slower rhythm about him, like his thoughts travelled in longer lines. He didn't seem to care that the screen on his phone was broken.

After the waitress cleared away the plates, Dylan spread some crumpled notes and coins out on the table. Fin could see there was a lot less than a hundred and fifty dollars.

'Is that…?'

'Yes, I'm afraid. And there'll be a lot less of it in a minute when I pay this nice bacon lady.'

'But wasn't there a hundred and fifty?'

'There was. But things cost. And it looks like we're not going to get far eating bacon continually.' He giggled. 'I just sounded like Antonella.' He pushed his lips forward and spoke like an old woman. 'Bacon continually. Continually bacon in continuality!' He pointed his nose in the air as if avoiding a bad smell, and Fin realised he was talking about Gran – *Antonella*.

Fin reached down to check that her driver's licence was still securely in his underpants; he couldn't bring himself to throw it away. They paid and Dylan bought a little packet of tobacco from a grocery store. Fin tried to add up the handful of gold coins left. It wasn't much.

By midmorning, the road was so hot that it made silvery mirage puddles that stretched almost all the way from the horizon to the front of the car. Fin had heard about these sneaky pools in the desert, but he'd never seen one. They were so wet-looking that they reflected the oncoming colours of the big trucks carrying cattle and grain.

The traffic stopped as they entered another highway town. Up ahead, a long freight train was passing between dinging boom gates. The thunder of motorbike engines approached from behind and swarmed around. A large group of bikies in leather and denim revved and surged up the wrong side of the road, pushing their way to the front of the queue of cars. As they passed, one of them turned and looked menacingly over his shoulder. His teeth were yellow and broken, with gaps at the front.

Dylan shrugged and looked at Fin. 'Hopefully, all that hurry's to get him to his dentist on time. Full-on breath cancer!'

The train passed and the slow traffic moved away behind the roaring engines of the motorbikes. Fin closed his eyes to stop the stinging sweat and drifted off to sleep.

~

When Fin opened his eyes, he saw a sign that read – *Welcome to Moree – Artesian Water Country*. Behind it was a tall green road sign listing the names of towns and distances.

'How do you spell Darwin?' Fin could taste the stale saltiness of his sweat.

'Well, spelling's never been my strong suit, but I think you'll find it's D-A-R-W-I-N.'

'Why don't we ever see it on the signs?'

'Not near enough yet.'

They pulled off the highway and drove into the town. Although it was only mid-afternoon, most of the shops were closed and a lot of them had *For Lease* signs in the window.

'Last time I was here, I wouldn't have been much older than you. Maybe twelve. There's a big volcano under here. It's so hot it squirts up boiling water.' He paused and seemed to make a decision before continuing. 'I came up here with my mum, your grandma, when she first got sick. Some people say that sitting in the volcano water cures cancer. It doesn't, though.'

Fin had been so focused on his dad, he'd never thought about other grandmas and grandpas, and possibly aunties, uncles and cousins.

As they drove through the town, Fin imagined a bubbling lake of lava below the surface. The thought seemed to make the ground unsteady, and the wide, dusty streets felt like they were about to explode.

'You ripper!' Dylan turned a corner, following an arrow on a sign that read – *Moree Artesian Aquatic Centre*. He circled around, looking for a parking spot in the shade.

They changed into their boardshorts behind the open doors of the car. Fin felt shy getting changed in public, so he left his underpants on. The surface of the road was so hot that he had to stand on his own discarded clothes to stop the soles of his feet from burning. While Dylan was looking the other way, Fin slipped Gran's driver's licence into a gap beside the passenger seat.

'Whoa! You could fry an egg on this!' Dylan sat down to get his feet off the hot road.

They slipped their shoes back on and Fin carried the only towel.

MOREE ARTESIAN AQUATIC CENTRE

'What's artesian?'

'It's that volcano water I told you about. This is one of the places where it bubbles up.'

The reception area was dark and icily air-conditioned. The contrast from the burning air outside was such a relief that Fin would have been happy just sitting in there. A lady in a green shirt smiled at them, her face was freckled and wrinkly.

Dylan retrieved his coins. 'Two tickets for two travellers, please. What's the damage for that?'

'It's eight dollars for you and six dollars for the young man.' She winked at Fin.

He liked the idea of being a 'young man'. His mum often called him 'little man', but he'd never thought of himself as anything other than a kid.

'I think this chunk of shrapnel ought to stretch to that.' He counted out the coins and slid them across to her. 'There.'

'Then it's four dollars each for the waterslide. But that's for unlimited.'

Dylan counted out the rest of the coins. There was only five dollars and twenty cents. 'We'll just have one in that case.'

She tore off two coloured-paper wristbands and handed them across the counter. 'On the house. We wouldn't want the two of you missing out after making it all this way.'

'Thank you so much.' He pushed the mess of remaining coins towards her.

She waved them away. 'Like I said, on the house. The two of you are going to need a cool drink sooner or later.'

Dylan nudged Fin in the side. 'What do you say?'

Fin felt shy and pulled closer to his dad. 'Thank you.'

'Any time.' She winked again.

They stepped back out into the scorching heat.

There were three large pools with silver railings and pipes like goose necks spraying water in wide falls. Shade sails provided some refuge from the sun. Rising up from a patch of green grass at the far end was a corkscrew waterslide. The look in Dylan's eyes showed that he was excited.

Fin noticed that, apart from one large family group on the far side, everyone swimming and sitting in the shade around the pool had the brown skin of Aboriginal people.

'You'd better get some suncream on that boy.' A bright-eyed woman in an old black swimming costume was holding a pump pack of suncream towards them. The skin on her face had an almost glittering sparkle to it in the hot sun.

Fin realised how he must look, still patchy pink and peeling. He hadn't been in front of a mirror for a couple of days. It seemed impossible that it had only been a week or so since he and Rory had tried to paddle to New Zealand.

'Come on. It's the good stuff. Take it.' She slapped the big pump pack against Dylan's belly.

'Yes. Thank you.' Dylan took it and squirted some directly on Fin's shoulders.

The woman turned her back and stepped heavily down a few steps into the pool.

Dylan looked around nervously as he rubbed the suncream over Fin's shoulders and down his arms. He was rushing and clumsy about it. It seemed like he was worried other people might think he was doing it wrong. Once he was finished, he looked for the woman so he could give the suncream back, but she was gone. He put it down with their towel, and they walked to the edge of the pool.

Sitting side by side in a steaming hot pool of volcano water felt right. Fin shifted closer to his dad so they were almost touching. Dylan stayed looking at the crowd of people enjoying the water; he didn't move away.

Fin thought about how all the answers he'd wanted his whole life were inside the man sitting beside him. But it felt too new to risk questions. One way or another, his mum would get out of hospital and Dylan would leave. He missed Lindy, but he found himself half wishing the hospital would keep her longer. She'd be safe from Gran there, and he had a hopeful, rising feeling that, even if his dad disappeared again, it would be different now, and he'd still be out there. They'd know each other and Fin might be able to call him on his smashed-up phone if he needed to.

Fin leant back against the tiles to let the oily heat of the water soak into him. 'Mum would love this.' He hadn't meant to say it out loud. It was as though he'd relaxed enough for the words to fall out of his mouth.

'It's different to when I was here with my mum. It's more fancy now.' Dylan was speaking with his eyes closed. 'I think I prefer it the old way.'

'Anyway, Mum would love it. She loves anything like this.'

'She likes fancy, that's for sure.' Dylan looked down and winked, as if to make it clear he wasn't being critical of Lindy.

Fin had never really thought of his mum as fancy, especially not when she was in her gumboots, shovelling cow poo at Old Bin.

Dylan continued. 'I think she maybe gets it from Antonella.'

Again, the words seemed to slip out of Fin. 'Thank you…I mean, for coming to get me.'

'Any time.'

Any time sounded like a promise.

'I mean, it was important.' Fin felt as if the great dam of words that had built up inside him had found a gap and everything was just going to squeeze out until he was empty. 'Gran, sorry, Antonella had already got to Josie, and Mum said I was going to be the next one because she was still in hospital. She was safer from the poison there.' The words continued flowing out of him. 'I made sure I wasn't eating anything she made because of it, but Gran gave Josie a cup of tea and that's when she was killed. I caught her, I just managed to catch her before her face cracked on the bricks. But it didn't matter in the end.'

Dylan sat quietly, not interrupting, with a calm expression. His silence created space for Fin to keep talking.

'And then I was thinking, what am I going to do? Because I knew the police would just bring me back if I tried to run, like they did when Rory and me tried to get to New Zealand, and so I…' He stopped mid-breath. It occurred to him that Dylan might not think it was okay to kill your grandma. 'Anyway, thanks. It's good. I'm glad.'

'Like I said.' Dylan nodded.

Fin felt like he had said too much but he couldn't restrain the urge to talk more. 'Anyway, how long do you think it will be? I mean, how long do you think until they unlock her out of hospital?'

'Not sure, Golden. It's usually not more than three weeks or so. That's always been enough to get her sorted out.' Dylan closed his eyes again. 'But you might not… You wouldn't know much about that, would you? You were only little.'

'No.'

How could it be that Dylan knew things about his mum that he didn't? And, if he knew, how could he sit there with his eyes closed not telling him?

'So it's not the first time Gran has tried this? I mean, the first time with poison? Why does she?'

Dylan's posture crumpled forward. 'I don't know. I don't mean to criticise. I don't want to disagree with your mother. And I know what she's told you and that's fine. But I'm not sure. From what I know, the only poison Antonella dishes out is from her tongue. She looks harmless enough, but that mouth of hers can turn into a deadly weapon. You must know what she's like.'

Fin imagined the sea of boiling lava that was bubbling underneath them. 'You mean the poison's in her spit or something?' He imagined Gran spitting into sandwiches and cups of tea.

'No. I don't mean it's in her spit. That's not it at all. When it comes to poison, I mean it's what she says. Her words are the most dangerous thing about Antonella. That whole poison stuff is just a big misunderstanding.'

Fin sat looking at his father. There were beads of sweat showing along the line of Dylan's black hair.

'So you're not going to tell me?'

'Yes, Griffin. But there's no point getting shirty. We're a long way north of it all now. I'm not sure I know any of this better than you, anyway. I've been in… I've been out of the picture.'

'So it's not in her spit then? So what is it? Is she like a snake or something?' After Josie had confirmed Lindy's warning with her horrible shaking, Fin wasn't going to be easily convinced that Gran only had nasty words.

The corner of Dylan's mouth lifted in a gentle smile, as though he liked the idea there might be half-snake, half-human people out there. 'No, she's not like a snake. It's nothing to do with you, all this. It was way before you.' Dylan looked down at him and then back at the pool. 'There was a point there. You know your mum. I'm sure you know. She gets a thought stuck in her head sometimes and it jumps around and around. Like a frog in a sock. It keeps hopping but can't find its way out.' Dylan looked at Fin for some confirmation he understood.

'Yeah.' Fin desperately wanted to hear what his dad had to say, but the sizzling need to defend Lindy was also spreading through him.

'Well, there was a point there when there were all sorts of these thoughts hopping around in her head and it got so bad she wouldn't get out of bed, but no matter how long she lay there, she couldn't sleep. She was so confused.'

'Yeah?' This sounded familiar.

'So the doctor gave her some medicine to help her think her way out of it. But she refused. No matter what, no matter how scared she was, no matter how much trouble she got in, she wouldn't take it. And she was so scared, and she was getting worse. She even thought I was trying to get at her. So eventually, Antonella started grinding up the tablets and putting them in her dinner.' Dylan looked again at Fin to check he should keep going. 'I didn't know what to do either. She wasn't even leaving the house. But as soon as that started, it was like a whole new story. Within a couple of weeks, it was like she was her old self almost. And then she started saying she was fine and she didn't need medicine and she'd proved it. And the runes and all that were the reason. Then she said she wanted to move, and we moved around a bit. And then Antonella told me. She gave me the tablets and she told me how to do it. I knew it wasn't right. I was going to tell your mum, but I could see the difference. I didn't want to lie about it, but when I saw she was getting scared again, I tried it a couple of times. But she always did the cooking.' Dylan put his arm around Fin's shoulder. 'And then you were coming and I wasn't going to do it, in case it wasn't right. You know, for the little baby inside her or whatever.'

Fin felt as though someone had whacked him in the back of the eyes. He didn't move. Dylan stayed close and quiet and they both watched the steaming chaos around them. The heat was suddenly suffocating. Fin took two deep breaths to settle himself.

'Anyway, I know two travellers who've got unlimited tickets on the waterslide.' Dylan patted him on the head.

The shock of what he'd just heard felt like a weight on Fin. He felt like he needed to sleep. He wasn't sure he could even stand up.

They climbed out of the pool, and Fin slipped and nearly fell; an oily coating from the volcano water covered his body and the ground. Questions filled his head as they hurried over the hot concrete to the bristling relief of the grass at the base of the slide. How had things become so confused? And why did Josie shake like that if it wasn't true? And what if he'd tripped Gran down the stairs? And then they began climbing the hot stairs. As he rose with each step, the roofs of the surrounding town revealed themselves. The buildings were scattered in huddled patches on a perfectly flat landscape. The distant farmland beyond the train line was blurred by the heat. Fin had never been on a waterslide.

When they reached the top, Dylan mimed holding up a pair of binoculars and spoke with an old-fashioned English accent. 'I think this is the place, Golden Boy. I think we should put our waterslide right here.'

Fin felt a weary smile make its way through the shock.

Dylan continued with his English accent. 'I think I'd best conduct a safety inspection before His Highness attempts…' And with one leaping step, Dylan was carried into the dark by the rushing water.

Fin heard a long, cheering 'woot!' echoing up. He hurried to the railing to look and Dylan emerged at the bottom, sending a huge splash out onto the grass. He leapt up, wooted again and leant back in a double thumbs up.

Fin stared into the darkness of the waterslide. He sat down between two powerful jets of water and froze. He suddenly felt very high up, a very long way from home, and very alone.

The rushing darkness ahead of him transformed into another dangerous mistake. He knew he couldn't go through with it. Not now. It was time to stay still. To wait and think and not do anything. If he didn't do anything, at least it couldn't be wrong. He stood up, taking care not to slip in the rushing water and walked back to the railing. He saw Dylan hunched over, waiting for him to splash out at the bottom. Fin felt as though the tower was hovering in the air. His heart began thumping in his neck and the ground below stuttered in a glitching spin. He looked away from the dizzy edge to stop himself falling.

And then he took one step, and another, held his breath and used the momentum of his running legs to launch himself into the waterslide before he could change his mind. A moment later, he was swallowed up by the rushing dark.

The slide disappeared beneath him and he dropped. Then, back in the gushing water, he was carried at a chaotic speed around a long corner. He was travelling so fast that he rode up high on the side of the tube and felt the joints between each segment of the slide thumping under his ribs – *dook, dook, dook.* He dropped again and the slide curved left. The dark was swept away by lines of coloured sunlight through plastic. He was flying through a circular rainbow. And for that moment, he had no decisions to make, nothing to do other than to let himself be carried by the water.

The slide dropped away and there was one arcing turn through the darkness before he emerged out into the sun.

'Woooot!' Dylan cheered as Fin splashed into the little pool at the bottom. 'How was it?'

'Wow!'

'Cop a look of that face! You'd think you'd never been on a waterslide before.' Dylan hurried back towards the stairs for another slide.

They climbed the stairs and whooshed down another three times, none quite as special as the first. Then they crossed the slippery concrete and waded into the bigger swimming pool, between the tumbling and splashing of Aboriginal families. The water in this pool was cool and the sails suspended above caught most of the sun.

Dylan leant back into the water. 'That's what the doctor ordered.'

'Can we go on the slide again?'

'All in good time, Goldy. It's not called an unlimited ticket for nothing. Let your old dad cool down this hot blood he's got.'

Fin lay back in the water, checking that he was doing it the same way as Dylan. He closed his eyes against the glare and took in the sounds of the giggling chaos, shouted challenges and splashing. He could hear Dylan's wheezy breathing beside him and, again, he thought of how quickly things had changed, how far from Gran and Rory he was, and his mum and poor Josie. But the Darwin man and his Chinese fruit trees didn't feel much nearer than when they had set out.

Dylan moved close in beside him and began speaking in a low whisper. 'You know, we put this pool and waterslide here. All this stuff, we put it in. But it's their land. They were here before. Before we built it. And they're still here, only in swimming pools instead of the bush.' He looked to Fin for a sign of acknowledgement before continuing. 'How do you think you feel about that?'

'I don't know. I like swimming pools.'

'But it's different because you've got a choice. If someone came and knocked down your house to put a waterslide there, even if you didn't want them to, how do you think you'd feel about waterslides then?'

'I wouldn't like them.'

'And what would you want the people and their waterslides to do?'

'Go away, I guess.'

'Exactly. And we've got to remember that. And we've got to give respect.' Dylan looked again for an acknowledgement.

Fin nodded subtly. He was conscious that Dylan was whispering and there were a lot of Aboriginal people around.

Dylan leant right back and floated in the cool water. Fin dunked under and pushed hard off the bottom to send himself rocketing up into the air. A few of the kids and mums around him turned when they heard the splash, and Fin felt very conscious of the colour of his skin.

They stayed paddling as they gradually cooled down. Dylan seemed very focused on the sensation of the water. He kept splashing it on his face and cupping it up to rub on his chest and arms, almost like he was in the bath, while Fin looked at the kids and adults around them. One Aboriginal dad had bright blue eyes and grey tattoos all over his chest and up his neck. He had strong arms and big muscles. His strength meant he was the main 'thrower in the air'. He had a queue of kids in front of him. But each time he turned towards Fin and Dylan, he seemed to look right through them, like their pinky-white skin camouflaged them against the water.

Dylan splashed his face again and spoke quietly. 'Now the tank's nearing empty, we'll have to sort out some cash. And you'll need some bacon, won't you?'

'That would be nice.' Then he remembered Dylan counting out the coins at the front desk. 'But no big hurry or anything. I'm fine. If there's a pool comp somewhere or whatever.'

'You'll get your bacon, don't worry.' Dylan flashed him a quick wink. 'I'm your dad, aren't I?'

'Yes.' He had wanted to say, 'Yes, Dad,' but the word seemed to catch in his throat.

'Your old man's hot blood is just about cool enough for another slide. What do you say to that?'

'Yes, Dad.'

Dylan smiled big and Fin saw the black gap of his missing side tooth.

'Well, you'd better get your sliding shoes on because...'

There was a shriek to their right and Fin looked to see an old Aboriginal man tilted over at an impossible angle. His arms flung out. His wet feet slipped. His shoulder and his big belly slapped down hard on the concrete beside the pool.

The happy chaos of the pool was instantly silent. Fin could hear the ripples breaking against the edge of the pool. Everyone seemed to look in different directions – down or away, anywhere but at the old man. Even the littlest of the kids.

Fin and Dylan watched as a woman in a saggy, rose-patterned swimming costume attempted to pull the man to his feet. The blue-eyed man with tattoos was looking straight at Dylan now. It was as though the silence of the crowd had made their white bodies visible.

The blue-eyed man's face was slack and his lip curled in an expression of rage. He snarled in a toothy shout, 'What are you looking at, you dying Jesus?' His words echoed around the concrete.

Dylan slouched forward, fixed his eyes down and turned away. He grabbed Fin's hand and pulled him towards the pool stairs. They walked silently across the hot concrete and gathered up their things. No-one spoke.

Fin looked up at his dad and whispered, 'One more slide?'

'No, boy.'

Fin didn't understand what they'd done wrong.

They stepped, still dripping with oily water, into the reception area and made their way past the desk.

Dylan went to push the door open and then turned back to the lady behind the desk. 'You wouldn't know of any pool competitions in town, would you?'

'There used to be one at the Royal, but the sergeant abolished it. There's still one at the Harvest. Or there used to be. But entering that one might be,' she searched for the words, 'contrary to your interests.'

'You have a nice day.' Dylan pushed open the door and the hot air outside nearly knocked Fin over.

They stopped to pull their shoes on to protect against the scorching concrete and then climbed into the car without getting changed.

Dylan steered them onto a flat road that led out of town through dirty farmland. Fin leant across to look at the fuel gauge; it was deep into the red section, almost at the bottom.

They drove through a small town with a sign that said it was called Ashley, and Fin noticed a jumping castle deflated on the front lawn of one of the houses. There were no shops and no people, only dust. Soon the town was gone and they were back out in the open.

Dylan looked left and right as they drove. He seemed to be searching for something between the scrubby trees on the horizon.

'Where are we going, Dad?'

'Well, I'm no blackfella, but I'd say we're headed north-west.' Dylan was calm, but it was clear that his head was full of something, and he wasn't in the mood for talking.

They passed a little general store. It was weatherboard with beer advertisements and two old pumps. There was a sign with petrol prices in white numbers. Fin calculated they'd get less than four litres for their five dollars twenty, and that didn't seem like it would get them very far. He saw a truck reflected in the mirage on the road ahead, and he caught a glimpse of the peering eyes of cows in the back as the long trailer passed.

Dylan looked left through the heat haze as they approached a line of denser dark green trees. He slowed the car and his eyes ranged back and forth across the landscape. He pulled over at the gravelly entrance to a driveway and tapped the fuel gauge as though he was checking it was working before turning the engine off. 'You've always got another fifteen kays when it hits the bottom.' A hot, dry silence flowed in as he opened the door.

There was a rusted white gate across the drive. It had dark blue letters cut out of wonky metal on it – *CORELLA*. Above that, a black sign that read *Trespassers Will Be Prosecuted*. Dylan waved his arm and called out a couple of times before he lifted the chain and swung the gate open. He drove slowly down the dirt track along the line of trees to a huddled stand of taller trees ahead. They were a strangely green contrast to the rest of the landscape. The little paddock on the right was all lumpy dirt and struggling stalks of grass.

Dylan winked and said, 'Better keep your head down. Blokes can get a bit shooty this far out.'

Fin slid down in his seat and Dylan slowed almost to a roll as the driveway curved towards an old farmhouse. It was surrounded by close trees, and its tin roof was so rusted there were only a few patches of silver showing through the brown. Its white weatherboard walls had peeled bare in long curls.

Fin heard the buzzing of insects and the zipping twinkling of little birds singing.

'You wait a tick.'

Dylan made his way around the side of the house, and Fin stayed out of sight, holding himself just high enough to see over the dashboard.

The green front door swung open. Fin's mind was overwhelmed by an image of a gun barrel rising, aimed at him through the windscreen. Then, as though his eyes had got it wrong, the figure transformed into Dylan, smiling and tossing his long black hair from side to side as he emerged onto the veranda.

He gave Fin the double thumbs up. 'It wasn't even locked.'

Fin jumped out and hurried to join Dylan on the veranda. Standing side by side, wearing only their boardshorts and shoes, they peered into the inviting shade of the house.

'It gets better.' Dylan led the way inside.

Fin hesitated. He wasn't sure about going into a stranger's house, even if it was unlocked.

Dylan nodded his head, beckoning. 'Come on. It's okay. Squatter's rights.' He turned and walked down the corridor.

Fin hurried inside. He could feel the narrow floorboards stretching under his feet. 'What's squatter's rights?'

'It means we can stay here until someone tells us to leave. Simple as that. Have you heard anyone tell us to leave?'

'No.' Fin remembered the sign on the gate – *Trespassers Will Be Prosecuted*. He didn't know what 'prosecuted' meant, but he hoped it wasn't another word for 'shot'. Also, Dylan's idea of squatter's rights didn't sound right. Otherwise, you'd find people sitting in your living room every time you came home.

Dylan led the way through the kitchen and out the back door. 'Check this out.'

Fin noticed freshly splintered timber on the door frame.

As they stepped into the light, Fin saw a thick metal pipe rising from the ground on the side of the lawn near a stand of taller trees. The pipe had a long elbow-shaped turn in it, like an upside-down 'L', and a big red valve wheel. The horizontal side of the pipe had rusted out in a long gash, and a wide sheet of water was spurting out. It had turned the whole backyard into a shallow waterhole. It even had its own little creek that trickled away at the back.

Dylan stepped into the water. 'When I saw all these trees, I thought it must have been a spring. But it's just an old bore pipe.' He knelt down and splashed some water up onto his arms. 'It must have been going for years to do all this.' He crossed to the other side of the pond. 'I don't believe it.'

Fin made his way carefully through the water to join Dylan in the shade of a big tree.

Dylan winked at him and spoke in a hushed voice, as though he didn't want to disturb the tree. 'The ones on the outside are a bit chewed. But look at that. Further in, they're perfect.'

Fin looked through the branches and saw mango after mango shaded by green leaves.

Dylan climbed, snapping leaves and little branches to clear the way, and began tossing mangoes down for Fin to catch. As each one landed safely in his hands, he laid it on the ground and waited for the next one. He wasn't sure about squatter's rights, but he knew from up at Gustav's that you're not allowed to take fruit from other people's trees.

Dylan climbed down and they began ferrying the mangoes across the waterhole to an area of dirt and cracked concrete beside the back steps. Dylan retrieved a long-bladed knife and a chopping board from the kitchen and set about slicing the mangoes into chunky porcupines.

They ate a few mangoes each and then sat in the warm bore water to wash the juice off their arms and bare chests. Fin leant backwards, closed his eyes and listened to the birds. He thought back to the flashing rainbow of the waterslide, and it already seemed like a long time ago.

He was worried about the owners coming back and things getting 'shooty'. But he also thought that Dylan was probably right. The pipe would have needed to leak for years to make the backyard like this, and the stillness inside the house felt like it hadn't been disturbed in a long time. He also thought how clever Dylan had been to search out the little waterhole by noticing the different trees; he'd remember that.

'We'd better get you out of the sun.' Dylan's voice was relaxed, like his head had emptied out of things to do.

They left wet footprints on the floor as they explored the house. The sitting room and kitchen as well as one of the bedrooms were in the main part, and another two bedrooms were in a section that looked like it had been joined on later. The floors in the new section were higher than the main house, and all the beds were just bare mattresses with yellow stains from where people had sweated through their sheets.

Dylan retrieved his half-broken phone and charger from the car. He tried a few light switches and then plugged his phone in. 'No such luck.' Then he and Fin went around the side to find the fuse box and Dylan confirmed the power was off at 'the mains'.

'What does that mean?'

'It means I don't think we're expecting visitors. But we've also got no power for the phone.'

They walked around to a wonky shed where the driveway ended. The whole thing shook so much as Dylan yanked the barn doors open that it seemed like the doors were the only thing holding the roof up. When they got inside, Fin saw that the back wall had fallen in and was leaning against an old car. The car was covered in years of red-brown dust.

Dylan wiped a patch clean low down on the side. Fin was surprised to see that its dark blue paintwork looked shiny, almost new underneath. Dylan pressed his ear to the metal and rocked the car from side to side with his shoulder.

'You ripper!' He moved across and squatted under the edge of the collapsed timber wall at the back. He beckoned Fin over with his red-dusty chin. 'Come on.'

Fin went around the other side and they pushed hard to straighten the wall up and, with a bit of wiggling and shoving, it fit right back into place. Once it was up, Dylan told Fin to hold it steady while he wedged in bits of timber. He finished the job with a hammer and some rusty nails. 'Good as new.'

Dylan opened the driver's door and then began searching around the shed. The benches had been hammered together from wood that looked like it had been collected from different places and then coated in brown oil. There were hooks on the wall with tools, and old coffee and Milo tins lined up on uneven shelves. Dylan seized a set of car keys from a hook and jumped in and tried the engine. Fin hoped Dylan wasn't planning to drive someone else's car.

There was a loud click, then silence. Fin was flooded with both disappointment and relief. He was sure that squatter's rights didn't extend to driving around in other people's cars.

Dylan climbed out and began wiping the settled dirt off the bonnet with his sweaty hands. 'She's a beauty though.'

Fin watched the dark blue metal emerge from the dirt. It was as if the thick layer of dirt had prevented it from ageing.

Once the car was more or less dusted off, Dylan clicked it out of gear and the two of them pushed it into the shade of a tree. Dylan lifted the bonnet and pointed to each part of the engine, saying its name. Then he mimed drawing a pointing-finger pistol, like a cowboy, and Fin had to call out the name of each engine part he pointed to. Even though Lindy was good at fixing cars, she had never taught him any engine parts.

Dylan checked the leads, the hoses and the battery, and they pushed the dusty car alongside their station wagon. Dylan hooked up some long jumper leads. He told Fin to sit in the driver's seat of the wagon and explained again which pedal was the brake and showed him the accelerator.

Fin started the engine and Dylan jumped into the blue car. There was a scraping, whining sound, but the engine didn't start.

Dylan called out, 'Push the pedal down. Give it a rev.'

Fin pushed down on the accelerator and the wagon's engine roared. Dylan tried the blue car again and again. Suddenly, its engine whirred into life, and a big cloud of light blue smoke appeared at the back.

Dylan signalled for Fin to kill the engine in the wagon. 'You ripper!' His eyes widened with excitement as he disconnected the jumper leads. 'It looks like there's about a third of a tank.' He slid the seat forward and told Fin to climb into the driver's seat of the blue car. Fin had to sit up straight to see over the steering wheel.

Dylan explained that they'd have to drive around for a while to recharge the battery. 'So, want to? It's okay. I'll be right here. And I can do anything with the gearshift. You just have to do everything real small and gentle. Not like a cartoon.'

Although Fin had driven the station wagon around behind the lion park, this seemed very different – the car was stolen. But Dylan had such a look of joy that Fin felt he couldn't say no.

'Okay.'

Dylan clicked on both of their seatbelts and explained they were going to have to reverse to make the turn. He moved the gearshift and Fin was able to back the car in a long curve until they were pointed down the driveway. Dylan moved the gearshift again.

Fin lifted his foot from the brake and the car began creeping forward.

'See? Like I said. You're a natural. You know it, anyway. But remember which one's the brake. That's the important one.' Dylan winked and then pointed ahead with two fingers, which meant – *eyes on the road*.

The driveway seemed to have grown longer since they'd arrived. Fin focused on every rise and fall, every rock on its crumbly surface.

'You can give it some gas.'

Fin felt like he was driving as fast as the surface allowed. He pressed down gently on the accelerator and the car lifted into a rolling glide. The ground disappearing under the bonnet was moving too fast now; he had to trust the road.

The big gate approached and he eased off, bringing the car to a stop. There wasn't enough space to turn around, and Fin hoped that Dylan didn't expect him to reverse it all the way back.

Dylan clicked the gearshift into *P*, climbed out and approached the gate. He lifted the chain and swung the gate wide open.

Fin was frozen in disbelief. It seemed impossible that his dad would direct him onto a real road, especially in a stolen car. Dylan approached, smiling, and Fin relaxed. It had been some kind of test.

'You've got to put it into gear. See there? D is for driiiive!'

Dylan walked back to the open gate and Fin looked down at the gearshift. The top of the shifter was worn shiny smooth by years of the owner's touch. He reached down, pushed the button and moved it into gear. He was determined not to seem weak.

The car lurched and he guided it forward. He stopped at the edge of the highway. Dylan replaced the chain on the gate and climbed into the passenger seat.

'Am I allowed, Dad?'

'Well, it's not really driving unless it's on a road. And, anyway, you're not going to find anywhere flatter and emptier than out here.'

The cattle truck Fin had seen earlier didn't make the road feel very empty.

'It's not like you're doing it on all those bendy roads up near Old Binnalong.'

Fin's head and jaw flooded with rage – *He's known where I've been all along. He could have just driven there himself.*

Fin lifted his foot from the brake and pushed down hard on the accelerator. He turned left and the wheels spun in the gravel as he swung onto the road. Once he had them straight, he pushed down harder on the accelerator until the car was flying.

'You ripper!' Dylan thumped twice on the dashboard and flicked a look over his shoulder to check for any cars behind them.

The car felt as though it wasn't even touching the road. Fin saw the wobbling hint of something coming towards them in the distance. 'Which side am I meant to be on?'

'Left side, Golden. Left. You're doing fine.'

Fin focused as the truck approached. Although they were travelling fast, Fin's eyes seemed to sharpen again and every imperfection in the painted centre line was clear. He could see the red of the big prime mover reflected in the mirage. He felt the shove of the air-pressure wave. He gripped the wheel tighter to stop them being forced off the road and held his eyes open against blinking. The roar of the truck's engine filled every little bit of space in his mind. Then the truck was gone, and there was melty silver all the way to the horizon.

They continued along the burning highway until Dylan said, 'I reckon the battery will be just about right.' He directed Fin into a dirt road with an entrance that was wide enough to turn around in.

There was a mottled grey horse in a fenced paddock beside the road. Fin looked closely at the horse, but Dylan signalled for him to keep his eyes on the road. He turned the car around in a slow circle and looked over his shoulder to get one more glimpse of the horse before turning back onto the highway. He forced the few distinct bits of the landscape here into his memory – the curve of the road, the line of taller trees, the red roof of a distant farmhouse. He felt like it was important to remember his way back to this place.

They didn't pass another truck or car. Dylan unchained the gate and Fin collected him on the other side. He took it easy along the driveway and parked under the shady tree.

Dylan let out a hot and weary groan as he climbed out. 'I don't know about you, but I'm jonesing for a mango.'

Fin went to climb out but stopped. They had just broken the law, and it seemed as though Dylan thought that rules didn't apply to him. He felt his heart slowing, his breathing became more regular. The sizzling rage he had felt at the realisation Dylan knew where they lived the whole time was fading now. He thought that he could just go, turn the key and drive, but then he felt a stickier acceptance. He was where he was; they were where they were. And there was nothing really to think about other than the current plan. He had no idea how their five dollars and twenty cents was going to get them to Darwin, but they wouldn't go hungry for a few days with the mango tree.

He thought back to the angry face of the man at the pool. It had only been a couple of hours. But, since then, his dad had taught him to drive.

CHAPTER EIGHTEEN

Dylan spent the afternoon searching every cupboard and old tin in the kitchen. He even went around knocking on the walls and the floor, looking for hidden compartments. All he found was a big bag of flour and a huge bottle he called a flagon. He said it had sweet sherry in it and was almost full. Dylan poured himself a mug and gave Fin a sip. It had sounded good, but it smelled like fruit bats and had a sickly sour taste; he preferred the eggy water from the bore.

As the sun began to fade, Dylan set about arranging some old bricks near the pond and gathering firewood. He said he wanted to get everything laid out before nightfall because they wouldn't be able to see once the sun set. He placed two wobbly wooden chairs beside the new fireplace but said he'd wait until dark to light the fire because the locals would notice smoke in an empty place like this. Fin took it as a sign that Dylan wasn't so sure about squatter's rights himself.

Once the bricks and wood were arranged, he retrieved a couple of pots from the kitchen. He poured in some flour, picked a few tiny bugs out of it, added some water and began mixing with his hands. He then gathered up some longer, thicker sticks and showed Fin how to shape the dough like a wonky sausage over the end. They both made two sticks each and leant them up against the side of the house.

Dylan filled some more pots with water from the spurting bore, carried them into the kitchen to cool, and moved the mangoes to a place near the fire bricks. He began peeling them and breaking the flesh into another pot. 'It might not look like much, but you can't beat it.' He kept going until the pot was full to the top with mushy mango flesh, and he lit the fire as soon as the long twilight began fading behind the trees. The fire crackled alight and cast a long shadow in the shape of the two of them, side by side.

The trees around the bore pond were alive with buzzing and chirping. Dylan brought the flagon and his mug out and sat on his wobbly chair, drinking mug after mug of sherry and smoking cigarette after cigarette until there were only little bits of tobacco left in the bottom of his packet. Just as Fin felt his hunger really rising again, Dylan pushed the flaming part of the fire back against the bricks and tucked the pot full of mango mush into the hot coals. He went into the dark kitchen and came back with a wooden spoon.

'You can stir.'

253

Fin had to lean back and stretch his arm out to avoid being scorched by the fire.

Dylan loaded another mug with sweet sherry. 'You have to keep stirring or it will burn on the bottom.' He winked. 'But don't worry. I can handle a bit of burntness in my mango jam. I quite like it, actually.'

Fin kept stirring, only stopping for relief from the heat. Dylan retrieved the dough sticks and leant them against the bricks so they were suspended over the coals.

'You'll have to keep them turning so they cook evenly.'

Fin stirred and turned until Dylan said it was ready. Then he showed Fin how to remove the dough from the stick without tearing a hole. He held it like a skinny cup and spooned it full of the hot mango jam. Fin waited his turn and filled his too.

'Bon appétit.' Dylan leant over and knocked his dough cup against Fin's as though they were clinking glasses.

The warm insides squirted into his mouth and the ashy taste of the dough was bitter and perfect. 'Mangoes are definitely my favourite fruit.' Fin spoke in a slow, important way, a bit like he imagined Dylan would say it.

'Me too.'

'This is a classic. That's what Rory would say.'

Dylan swallowed down another piece of damper. 'He sounds like a classic himself.'

'Don't suppose I'll be seeing him though.'

'You'll get your chance.'

'His pop says we're not allowed. Because of whatever, because of Mum.'

'Don't worry too much about old Coleman. His bark's far worse than his bite. He'd like a swig on this, I can tell you that.' Dylan took a big sip of sherry.

'What happened, Dad?'

'Oh, Golden, all this bull… Sorry, all this was a long time ago. Before Rory and you. And it was stupid, so stupid. So don't you get any ideas. But Angela, Rory's mum, they were young, and you know, she had too much…medicine. She nearly died, but she didn't though. And there was a big stink up because it was your mum that had given it to her.' Dylan was speaking faster now, as if he wanted to get it over with. 'And everyone was saying it was serious. And when the police came, they were going for your mum. And I told them it was me that gave the medicine to Angela.'

This made no sense to Fin – surely he could just have explained that the medicine was a mistake? 'Why do that?'

'Who knows why people do things. They were just trying all that medicine to see what it would do.'

'No, why did you say it was you?'

'Well, Angela was maybe going to die and, if that happened, your mum would have been in real strife, maybe even jail. And she was still sick, and she couldn't handle it. So I told them.'

'Did you? Go to jail, I mean.'

'No, not that time. Angela was all right in the end. And that was my first offence.'

Mango dripped down onto Dylan's bare chest. Fin saw a faded scar just under his collarbone; the skin looked discoloured, possibly from scratching. As Fin looked closer, he could just make out wobbly letters – *Griffin*. He hadn't noticed it in the daylight. For some reason, it showed up clearer in the light of the fire.

Dylan saw him looking at it. 'A mate did it for me. But he didn't have the right kind of ink.'

They filled up another damper cup each. Dylan chomped his down in a few mouthfuls, but Fin nibbled around the edges and licked out a layer of jam at each new level.

Dylan put another piece of wood on the fire and poured more sherry. 'You deserve better than damper and mango jam.'

Fin licked the last bits of jam out of the bottom of his damper cup. 'I like it.'

Dylan said the reason some people are rich and some people are poor is because the government and economic system is rigged to keep poor people poor so they don't rise up and change the system. 'If it was fair, why should the system say that one kid gets to ride to a private school in a Lexus and you've only got damper and wash it down with bore water?'

Fin understood what his dad meant, but he thought the other kid's parents probably had good jobs.

Dylan continued. 'Let me put it this way. If you were in charge of the system, would you have it that way around?'

Fin had to guess what his dad would most like to hear. 'No. If it was me running it, I mean, in charge of the system,

I'd give every kid a Lexus for school.' Fin didn't know what a Lexus was, but it sounded like a small helicopter of some kind. He decided to leave out the bit about private school. He'd heard that the kids who went to them complained a lot and didn't talk to other kids.

'Exactly! That's because the system isn't working for you. Where's your Lexus on its way to private school? I'll tell you where it is. It's tucked into some fat cat's wallet next to his big fat bum cheeks all full up with lobsters. That's where it is.' Dylan took a big drink from his mug. 'And it's him and his lawyer mates that make all these scams for getting rich and then they call them *laws*!' Dylan spat the word out. 'And they know that if they call them laws, they sound important and all the plebs will play along so we don't get into trouble. They'll say, "This is our big pile of gold over here and you can't have any of it because it's the *law*. You've got to go hungry and sick because it's the *law*. You've got to go to jail because it's the *law*." And then he turns to one of his toffy lawyer mates and says, "Write that down, will you? Make another law, will you? And pass me a couple of lobsters while you're at it, my bum cheeks are feeling a bit empty!"' Dylan was leaning forward now and almost shouting.

He seemed to notice that Fin was overwhelmed by what he was saying, so he spoke more calmly, but still with determination. 'Anyway, don't worry. But don't be too fussed about the laws these fat cats make. Right and wrong don't change, but laws change. And don't worry about taking things when you really need to. They were all yours to begin with. Birthright stuff. And the only reason you have to break their fu... The only reason you have to break their laws to take them back is because the system robbed them from you in the first place.'

Fin was scared of saying something wrong. 'Yes, I guess so.'

He thought about how dads are different to mums. Even when Lindy was really shouting, all wound up, he knew he could tumble forward into her arms for a cuddle, no matter what. He didn't feel like that now.

They stayed out there sitting and talking until Dylan stopped loading the fire with new wood. The heat of the day had disappeared.

Dylan ran out of tobacco and seemed to grow sleepy, hunching further forward in his chair. 'Throw me one of those mangoes, would you?' He gestured to the last two mangoes on the ground beside Fin's feet.

Fin handed one over. Dylan bit into the top and used his teeth to peel the skin away from one side. He took a couple of bites and then tossed it into the bore pond. 'If there's one thing I've learnt, you can get sick of anything.'

CHAPTER NINETEEN

Fin woke to the sound of floorboards creaking. He opened his eyes and saw the hemline of a floral dress disappearing at the edge of the doorway. He sat up in shock, jumped off the mattress and tucked himself in behind the door. One word kept repeating in his mind – *shooty*. The house was silent. This didn't make sense because whoever it was would have seen Dylan by now. Again, Fin heard the old floorboards creaking.

He peered through the crack in the door, trying to see the woman. He couldn't hear voices. And then, as if his veins had been flushed with iced water, he realised the owner had already got to Dylan. He heard the owner walking back and forth in the kitchen. Her footsteps were quiet and familiar, like Gran's.

He heard the footsteps approaching and all he could think was – *I've got to get to the car.* The footsteps drew closer, and Fin pushed his head harder into the crack behind the door to try to see. The early light cast the woman's shadow across the floor. She came closer. He could see the outline of her dress. She would find him for sure.

He looked up at her face – it was Dylan. He was wearing an orange and white daisy-patterned dress. He also had a pair of brown stockings upside down on his head. The twisty legs hung down over his shoulder like two long plaits. He looked into Fin's room. When he saw the empty bed, his eyes flicked to the crack behind the door. He said, 'That's a funny place to eat your breakfast.'

Fin came around into the doorway. 'What are you doing?'

'I got cold in the night. Do you think it suits me?'

Fin sat back on his bed. He could hear the blood pumping in his ears. 'It's a dress.'

'I like the pattern, but the sizing's all wrong. Whoever she was definitely had a fuller figure.' Dylan winked. 'I got up early to cook us a bit more damper before the sun came up. I didn't wait. Yours is on the bench in there.' He walked back into the bigger bedroom and lay on the bed.

Fin tried to calm himself after the fright. He chewed down some of the smoky damper and struggled to drink some bore water straight from the heavy pot; it had gone cold overnight and the eggy flavour had intensified.

Dylan kept the dress on. It made him seem like someone else, and the stockings on his head almost transformed him into a creature from another planet. Each time their eyes met, Dylan looked defiant. As though wearing the dress and keeping the stockings on his head was a protest against 'normal'. It was exactly the sort of thing Lindy would do.

As the day brightened, Dylan seemed to grow more restless. He prowled from room to room and even went back to banging on the walls, looking for secret compartments. He tried getting the electricity to work again but just ended up slamming the cover on the fuse box. It reminded Fin of how Gran had described Lindy just before the biggest Christmas fight – *like a bottled spider*. Again, Dylan seemed to have run out of words. He expressed himself through sighing, heavy-footed pacing and slouching. It was as though the house had shrunk overnight and was now too small to contain him.

Fin kept himself out of the sun so he wouldn't have to drink too much more of the bore water. But a couple of times he headed out into the scorching heat of the pond to listen to the birds and escape the pressure of the house. Around the middle of the day, just as Fin had managed to stretch himself out into a sweaty sleep on his mattress, Dylan appeared in the doorway with his hands on his hips. He was still wearing the dress. 'I'm going out. I'll be back in a while. We need a plan.' He turned to leave. 'I didn't want you waking up in an empty house is all.' He walked determinedly out the front and banged the door behind him.

Fin heard the car engine start up, then the sound was gone. The pressure of Dylan's sighing and pacing was replaced by dangerous quiet, and Fin couldn't help expecting another glimpse of a dress. This time it really would be the owner. And, despite his fear, he half wished she would come.

Fin searched through the kitchen cupboards for some more cooking pots and filled each one from the spurting bore pipe before setting them down in the shade of the house. As the day wore on, his head flashed with images of the grey horse he'd seen the day before. He imagined himself riding, following the powerlines. Each time he began planning a way out, he reassured himself that Dylan would come back, even speaking out loud sometimes. He'd say things like, 'Any minute now. No need to worry,' and 'Don't get your knickers in a knot,' and 'He knows where you are.'

As the shadows grew longer, he started preparing for nightfall. He gathered sticks for the fire and dragged the big bag of flour out onto the kitchen floor. Then he realised it wouldn't work because Dylan had the cigarette lighter. So he returned to his sweaty mattress to steel himself against the possibility of a night alone in the house.

He thought about how things must be at Gran's, imagined hurrying down the path to check the crab pot, flames crackling and the buttery smell of new crabs roasting on the fire. And then the chemical spots gradually spreading up his neck until they covered his face. He thought that Gran probably would have had a funeral for Josie, and he wondered if they would have let Lindy out of hospital so she could go. He imagined Lindy and Gran standing on opposite sides of the grave, and Lindy refusing any food and drink until the ambulancemen took her back to the jail-safety of the hospital.

And he drifted into sleep.

~

He woke suddenly, drenched in sweat, and it took him a few panicked moments to remember where he was. The light outside was fading. He pulled himself quietly to his feet. 'Dad?' The only sound was the trickling of the bore and the insects and birds shifting into their rituals of night-time.

He went out the front in the vain hope of seeing headlights on the driveway. He checked the ignition of the dusty car, and then the hook in the garage for the keys. They were gone. Fin thought that it was strange that Dylan had taken the wagon; it was almost out of petrol.

He thought of searching through the house for another set of keys. The tank probably had just enough in it to get him to where he could pick up the trail of powerlines that would lead him back to Gustav's.

He made up his mind to sleep in the car – at least he could lock it up against the night. And he'd have the inside light if he got scared. Then, if Dylan still hadn't come back, he'd drink as much bore water as he could and set out along the road towards the grey horse. He thought he'd probably have a better chance of reaching the powerlines on horseback.

He'd ridden a few times up at Old Bin. He knew it would be hard to climb onto the horse without stirrups, but he'd have to try. And although he didn't like the idea of taking someone's horse, he'd heard that horses were like cats – they always find their way home.

He clicked the car door closed.

The comforting silence wrapped around him. He locked each of the doors and stretched out along the back seat. The lining was starting to come away from the ceiling and it billowed like a tent. He rolled his hand back and forth, as if he had his golf ball, but he'd left it in the wagon.

There was a flash of turning headlights across the glass and Dylan's car pulled up behind. Fin unlocked the door and jumped out.

Dylan opened the door and stood up; he'd taken off the dress and was wearing jeans with no shirt. 'Going somewhere?'

Fin's words erupted out of him in a shout. 'I don't like it when you leave me! I didn't know if you were coming back.'

Dylan lifted his hands in front of him as though he was trying to calm a wild animal. 'It's okay, Golden. I'm here now.'

Fin couldn't resist saying what came next. 'No! It's not okay. No. It's not. My whole life you leave me. Just now you show up and then you turn around and leave me in somebody's stolen house! It's...not...okay! Don't even say it's okay.' Fin felt angry tears pooling in his eyes.

Dylan took a step closer and stopped where he was. 'Okay, Golden. You've made your point.' He looked straight into

Fin's eyes and nodded, as if to say, *settle down, little man,* like Lindy would.

Fin couldn't stop. He felt like Dylan still hadn't understood. He was angry again about the screwdriver man behind the lion park. 'Stop saying "okay". You weren't the one here all day with nothing. I could have got shot by the owner of this place. You weren't. And not even food. I was just going to sleep in the car.'

Dylan spoke over him with a resolute gravelliness. 'And you weren't the one down on the footpath begging change for hours in this heat. You weren't the one doing that.'

The image of Dylan begging came as a jolting shock.

'And no stupid good it did us anyway, barely eight bucks. And the only ones that even think about helping you in a town like this are the blackfellas. And when they hand it over, you can see they need it worse.' He took another step towards Fin and his voice softened. 'I didn't take you because no-one wants to see that. You don't want to see that. But we need cash and we need fuel. You know as well as I do this place is wearing out.'

Fin didn't know what to say.

'Anyway, if you insist, I'll take you next time I go anywhere. I promise.' Dylan pulled out his tobacco packet and sat down on the ground where he was. 'One way or another, we're going to have to raise some money.'

Fin sat down too.

Dylan upturned his tobacco packet and a dozen or so cigarette butts tumbled out onto the dry grass. He sighed as he looked at the charred ends on the ground. 'There aren't many bus stops in this town.'

He held his hand over the empty packet and began rubbing each butt so whatever ashy bits of tobacco remained sprinkled out. They sat in silence as the last of the twilight faded. Dylan rolled himself a cigarette and the smoke stank of ashtrays and garbage.

He smoked it right down to his fingertips. 'You and I had better drink some water.'

'I brought some more pots in for us.' Fin felt his stomach spasm in a hunger pain.

'Good thinking. That reminds me.' Dylan retrieved a whole loaf of fresh white bread from the car and they walked through the dark house to sit on the kitchen floor.

They ate slice by slice and drank water from the heavy pots. They reached into the bag until the bread was all gone. Dylan lay on the saggy floorboards in the living room, and Fin got on his bed again. They had run out of things to say.

~

'Come on, Golden Boy. It's next time.' Dylan was standing in the doorway of Fin's little room. There was something harsh about his voice. Fin realised he had fallen asleep after the bread. As his eyes began to make sense of things, he saw that the stockings were dangling from either side of Dylan's head again, and he'd stretched a woman's white cardigan over his shoulders. Its tight sleeves only came two-thirds of the way down his arms, just covering his tattoos, and it left a gap of bare stomach before his jeans started.

'You said you wanted to come.' Dylan turned and disappeared into the dark.

Fin found him out the front. He'd rolled the station wagon onto a scrubby bit of dirt and grass beside the driveway. The other car was parked on the driveway, facing the road. The passenger door was open, and Fin could see the stocking legs silhouetted against the shoulders of the white cardigan.

Dylan called out as he approached, 'Have you left anything inside?'

'No. I didn't bring anything in.'

'You're sure? Absolutely nothing?'

'Sure.'

'You're driving.' Dylan lowered himself into the passenger seat.

He dreaded the idea of driving at night. But from the way Dylan spoke, it was clear he didn't have a choice.

He sat in the driver's seat and Dylan slid it forward.

'Absolutely nothing left inside?'

'No, Dad.'

There was no moon and Fin sat up straight so he could see the shine of the headlights on the driveway.

Dylan climbed out to open the gate and got back in without waiting to close it. 'Turn right.' He pointed the direction.

Fin turned onto the road.

The orange cat's eyes on the centre line set a steady visual rhythm.

'Other side.' Dylan pointed to the left.

Fin guided the car across the centre lines.

'This right now?'

'Yes, Golden. You're doing it right. You can give her a bit more gas.'

Fin accelerated and the car seemed to lift. They were going fast in the dark. Out of the corner of his eye, Fin saw Dylan retrieve a black cap from the floor. He placed it on his head and began tucking his long hair and the stocking legs up under it. It made no sense to Fin that he didn't just take the stupid stockings off.

A dead kangaroo was sprawled at the road's edge and Fin moved the car towards the centre to avoid running over it.

Dylan held his hand up in a goodbye wave. 'Hoo-roo.'

Fin couldn't help a little giggle.

Dylan spoke clearly and calmly. 'If you see one of those hopping out in front of us, just drive straight. Running over a roo won't kill us, but swerving off the road to avoid one just might.'

They continued through the dark until Fin saw the lights of the little shop with the petrol pumps coming up on the right side.

'I'll get you just to head on past her and we'll make a U-bolt a bit further down.'

None of this made sense to Fin. He didn't think their thirteen dollars or so was going to buy enough petrol to get them very far.

'Here will do it.' Dylan pointed ahead to a dirt side road. Fin turned the car around on the gravel. It felt like the steering wheel moved automatically.

He drove slowly back towards the shop, scanning the edges of the road for kangaroos.

As he looked past his hands on the steering wheel, the whole situation suddenly shifted, seemed fake. It was like he was watching his life in a movie and an actor was playing his role, Fin Alverton – or was it Fin Martin? And these past few imaginary days were happening somewhere else and to someone else, and he was actually leaning back into the spongy comfort of a couch. Or even dreaming it all from his rattly room up at Old Bin. Yes, it was a dream, he decided. Just a weird dream. There was nothing connecting this to real life.

He steered the car into the shop's driveway.

'Keep her this side.' Dylan pointed to the right side of the petrol pumps.

Fin had come off the road too fast, and he had to brake hard to stop. He put the car into *P* and looked at Dylan.

'Okay, you kill the engine. But you start her up again the minute I finish filling, okay?'

Fin nodded.

Dylan pulled the hat down low over his eyes, climbed out and began filling the car with petrol. Fin leant across to watch the numbers ticking over on the fuel pump, litres and dollars. And as soon as the dollar amount reached thirteen, he knew Dylan expected him to drive off without paying. In that same instant, as the number twelve became thirteen, everything clicked back into a sharp reality. This was not a dream, not a movie. This was real. And, the same as when he'd driven fast for the first time, the edges of things seemed suddenly clearer, like they were much nearer than they could be.

He watched the numbers tick over – $43.25…$51.16… $67.81 – until they stopped at $73.98. He heard Dylan withdrawing the nozzle and putting it back into place on the pump.

As instructed, Fin started the engine. He planted his foot firmly on the brake and clicked the gearshift into *D*. He hated it, but he was ready. Dylan opened the passenger door but didn't get in. He smiled with his whole body and gave Fin a look of calm reassurance, like it was the end of a long day. 'That's the ticket. You keep her running. I'm just going to grab some smokes.'

Like a dad, Fin thought.

Dylan tossed his hat onto the passenger seat and, as he turned and began running towards the little shop, he pulled the stockings down over his head.

Fin's whole body clenched up to the point of shaking. He was gripping the steering wheel so tight it felt like his fingers might split open. He had his foot hard on the brake. He kept his eyes straight ahead, resisting the temptation to look at what was happening in the shop. He felt as though he could stay separate from it all as long as he didn't look.

And then he looked.

There was a golden flash of light and a single cracking sound. He felt his stomach twist up and drop; he felt wetness squirting into his pants and spreading over the backs of his legs. Dylan came running towards the passenger door. His arms were full of tobacco packets. He rolled sideways into the car, dumping the tobacco onto the floor. He pulled his knees up and yanked the door closed while still lying sideways across the gearshift. 'Drive!'

Fin pushed down on the accelerator and the wheels spun on the driveway. He had to steer hard left and right to keep the car moving towards the road until the tyres gripped and the car shot forward.

Dylan sat up and pulled the stocking off his head. His long hair tumbled down over his shoulders. He raised his arms and tore off the little white cardigan.

The road was vanishing beneath the front of the car and the centre line was blurred. There was only one word in Fin's mind – *kangaroos.*

Dylan wound down the window and the roar of the wind was so loud that Fin nearly swerved off the road. Dylan bundled up the cardigan and the stockings and tossed them through the open window into the dark. Next there was the metal thunk of something heavy dropping into the storage console on the passenger door.

Dylan took a deep breath and let the air hiss back out through his teeth. 'It's okay, Golden Boy. No-one's chasing us yet.'

In the far distance, to the left, beyond where the headlights shone out into the black, the outline of a tree caught his eye. It was rising up out of the flat land and it was silhouetted against the sky. Its branches were cut off and stumpy halfway along. He was overcome by a sick familiarity and the old feeling of Ψ – *Algiz*. Although the headlights shone clear into the night, it felt like the road was fading, like he was being pulled backwards into sleep.

He pressed down hard on the brake. The car began to skid and the back wheels drifted around to the right to the point the car was almost sideways across the road. As they skidded, he eased off the brake and managed to straighten up just as they came to a sudden halt. Fin's head whipped forward and nearly whacked the top of the steering wheel before it was flung backwards against the seat. Dylan was thrown forward. He swivelled and managed to grip the side of the driver's seat as his ribs and arm thumped into the glovebox.

There was a second of silence. Dylan turned his head to look out the back window. 'Jesus, Golden! What are you doing?'

Fin kept looking forward at the silhouetted tree in the distance and the illuminated road ahead. Dylan looked out too and, in the furthest reaches of the headlights, they watched as three kangaroos rushed across the road. They were hurrying like they were escaping from something, two big kangaroos leading with a smaller one following behind.

Dylan pulled his seatbelt on. 'Jesus, your eyes are good. You must get that from me.'

Fin watched until the tail of the smaller kangaroo disappeared into the dark.

'Come on, Golden Boy. We're sitting ducks here.'

Fin lifted his foot off the brake and steered them along the empty road.

He began to slow down when he saw the outline of the taller trees around the mango house.

Dylan waved his hand in front of his face. 'Whooo! It smells like someone's got a full-on fart crisis. And I'm not just talking an anal volcano.' His use of these words seemed to change the happy memory of their first funny breakfast in the café.

Dylan pointed ahead and Fin slowed just enough to turn through the big gateway. He hurried down the bumping driveway towards the house.

'I don't think those mangoes agree with you. You're brewing some sort of chemical weapon in there.'

Fin wasn't going to admit he'd pooed his pants. Instead, he focused on navigating each rise and fall of the driveway.

'Okay, bring her up. Right next to the other one.'

Fin pulled the car up beside where the wagon was parked beside the driveway. He switched off the engine and felt the beginning of tears, but it was like they were stuck inside his head, soaking back down his neck.

Dylan waved his hand in front of his face again but then seemed to realise that it wasn't right to keep making jokes about farts. 'Oh.' He climbed out and busied himself with a coiled hose that was on the ground beside the wagon.

Fin stepped out and stood beside the car. He felt the ooze of poo starting down the insides of his legs. The first part of the moon was just clearing the horizon. It was a thick, lopsided crescent, and its soft light revealed the house and garden.

Dylan began feeding one end of the hose into the fuel tank of the dusty car. 'You might want to get cleaned up. We're leaving.'

Fin walked towards the house.

'Remember, leave nothing behind,' Dylan called, and then began sucking on the other end of the hose.

Fin navigated the darkness of the house by memory. He went down the back steps and dropped his shorts by the edge of the bore pond. The runny, fruity poo was most of the way down his legs, and he could feel it stinging the backs of his knees. He stepped out of his shorts and saw the crumpled shape of them on the ground. He couldn't throw them away, he owned almost nothing.

He thought of just sitting in the bore pond to wash off and rinse out his shorts. But he felt he couldn't. The pond had been good to him and dirtying it would ruin it for the other creatures, and the next visitor.

He retrieved one of the big pots from inside and scooped up a potful of water from the shallow pond. He carried it around to the corner of the house, where he felt confident the pooey liquid would run into the dry dirt. He poured the water down the backs of his legs and scrubbed the poo away with his hand. It took a couple of trips to the pond's edge but eventually his legs and bum were clean. He rinsed out his boardshorts and undies as best he could, then pulled them on still wet. He didn't care if the bore water soaked into the car seat.

He thought about escaping, dodging around Dylan and running through the scrub until he found a horse to carry him away or a powerline to follow. Even with his sharp, dangerous senses, Dylan wouldn't be able to find him in the dark. And he'd have until the light of morning to creep as far away as he could.

He stepped inside and made his way back through the house. He knew he couldn't run. They were bound together, firstly by blood, and then by all that had happened in the last three days. Up until now, every wrong thing Dylan had done had seemed like an accident. Or, at least, a mistake. But, as he stepped out onto the dried-out front lawn, Fin knew it was different now. And he too had done bad things.

Dylan was rolling the dusty car back into the mouth of the shed. He tossed the hose aside, pulled on his old black T-shirt and climbed into the wagon. He revved it up onto the driveway and leant across to open the passenger door. 'I'll drive this time. Give you a chance to get some rest.'

Fin sat down and clicked on his seatbelt. Dylan tugged at the belt to make sure it was fastened securely.

Like a dad, Fin thought.

Dylan kept the headlights off and followed the driveway by the light of the moon.

He paused as he approached the road and made a survey of the dark. He began edging forward once he'd satisfied himself that no-one was watching. 'There's no feeling like a full tank of petrol.'

Fin couldn't help finishing the line in his head – *you can keep driving until you run out of road.*

Dylan turned the car onto the empty road and didn't click the headlights on until they were already up to speed.

CHAPTER TWENTY

Fin half opened his eyes and saw the familiar road markings that led the way to Gustav's. He could feel the presence of his mum, steering them purposefully towards home. He breathed slowly through his nose, expecting Lindy's butter and toast smell. Instead, there came the dirty harshness of cigarette smoke. His eyes sprang open, and he was shocked from the safety of his dream.

'Get some sleep?' Smoke puffed out of Dylan's nose with each word.

The car was hurrying along open road. Fin surveyed his surroundings to work out how far they'd travelled. 'Yeah.'

The landscape was all dirt with wonky irrigation sprinklers on big tyres, and the sun was just about to rise. Dylan had a sleepy, contented energy about him, and he looked at Fin a lot.

Ahead, almost at the horizon, Fin could see a mysterious body of water. It looked as though it could only be the distant ocean. He sat up high in his seat, straining to bring clarity to the rippling blue in the distance. As they drew closer, it became more and more impossible. It was a hill of pale blue water with rippling waves running across its face and disappearing into air. Fin saw a lone figure walking by the side of the road, far ahead. It had to be someone lost or run out of petrol.

When they were within a couple of hundred metres, Fin saw the mountain of water for what it was – a giant blue tarpaulin stretched over a huge pile of something. Long peeling waves flowed through the shiny surface as it was shifted by the wind. Dylan slowed the car, and Fin made out the figure of an old lady hobbling on the gravel beside the road. She was wearing a pale blue cardigan over a white dress. She had a pink felt hat pulled down low on her head and a white handbag slung over the crook in her arm. From this distance, it could have been Josie's ghost.

'Should we check she's all right?' Fin brightened at the prospect of helping someone.

'What do you think?' Dylan meant 'no'.

Fin persisted. 'I think we should. What's she doing all the way out here? Anything could have happened or whatever.'

It was clear Dylan wanted to keep moving, but he relented. 'Shovel that stuff under the seat then.'

Fin unclicked his belt and began stuffing all the tobacco packets into the low gap beneath the passenger seat. Dylan pulled over just ahead of the old lady. They both climbed out and stood beside the car. The sun still hadn't cleared the horizon and there was a cold edge to the earthy air.

'You okay, love?' Dylan nodded, as if to suggest the answer.

She spoke with a clear voice, like she was on the radio. 'Fine, thank you.'

'Anything we can…? Cold morning out here for a walk.' Dylan seemed to struggle to find words.

'Mornings are often cold.'

Fin noticed that her brown stockings had a hole over one knee, and dark blood had soaked around it.

Dylan looked around at the empty fields. 'Live around here, do you?'

'I'm headed for the railway, Flinders Street. I'm meeting my husband there. Just so you know.'

Dylan flicked Fin a quick, cheeky look and then returned his gaze to the woman. 'Flinders Street, Melbourne? Is that where you're meaning?'

Fin was startled by this. He looked out again to orient himself. The glow of the almost-risen sun was on the right of the car so he knew they were still going north. As he'd done when he and Rory set out for New Zealand, he tried to fix the position of the brightest part of the glow in his mind so he'd know which way to walk if he found himself alone.

'Yes, sir. And I'd best not be late. Harry's not much of a waiter. So I'll wish you gentlemen good day.'

Dylan shrugged his shoulders at Fin as if to say – *no point arguing.*

But Fin pleaded with his eyes and mouthed 'please'. They couldn't just drive off and leave her, especially not heading in the wrong direction.

Dylan relented. 'Well, ma'am. As it turns out, we share a destination. We're also headed for the railway. May we drive you?'

The old lady furrowed her brow and stayed silent for a while before speaking. 'I'd be obliged, under the circumstances, very gratefully. I seem to have a splinter in my knee and it would do well for a rest. But I do stress it's my husband I'm meeting. He won't suffer any hijinks.'

'Naturally.' Dylan moved around to the passenger side and opened the door for her to climb in. He stuffed Fin's sleeping bag out of the way as he unfolded the rear seat to click it into place.

Fin climbed into the back and noticed that the tobacco packets had dislodged his golf ball from its spot under the passenger seat. He picked it up and then reached around and retrieved Gran's driver's licence from where he'd wedged it at the volcano swimming pool in Moree. He tucked it down the front of his undies as Dylan sat down.

'All buckled in?' Dylan winked.

Fin nodded and Dylan steered onto the highway.

As the rippling tarp disappeared behind them, Fin felt the car slow. He looked up to see flashing police lights. They'd only been driving for a few minutes.

There were two police cars parked diagonally across the road with a sign directing traffic to the side.

Dylan whispered to himself, 'Here we go.'

Fin heard the heavy scraping of metal against the plastic of the driver's door console, and Dylan leant forward in his seat as he shoved something in behind him. He settled back and turned to Fin with a reassuring nod. 'It's sweet.'

Dylan pulled the car over as directed and wound down the window. A young policeman craned his neck and came close, almost poking his head through the open window. He looked around the inside of the car without speaking. The policeman's freckly face and blue eyes made him seem like a teenager.

Fin thought how lucky it was the tobacco packets were hidden.

He watched as Dylan kept both hands on the steering wheel and spoke in a relaxed, half-laughing way. 'It's a bit early for the breathalyser, isn't it, constable?'

The policeman's eyes continued to examine the car as he spoke. 'You have not been stopped... We are not currently conducting roadside breath analysis. This is in relation to an ongoing police operation.'

Fin noticed Dylan's hand drop from the steering wheel. It came to rest on the gearshift.

The policeman continued. 'Where are you heading?'

Dylan managed to maintain his cheerful calm. 'On our way to Brisbane. My auntie, actually my great-auntie. She's booked in for her medical.'

The policeman stepped back and his eyes darted over the outside of the car.

Dylan's hand moved slowly to his side as he spoke. 'But at this rate, we're already under the pump getting her there by nine-thirty, especially with all that city traffic.'

The policeman kept his eyes on the car as he walked around to the passenger side and tapped on the glass. Fin watched as Dylan's hand tucked in beside his left hip. The old lady wound down the window and said in her clear voice, 'Two tickets to Flinders Street, if you'd be so good. First class.'

There was silence for a moment and the policeman laughed. 'I haven't heard that one before.'

Dylan chuckled along with him and his hand drifted back to the gearshift. 'Like I said, medical. My auntie needs it bad.'

'Great-auntie, didn't you say?'

'You got me there, officer.'

Fin watched as Dylan's hand moved slowly towards his side again.

The policeman kept his eyes on Dylan as he called to Fin, 'You got your seatbelt on in the back there?'

Fin stretched it out to show him, but the policeman didn't take his eyes off Dylan.

Dylan spoke with a chuckle in his voice. 'Opportunity for the boy to have a day out in the city.'

The policeman paused as if he was fitting pieces of a puzzle together in his mind. He took a step back to look at the car again, and a low wave of his hand meant they could go.

Dylan navigated slowly between the police cars. He accelerated onto the highway and the old lady grabbed her hat to stop it blowing off as she wound up her window.

Fin heard the heavy thunk of metal dropping into the hard plastic of the driver's door console. He rolled his golf ball around in his hand and adjusted Gran's licence in his undies.

The sun rose. Its low glow made shadows across the road, cast by the occasional wheat silos they passed. They came to a fork in the road. There was a large sign with a curving arrow pointing right to Brisbane. The left arrow pointed to Toowoomba. Fin watched a big truck veering away to Brisbane as Dylan steered them onto the left fork.

The old woman began humming quietly to herself. It was a familiar melody and sounded like an old, happy song. The sort of thing Gustav might have had on one of his records.

The landscape became gradually greener and big trees lined the road. They passed another sign – *Allora Town Centre – Sunflower Route,* which made it sound prettier than it was. There were dried-out wooden telegraph poles next to the sign. They were nothing like the sturdy goat-head-shaped metal that could guide him back to Gustav's.

They drove towards the town and Fin's stomach tightened as they pulled onto the gravel driveway of a petrol station. He listened for metal scraping on plastic, but the sound didn't come. Dylan topped up the petrol while the old lady hummed quietly. She didn't seem to object to them driving in any particular direction. Fin wondered if she had already forgotten where she was going.

Dylan finished with the petrol pump and knocked on the window. 'Come and get yourself an iceblock or something.'

The glass doors opened automatically, and they stepped into a cool shop with a few rows of stumpy shelves full of lollies and magazines. The shopkeeper was a brown-bearded, chubby man holding a coffee mug. He set his coffee down as they approached. 'You gentlemen are out of bed early.'

'Best part of the day.' Dylan waved Fin towards the iceblock freezer.

Fin obeyed, but he was terrified at the thought of what might happen next. He didn't take his eyes off Dylan. He felt the cold of the freezer on his arm and, without looking down, grabbed the first iceblock his hand landed on. He joined Dylan at the counter. He'd chosen a chunky chocolate one with vanilla ice-cream.

'That will be twenty-four dollars seventy altogether.'

Dylan retrieved a thick fold of fifty-dollar notes from his pocket and Fin breathed out; he'd been holding his breath.

The shopkeeper pointed to the car as he handed back their change and Fin's ice-cream. 'I see you've got old Lillian Temple there. Driving her poor daughter spare with all this running about. She can cover miles in a day.'

Fin was startled by this. 'Do you know where she lives?' It seemed impossible that Dylan had chosen the correct fork in the road to take her home.

The shopkeeper directed his response to Dylan. 'You bet. Up on Jubb Street, round behind the golf course. Brick house. Couldn't tell you the number, but there'll be a yellow Commodore out the front this time of day. Unless they're already out looking for old Lillian.'

Dylan sighed as he tucked the change back into his pocket.

The shopkeeper continued. 'I reckon they should put one of those things on her. One of those tracking devices like they do with criminals. Save everyone a mountain of bother.'

As Fin and Dylan stepped out into the warm morning air, the word 'criminals' stayed in Fin's head.

They climbed back into the car, and Fin leant over from the back seat to place his hand on the old woman's shoulder. 'Lillian?'

She turned her head towards him.

'Seatbelt, Golden.' Dylan waited for Fin to sit back and he steered them out onto the road.

They circled around the golf course and turned into a smaller street. Fin saw a yellow car in front of a brick house. Dylan pulled in behind it. Lillian climbed out and walked towards the house without looking back.

Dylan flicked his eyes towards Fin. 'That was easy.'

'We've got to make sure she gets in.'

'Last thing we need is complications. We got this far.'

Fin clicked open the back door and held it ajar so Dylan couldn't drive off. He was determined not to let his dad get in the way of a good deed.

Lillian retrieved a set of keys from her handbag as she approached the front door. She struggled with the lock before the door was opened from the inside and swung wide. Lillian stepped inside, and a broad-shouldered woman came out and hurried across the lawn towards the car.

'Complications.' Dylan was speaking to himself, but there was no scraping sound or thunk of metal.

The woman was almost running towards the car. She was wearing undersized pink shorts and a white T-shirt. The shorts were bunched up at the top of her chunky legs. Her straggly brown hair hung down to her shoulders; it looked like she was wet from a shower. She had brown eyes and her face was an almost perfect circle.

She spoke to Fin first. 'Thank you! Thank you! Thank you so much for bringing Mum back.' She hurried around to the driver's side. 'Thank you. This is all so crazy but you've actually saved us a nightmare this time.'

Dylan spoke with a smile in his voice. 'No worries. Melbourne on foot didn't seem likely.'

'Ugh! The bloody trains. They call to her in the night.' She leant forward and rested her head on the roof of the car in a gesture of exhausted relief. 'My husband's on the road and I couldn't get out with all the kids in the dark. I've just got off the phone to the highway patrol.'

Dylan's neck and shoulders visibly stiffened at the mention of police.

The woman continued rapidly. 'Anyway, you must let me get you something. You must. I've got a house full of breakfast and coffee and all kinds of tea.'

'No, I think we'd...'

'I simply won't take no for an answer. You must have room for a cup of tea? I got all these packets for my birthday, not the cheap ones. I can't tell you what a miserable day we all would've been in for without you. And Mum, of course.'

Dylan looked over his shoulder and Fin nodded as keenly as he could. He'd finished his ice-cream, and anything else to fill his stomach seemed like a good idea.

'Okay, then. You've won over the boss, at least. A cup of tea, maybe just one.'

'What a sensible young man your boss is. Anyway, please call me Bev. And?'

'Dylan. And this is... He goes by Fin. He might look young but don't be fooled. He's got a head on his shoulders.'

Fin wasn't sure what it meant to have a head on your shoulders but it sounded like a good thing. He clutched his golf ball hard and crossed the lawn to the front door; his head felt even more on his shoulders than usual.

The house was all closed up with ceiling fans going. The walls that weren't covered by floor-to-ceiling bookshelves were painted a yellowy off-white, and the door and window frames were dark wood.

Bev led them into the kitchen. Lillian was already pouring herself a cup of tea.

'Oh, Mum. And you've done something to your knee.' She turned to Fin to explain. 'She makes the tea and then just leaves the cups on the bench to go cold. She can make two dozen in a day. My husband reckons she doesn't drink them because she's making them for someone else. I'll just ring to let the highway boys know you found her, and I'll make sure the back's locked up while I think of it.'

She disappeared through a doorway and Lillian followed behind.

Dylan spoke through a nervous smile. 'That's not bad, hey?' He lifted a finger to point through the kitchen window. There was a swimming pool beside a small patch of yellow lawn. Although it was still early morning, four kids were jumping, splashing and running around the pool. Fin couldn't hear what they were saying but they seemed to be engaged in a shouted argument.

'Cool pool.' Fin would have liked to jump in with them.

'And how are the books? Those bookshelves. It's a really good sign.'

Fin looked across the crowded bookshelves. Right at the end, he saw the spine of a Mensa IQ test book.

Bev reappeared and hurried towards the kettle. She tipped the cup of tea Lillian had made down the sink. 'Now, tea? Or maybe, by the look in your eye, you strike me more as a coffee man.'

'Yes. Thank you. I'll have a coffee, thank you. With just a little milk and sugar.' Dylan's hands trembled as he spoke.

It was hard for Fin to imagine Dylan being scared of anyone.

'And what about you, Fin? All the kid stuff gets hoovered up pretty quick with this lot. We've got plenty of milk. How about a hot chocolate? Or a cold one if that's more likely?'

'I'll have one of those. A hot one.'

'Manners, Golden.' Dylan was still nervous.

'Please.'

Bev winked at him and set about making the drinks. Dylan pulled out a bar stool for Fin to sit on at the bench and he propped alongside.

Bev said, 'Yes, Darren and Alex are Gidhabal mob. They're twins. They've been here since school finished but there's been a few dramas finding them a kin spot. One together, anyway.'

Fin thought she must be talking about two dark-skinned boys out in the pool. They were both a bit older than Fin, maybe ten. Their wet brown hair was cut short and stuck to their heads. Their bony shoulders showed through their dark blue rash vests.

She handed Dylan his coffee.

'There's a lot of kids out there.' Dylan seemed to be speaking more to Fin than Bev.

'Yes, we're lucky.' She turned to Fin. 'We foster. Yep, we foster. Tarsha, the older one, she's been here almost a year now. And Amelia, it's been about three. She's not going anywhere, not if we've got anything to say about it, anyway.'

The older girl looked about fourteen. She was skinny, in a black bikini with blue and blonde streaks in her hair. The other girl was younger than Fin. She was wearing bright flower-patterned boardshorts and a black rash vest. Her brown hair was in two tight plaits at the back.

'Do you get what she's saying, Golden Boy? I mean about fostering?'

Fin nodded, but Dylan explained anyway.

'Well, fostering, foster parents. They look after kids for a while if the kid's parents can't look after them. That's right, isn't it?'

Bev handed Fin his hot chocolate. 'Careful, I might have over-microwaved it a bit. Yes, that's right.'

Fin looked out the window and wondered why these kids were on loan to Bev, and where their parents were now.

'You must let me give you something to eat. I can't tell you what an ordeal this could have turned into if you didn't bring her back. We've got toast and cereal. I could even do you some baked beans if you fancy?'

Dylan's hands were unsteady as he took a sip of his coffee. 'I'm on a promise to get this boy some bacon.'

'Well, we don't have that, unfortunately. And if we did, it wouldn't survive long. Vroooom! That's how food goes around here, especially good stuff. Like a race car. Vroooom!'

'That's okay. I don't mind, whatever. Anything is okay.'

Dylan raised his hand and began talking over Fin. 'No, no, no, you don't. We both know how you get without your bacon. And it's good for the muscles. Protein and all that, anyway.'

Bev seemed very confused. 'Okay, well...'

Dylan interrupted again. 'I'm not sure if this would be too much. Overstepping, I mean. But you know how it is with these things. And kids. We've been on the road a few days now. No stove. So maybe, if it's no trouble, I could dart out and grab us a nice big bag of bacon? I'll do the cooking, mind you. When I get back.'

Bev's voice was quiet. 'I guess. I mean, if Fin needs bacon that badly...'

'Well, it's settled then. I'll just be a minute. There's got to be an early supermarket, yeah?'

'We've got two. Just left at the corner and follow Forde Street all the way into town.'

Dylan hunched over so his eyes were level with Fin's. 'And how about one of those hash browns? The little ones. Like that first morning in the café. I've seen them in boxes in those big freezers.' Dylan's eyes grew shiny. 'And tomato? You really wolfed that down. How about some of that? And I'll be sure to cook everything up nice and crispy.'

Fin understood that Dylan wasn't coming back.

'Well, then. Bacon it is.'

'Okay, Dad. Bacon.'

'And I won't forget the hash browns and the tomatoes. It'll be like that first day. And eggs, of course.'

Fin angled his face back to stop the tears falling out. 'And eggs, yeah.'

'Okay, Golden. I'll just be a tick.' He winked, stood up straight and turned his back to go. He didn't say anything more to Bev.

She was watching from the kitchen with her shoulders down.

Just as Dylan reached the front door, Fin called out to him, 'Dad, I'll see you soon.'

'You bet, Golden Boy. You bet.' And he was gone.

Fin sat looking out at the pool. He didn't try to stop the tears dripping now. Bev stayed where she was. Quiet, looking out the window too.

When he felt like he could talk again, he climbed down off the stool, rounded the bench into the kitchen, reached down the front of his undies and retrieved Gran's driver's licence. He held it out steadily to Bev. 'I'd like you to call my grandma.'

'Do you want to speak to her?' She took the licence.

He knew Gran would be furious that he went with Dylan. 'Um, no. Not now. Could you please just call her and tell her where I am?'

Bev nodded and her words sped up. 'Yes, of course. Do you know her phone number?'

'No.'

Bev looked closely at the licence and disappeared through the doorway.

The sun sparkled off the surface of the pool and Fin watched as the kids splashed and shouted.

Bev returned and gave him the licence. It was damp, like she'd washed it. She had a blue rash vest in the other hand. 'I spoke to your grandma. She said she needs to organise a few things first but she's going to drive up to get you. I think that's what you want? I gave her the number here too.'

'Thank you.' Fin felt empty.

'I thought you might like this.' She held the rash vest out to him and reached for a big bottle of sunscreen on the kitchen windowsill. 'Do you need any help with suncream?'

'I can do it.' He held out his golf ball and gestured to the windowsill. 'Can I leave this up there for now?'

'Yes, of course. I'll make sure it stays put.' She carefully placed it on the windowsill. 'And before anything else, how about a bit of toast?'

'Thank you. I'd love some toast.'

~

Fin finished four pieces of toast with Vegemite. He spent the hot part of the day jumping in the pool and spinning a frisbee out to Darren and Alex. The kids shouted happily, swearing and fighting sometimes, but they were kind to him. They all ate cheese and Vegemite sandwiches for lunch and shared a whole carton of chocolate milk.

The three boys jumped into the pool as the day began to fade into evening. Fin tried not to wobble on the surface of the water as he lay back on the torn half of a boogie board.

The sky was pink-silver, and there were gnarled columns rising up from the top of an arrow-shaped cloud. He could see a sheet of greenish rain falling on the low hills in the distance, but the storm looked like it was going to pass by without getting them. It was still too early for stars.

There was a roll of thunder and Fin heard a phone ring. He balanced carefully as he cupped one hand and rubbed the water on his arms, the way Dylan had done in Moree.

Bev came to the edge of the pool and spoke softly. 'Griffin, maybe hop out for a sec? We need to have a word inside.' She held up a towel and wrapped it around him. It was the first time she had called him Griffin, so he knew it had been Gran on the phone. Fin suspected she'd said she wasn't coming.

He followed Bev into the house and then she turned and led him into the laundry. There were two old washing machines side by side and a door at the far end.

'That was your grandmother on the phone. She's past Coffs Harbour, but there's really bad weather on the highway. There's some flash flooding, and she's worried about pushing on. So she asked if it would be okay with you if she stops for the night and heads off first thing in the morning. She's given me the mobile number and asked for you to call. I mean, if you want? I think she just wants to check everything's right with you. You know, being here.'

Gran would have seen the cup hook by now; he really didn't want to call. 'Is it all right? Me being here?'

'Um, I'm supposed to register you if you're spending the night.' She paused and seemed to search his eyes for a reaction. 'But you don't want to get on the department's radar if you can avoid it. Once you're in that computer, you never get out.'

The thought of his name, Griffin Alverton, trapped in a computer somewhere seemed horrible – or was it Griffin Martin? And, as though wishing alone could make it real, he wished painfully for the sound of Dylan knocking on the door. This time with a real umbrella, soaking wet, with enough bacon for everyone and saying the first shop was closed so he went on and got caught in the storm.

'But what does that mean?'

Her cheeks rounded in an apologetic smile. 'We've only got a yoga mat to spare, but you can bunk in there with the boys.' She pointed to the door at the far end of the laundry.

'What about the computer?'

'I won't tell if you won't.' She held his gaze for a moment.

He nodded quickly.

She reached into a plastic basket and handed him a folded set of pyjamas. They felt warm, like they'd just come in from the washing line. 'These ought to do the trick. I washed your T-shirt too.'

'Thank you.'

'You're very welcome.' She turned to leave but then stopped and leant down so she was looking him in the face. 'You okay, Fin? Want to talk about anything?'

Fin thought of all the things he wanted to talk about: the sound of metal scraping and thunking in the front seat when they were stopped by the police, the angry eyes of the man shouting at them in the pool in Moree, the bore-pipe waterhole and the mangoes, the flash in the little general store, New Zealand and Lindy on the roof. 'It's okay. I'm fine.'

She stepped back out of the laundry and began sliding the door across. 'I'll let you get changed.'

He stood for a moment and looked at the baskets of folded clothes. They reminded him of the way Lindy used to cross her legs on the lounge-room floor at Gustav's and make little islands of T-shirts, shorts, socks and undies. He wanted the hospital people to let her out so he could have her back. He knew he'd be able to look after her if they could just get home.

He stretched off his rash vest and dropped his boardshorts and undies. Gran's drivers licence toppled out onto the floor. He wrapped the licence in his wet undies and pushed them into a gap beside one of the washing machines.

The pyjama pants had a pattern of black and white starfighters on them; the top was grey with *STAR WARS* written in black letters, the same writing as his breakfast set. When he was dressed, he hung his wet boardshorts and the rash vest over the pool fence to dry. The last of the twilight was fading now and the storm had moved closer, swallowing up half the sky. Fin knew Dylan would push on no matter how hard it rained, and he wouldn't need to find a pool competition for a while.

~

Bev baked a huge frozen lasagne and put chopped-up carrots and cucumber on the side of each plate. The kids sat at a table with a big sheet of plastic stretched under it like a rug. After dinner, the girls went into their room, and the three boys pushed their heads together to play on an iPad until Bev told Darren and Alex they had to brush their teeth.

She led Fin through the laundry and swung the door open at the far end. There were concrete steps down into a tiny room made of plain timber beams and wide blue sheets of plasterboard. The room was lit by a bulb with a little shade over it, dangling from a wire. Bev had unrolled a red yoga mat on the floor and put a pillow and an empty doona cover on top.

'Noel knocked this up as a spare when Mum moved in. It's not exactly... Well, anyway, it keeps the rain and the toads out, mostly. I'm sorry I don't have anything thicker for you to sleep on. I hope you'll be all right on the floor there. The boys will sort it out if you get a toad.' She paused to look at him. 'You all right with the dark?'

Fin nodded and she walked back out through the laundry before calling out, 'Lights out at nine.'

Darren and Alex jogged in wearing their pyjamas. Alex shoved the door closed and climbed onto the top bunk. Darren sat down on the lower bed with his feet on the edge of the yoga mat. His pyjama pants were too short for him, and Fin could see the dark skin of his shins in the lamplight.

Darren lay down and tucked his legs inside his empty doona cover, like a thin sleeping bag. 'Get inside. There's no switch in here. She pulls the plug in a minute and you can't see anything once that thing's off.'

The bottom of the doona cover bunched up and caught on the yoga mat, but Fin managed to get his legs inside just before the room went dark.

Bev's voice came from the other side of the door. 'Night, boys.'

Darren and Alex were quiet as Bev walked out through the laundry and slid the door closed. But as soon as Bev was gone, they started giggling and shooshing each other. Then there was the slow crunching of plastic wrapping being carefully opened on the top bunk.

Fin felt something light fall onto his doona cover.

Alex said, 'That's your bit. Make sure you lick your fingers right off or she'll know.'

Fin patted his doona cover and found a piece of chocolate. He bit into it and it tasted like it was filled with jam. He ate it carefully, without speaking.

Alex whispered, 'Do you live here now?'

Fin replied as quietly as he could. 'No. My gran's coming to get me in the morning.'

'You're lucky. What's your name again?'

'Fin.'

'No, your name name. The proper one with your family one and that.'

'Oh, Griffin…Griffin Martin.' Fin wasn't sure why he used his new surname; it felt it might be his last chance.

Darren whispered, 'So your gran's coming? Where's she taking you, anyway?'

'Back to Sydney.'

Alex spoke from the top bunk. It seemed like they were taking turns. 'So how'd you get all the way to Allora?'

'Drove.'

There was a long silence.

'We've got cousins in Sydney. I've heard it's mega.' It was Darren this time.

'Yeah, it's pretty mega in the city, but not where my gran is.' He kept his voice low as he told them about trapping crabs and stealers in the river.

'And you eat them?' Alex seemed doubtful.

'Yep. Cook them on the fire there, right on the rock.' Fin remembered the spots on Rory's neck and what Dylan had said about the chemicals and the old factory.

Alex said, 'I ate a crab once and it tasted like a dog had pooed on it.'

'You have to scrape the gills out before you put it on the fire or it tastes like that. I can show you how to do it. You use a stick.'

'Sounds right.'

Darren started to speak more freely, like he knew Bev was too far away to hear them now. 'Our pop used to take us on the Condamine. He said we, you know blackfellas, used to be able to reach in and grab them. Big fish, just with our hands. Sounds all right, doesn't it?'

'Yep.' Fin was worried he might say the wrong thing. He remembered the Aboriginal man in Moree – *What are you looking at, you dying Jesus?*

Alex spoke next. 'You know the Daleys? They live in Sydney. That's our cousins.'

'No, I don't think so.

'You know *any* blackfellas there in Sydney, Griffin Martin?'

'No, I don't. I think I don't anyway.'

Darren and Alex stayed quiet. The silence seemed too long, like Fin was supposed to say something obvious but important. As the silence continued, he felt like there might be an argument unless he showed that he knew something about Aboriginal people. So he said, 'My dad told me that thing about waterslides. How, you know, you guys... How Aboriginal people own the land and they hate waterslides because of how they got built there when you didn't want them. You know?'

The silence continued.

Fin said, 'Do you hate waterslides?'

Both boys laughed, hissing through their teeth before Darren spoke. 'Griffin Martin, you've got to be joking.'

They giggled in muffled whispers and the boys occasionally made squeaking fart noises. The last thing Fin heard before he fell into a deep sleep was Alex whispering from the top bunk.

'You'd better not piss in those pyjamas, Griffin Martin. Aunt gave you the best ones.'

And Fin was asleep.

~

When he woke up, the bunk room was silent. His doona cover was bunched around his legs, and he could see a rainbowy triangle of light shining through a gap where a corner of the plasterboard had been snapped off. He untangled his legs from the doona cover, but he didn't get up. If he could stay there on the yoga mat, it would delay what was coming.

There was the sound of clattering plates and muffled voices. He lay a moment longer before he climbed to his feet, walked through the laundry and edged the back door open so he could step out into the morning air. He collected his shorts from the pool fence, and his shoes and T-shirt from the back step, and then retrieved his undies from beside the washing machine; they were still damp. He quickly undressed, pulled his undies on and tucked Gran's licence inside before putting on his boardies, T-shirt and shoes. He bundled his pyjamas under one arm and followed the sounds of breakfast.

The twin boys were already dressed in their boardies and rash vests, and Alex had his swimming goggles lifted up onto his forehead. They were sitting on stools at the kitchen bench. Tarsha, the teenager, was lying back on the couch looking at her phone and rubbing shiny ointment into her lips, and little Amelia was rolling from side to side on the carpet in her pyjamas.

Bev was in the kitchen holding a bag of bread. 'There you are. The boys told me you made it through the night without a toad.'

Fin nodded. 'No. Nothing got in.'

'Vegemite again?' She pointed with her chin. 'You can put them on the back of the couch there.'

Fin flopped his pyjamas onto the couch and sat on an empty stool between the boys.

'You coming in the pool, Griffin Martin?' Darren wiped his hands on the front of his rash vest.

'I maybe shouldn't. My gran will be here soon.'

Bev retrieved his golf ball from the window sill and handed it to him before she put down a plate of Vegemite toast and a mug of milk. 'I'm just going to check on Mum.' She walked to the door in the back corner and had to unlock it to get through.

Fin tucked his golf ball into the pocket of his shorts.

Darren pointed to the lump in his pocket. 'So that's your golf ball?'

'Rory, the one I told you about. He gave it to me.' He took a bite of his toast and a sip of cold milk.

Alex tilted his head to the side. 'Is that all still a goer? Your gran coming to take you to Sydney and that? It's still happening? Is that what Aunt said?'

'Yep. I think it's happening.' Fin felt as if Alex must have heard something.

'You sure about that?'

'Yesterday, Bev said she was.' Fin continued eating his toast.

Darren burped loudly. 'I'll bet she's got a good big car if she's driving all the way from Sydney.'

Fin tried to think of what would happen to him if Gran didn't come. 'It's a silver one but it's not that big.'

This time Alex burped. 'Nice of her to come all that way for you.'

The thought that Gran might not come felt like it cut a hole below his ribs. He and Dylan would still be on their way to the fruit trees in Darwin if he hadn't insisted on stopping to pick up old Lilian. Now, Gran would have seen the cup hook and understood what he had planned to do to her, so he'd probably end up on loan to someone, like these kids, at least until the doctors let his mum out.

'Our uncle was going to come get us from Townsville once.' Alex swallowed down the last of his toast. 'But I'd go out of my mind. You know, being in a car that long.' He reached out as if he was going to snatch Fin's plate. 'You'd better eat up that toast if your Gran's driving you all the way to Sydney.'

Fin now felt certain they'd heard that Gran wasn't coming. He chewed up some more toast. 'Maybe I could come in the pool.'

Alex stretched out his goggles and placed them over his eyes. 'Yeah. It's going to be a hot one.'

The doorbell rang and all three boys stood up from their stools. The twins turned towards each other, and Darren reached out like he was trying to shake Alex's hand.

Little Amelia sat up and said, 'We're not allowed to answer the door.'

Alex shook his head, 'I'm not shaking your hand yet.'

'I told you.'

No-one moved.

'And shaking your brother's hand just feels wrong.' Alex moved his goggles back up onto his forehead

'Don't knock it till you've tried it.' Darren grinned.

Bev reappeared and hurried through the living room. 'I'll get it.'

She swung the front door open and, from where he was standing at the kitchen bench, Fin could see it was Gran standing in the doorway. She was wearing her light-blue shirt. But she looked crumpled, like her edges were softer. He was so convinced that she wasn't coming that he'd half expected it to be the police.

'Beverly?' Gran puffed the word out, like she was catching her breath.

'You must be Antonella. Griffin's here.' She stood aside so Gran could see him at the kitchen bench.

Gran squinted as she looked into the dark of the house. When she saw him she said, 'Hello,' stretching the word out like it meant something else.

He went to speak, but he felt like he was frozen. All he could think about was the cup hook beside the stairs.

Bev said, 'We should have a quick chat,' and she led Gran into a room at the front of the house.

Alex held out a little chocolate bar in a red wrapper towards Darren.

'Told you she'd come.'

Alex shrugged and looked at Fin. 'Sorry, Griffin Martin. Most grandmas don't make it.'

It took Fin a moment to realise that Alex had just lost a bet.

Alex pulled the chocolate bar back close to his chest. 'Your face makes me feel bad now. You can have it.'

Darren held out his hand. 'What about me?'

Fin said, 'It's all right.'

'I'll give you half.' Darren took the chocolate bar and, in one quick motion, he unwrapped it and snapped it in half. He handed a piece to Fin, then he paused and broke his own piece in half to give some to his brother. 'There's never any point betting with you.'

They heard the sound of a door opening at the front, and the boys quickly popped their pieces of chocolate into their mouths.

Gran walked back towards the front door and pointed at the plastic sheet on the carpet under the dining table. 'That must simplify things.'

Bev called out, 'Fin's going home.'

Fin walked towards Gran and she reached her hand out for him to hold. Bev and the other kids followed them onto the front lawn.

Bev bent down and pulled him into a quick hug. 'Take care, Fin.'

Tarsha waved and said, 'Bye,' almost silently. She seemed really upset that he was leaving.

Amelia planted her hands on the ground and flicked her legs up into a handstand. 'Bye, Fin.'

Tarsha grabbed Amelia's ankles to steady her.

'Let go of my legs. I can do it on my own.'

Tarsha let go and Amelia toppled onto the grass.

Alex waved and said, 'You be careful of those waterslides, Griffin Martin.'

Gran glanced down sternly at Fin. He could tell she hated that they'd used Dylan's surname.

Darren smiled and said, 'See you somewhere, Griffin Martin.'

Gran led him along the path to where her little silver car was parked behind Bev's yellow one. He walked around to the front passenger door and climbed in. Gran sat down heavily in the driver's seat. She didn't look at him. Her shoulders were tense and her eyes were fixed forward. 'Back seat, young man.'

He was certain now that she knew what he'd planned. He got out and opened the back door to climb in. As soon as he sat down, he found his bright orange hat on the seat beside him. There was a note inside, written in purple ink.

Dear Mr Golden,

Next time you go running off, don't forget your hat.

Ever yours,

Josie

His throat was so tensed up that he coughed before he could speak. 'Josie?'

'She wouldn't let me leave without it.' Gran was still looking out through the windscreen.

'Josie? Really? She's all right?'

Gran gripped the steering wheel. 'She's on her way to all right. The minute she regained herself she was like a spider in a bottle. The doctors eventually relented and let her out.' She started the engine. 'Belt on, Griffin.'

He pulled his hat down on his head and clicked his seatbelt on.

Gran moved the gearshift into *D* and steered the car off the gravel and onto the road. She raised a hand to wave to Bev as they pulled away. Fin turned to look out the back window and saw the twins facing each other on the lawn. It looked like they were shaking hands.

Gran turned left onto a long street and, as soon as they'd gone a few houses down, she pulled over onto the gravel again. Fin's whole body stiffened. He looked around for the best direction to run. There was a dusty path between two houses with a small caravan parked beside it. He reached for his belt buckle.

Gran clicked the car into *P* and stopped the engine. She let her head fall forward onto the steering wheel and held it there for a moment before she began weeping. She cried and cried, rolling her head back and forth. Eventually, she turned to look at him. 'What on earth are you doing here?' The whites of her eyes were pink around the blue.

'I'm sorry, Gran.'

'Oh, dear boy. Of us all, you're the one who's blameless.'

'For what I did, Gran. I'm sorry.'

'Whatever it is. It's all right now.'

Fin nearly vomited with relief. She mustn't have seen the hook or, if she had, she hadn't known what it was for.

She sobbed out a short laugh. 'That hat. You look like a roadworker.' She unclicked her belt, climbed out and walked around to open his door. She beckoned him out and they stood beside the car for a moment before she leant down and looked him all over, like she was checking for parts that had gone missing. She pulled him into a long squeezing hug.

'You smell nice.' Fin could hear her curls moving against the brim of his hat.

'I guess that's one thing. I've come a long way.' She squeezed him again. 'You smell nice too.' She stood up and took a deep breath before she walked back to the driver's door. 'Come on. You can sit in the front if you prefer it.'

He climbed into the passenger seat beside Gran.

'How's Mum?'

'She's having another check-up on Friday but seems better.' Gran started the engine. 'More...continuous.' She clicked the gearshift into *D* again. 'Old Binnalong's not far out of our way. I thought we could stop in at your place. It's only a couple of hours from here, and it would be good to check on things. Okay with you? The Northern Rivers caught the worst of the storm.'

Fin nodded. It felt as though the car suddenly filled with the clear air of Gustav's.

'I thought you might like to pick up a few things to see you through until your mum's recovered. And she can get you both home.'

Gran steered the car off the gravel, and Fin sat up and concentrated on the surface of the road. But then he relaxed back to look up at the storm clouds ahead.

Gran pressed a button on the radio and slow classical music began playing.

'Josie's really all right?'

'Well, sort of. She loses track of her thoughts quickly. She remembers nothing at all about what happened.' She flicked a quick glance at him. 'But I told her what you did, catching her like that.'

Fin remembered that horrible moment on the patio, and he could almost feel the floppy weight of Josie on his back. 'This sounds like her music.'

Gran hummed along for a moment. 'I suppose it is.'

Soon after they turned onto the freeway, Fin drifted off to sleep, and when he opened his eyes again, the sound of water was heavy under the car and the windscreen wipers were working hard to clear the blur. There was a break in the clouds ahead, just enough to let the sunlight through.

He sat up tall in his seat and, in the distance, he could see a grey smudge on some low hills. As the wipers cleared away another slosh of rain, it was unmistakable – a line of goat-head powerlines running all the way along the ridge. And they were moving closer.

ACKNOWLEDGEMENTS

This book was written on Gadigal land, Darramuragal land and Kamilaroi land. I pay my respects to Gadigal Elders, past, present and future. I pay my respects to Darramuragal Elders, past, present and future. And I pay my respects to Kamilaroi Elders, past, present and future. I also acknowledge their living cultures and the stories that continue to be told by Gadigal, Darramuragal and Kamilaroi peoples on the lands where this story was written.

I would like to thank the following people for their help.

Firstly, **Mini**, thank you. I adore you. You put the love in my heart and the petrol in my tank. You're the reason I can keep going. Thank you to **Grace Heifetz** for your bulletproof enthusiasm, good humour, energy, wisdom and for loving this book enough to make it real. Thank you to **James Kellow** for believing in Fin and Rory, and for guiding their little boat into the world. Thank you to **Fiona McFarlane** for your kindness and insight, and for caring enough to tell me when

I get things wrong (and right). Thank you to **Alex Craig** for the clarity of your editorial eye, your ability to see the big picture, and for piloting this book through the turbulent seas of 2021 into the calmer water of 2022. Thank you to **Brigid Mullane** for the energy you put into the edit and for making everything work. Thank you to **Vincent Kenney** for your dad jokes about swallows, roadkill and bikie dentists. But mostly, thank you, Vin, for your friendship, for recceing the waterways with me and navigating us safely to Moree and back. You're the perfect companion on a literary adventure. Thank you to **Jane O'Keefe** for your energetic support and eagle-eyed proofreading skills from the first draft to the last. Thank you to **Tim Ailwood** for your help with the original manuscript, and for your friendship. To **Amy Daoud** for your striking cover that captures the thrill and perils of boyhood. To **Simone Ford** for your sleuth-like attention to detail and for (eeek!) always being right. And to **Libby Turner** for the thought and care you put into the proofread. It was a big help and it allowed me to see other aspects of the book more clearly.

Thank you all. This book would not be what it is without you.

Jack